COLD DARK
IRISH MAFIA
ROMANCE

DANGEROUS DOMS

JANE HENRY

J. HENRY PUBLICATIONS

Copyright © 2020 by Jane Henry

All rights reserved.

No part of this book may be reproduced in any form or by any electronic or mechanical means, including information storage and retrieval systems, without written permission from the author, except for the use of brief quotations in a book review.

Cover photography by Wander Aguiar

Cover art by PopKitty Designs

SYNOPSIS

Aileen

They promised me as tribute.

Youngest of six, I'm untouched.

Unblemished.

And in the world of the Irish mafia...

Wanted.

I'm given to a man I've never met.

Forced into a union I didn't condone.

Owned by a dangerous rival.

He may take my body, but he won't steal my heart.

Chapter 1

Cormac

My mouth waters when the bartender places three large, frothy pints of Guinness in front of us. Christ, I need a pint like a newborn calf needs her mother's titties.

"Anything else I can get you boys?" Rafferty Kelly asks with a ready grin. The oldest son of a dirt poor family of ten, he's scrapped his way from the dank hovel he grew up in the Midlands to Ballyhock. A stone mason by day and bartender by night, word has it he still supports his mam and the little ones back at home. Rafferty runs a hand through his short, ruddy hair, and folds his arms on his chest. I down my pint in long, thirsty gulps, slam it back down on the counter and give him a chin lift. He grins in approval.

I tap the empty glass. "Another one, lad." He clucks his tongue and takes my empty pint with a wink. When his back's turned, I fold a tenner into the tip jar.

"Y'alright, Cormac?" Keenan asks, nursing his pint. His tone's casual, but I don't miss the way he drums his fingers on the table, or the ramrod stiffness in his spine. He knows I've been wrestling with what I have to do all week. Hell, he was the one that threw the fucking gauntlet.

"I'm alright," I mutter. I'm in the mood to drink, not talk.

The door to the pub section of the club swings open, and Nolan ambles in. I snicker to myself as every damn girl in the pub takes note. One girl tosses her hair back, and another straightens her shoulders to show off her tits. One even takes out a golden tube of lipstick and smears red on her pouty lips. Some whisper and point, and one even walks his way, but he walks past her without a second glance.

Nolan's single, and every damn girl in Ballyhock knows it. They don't care that he's the youngest McCarthy son. They don't care that he's the heart and soul of the Irish mafia closest to Dublin. How he gets his money or spends his time is of no consequence to them. He's rich, he's easy on the eyes, and he's a fucking charmer.

He walks past each of them and stalks straight toward us. Rafferty wordlessly slides a pint of Rock Shandy in front of him, the yellowish orange drink good enough without a drop of alcohol. A year ago Nolan would've have scoffed at a virgin drink and called the manhood of any bloke who drank one into question, but now, Nolan doesn't even flinch. I'm proud of him. He's been nearly a year sober, and it's only been in recent weeks he's even come near a bar. Takes fucking bollox to face your weaknesses and stay strong.

"What's the story, brother?" I ask him, tapping my pint to his in greeting.

He swigs his drink before speaking, places it on the bar top, and sighs.

"Christ, but it feels good to be back here."

Nolan was the first of the McCarthy brothers to frequent The Craic, the dual-purpose club now under new management and aptly named.

Rafferty wipes the counter in front of Nolan and nods. "Good to have you back."

Nolan was the one who recruited us all here to begin with. Beyond the bar is a members-only exclusive section of the club, reserved for those who've got what Nolan calls, "tastes of a particular nature." In Ireland, we hide our sex clubs well. I suppose we have to reconcile the ghosts of our Christian forefathers by keeping up appearances, or some such shite. But we have our demons, too, behind closed doors.

Keenan looks to Nolan with concern. He knows how Nolan's bout with alcoholism nearly destroyed him, and as the older McCarthy brother and Clan Chief, it's his job to be sure Nolan's alright.

"All good, lads," Nolan says with his signature grin. "I figure now that I've got control of myself, time to control some tits and arse."

I snort, and even Keenan's lips tip up.

"Sounds about right," he approves. "You're heading to the back, then."

"Aye." Nolan takes another long pull from his drink.

"Any word on the bitch you're trackin'?" Keenan asks.

Keenan assigned Nolan to tag the nosy reporter who's had her head up our arses, and it seems he's making headway with her.

"She's hot onto the Martins, it seems," Nolan says.

"Will you need to teach her a lesson?" Keenan quirks a brow, his pint to his lips.

Nolan grins, his voice lowering an octave to a lust-filled groan. "Christ, brother, I hope so."

I laugh out loud. I know exactly what he means.

Keenan shakes his head, but he smiles, his eyes crinkling around the edges, and for one moment, my heart squeezes. God but he looks like my father when he smiles like that. Seamus McCarthy, father to the three of us, has been dead now for nearly a year. He was a hard-headed son of a bitch, but a loyal man. I wouldn't be the man I am today if it hadn't been for him.

"Cormac, we said we'd talk about your decision this weekend. What will it be, brother?" Keenan shoots straight and is ready to move ahead with our plans. It's rare we discuss Clan business in a pub instead of one of the more private meeting rooms, but sometimes if we can talk discreetly enough, it's worth it.

I don't answer at first, but take another long pull from the cold, frothy Guinness. I welcome the thick, slightly bitter taste, my belly warming with the gulps I take. Up until now, we could've been any three brothers sitting at a pub with a cold drink. But few people have to wrestle the decision before me now.

My father was killed by a Martin clan sniper, an act of

war according to the iron-clad code we follow. But shortly after my father's death, our rival, Mack Martin, offered a virgin tribute to Keenan, to be given to one of our men. Marrying the Martin girl would ensure peace between the Clans. We agreed she wouldn't marry until she'd graduated, but now that she has, it's time.

Keenan raises a finger to Rafferty. "Another round, Rafferty."

"This one's one me, brother." Keenan's soon to be a dad, and I want to celebrate.

I take another long pull from my pint and mull over the choice before me. As the second eldest McCarthy brother, I'm next in line to the throne. There's no escape. If anything were to happen to Keenan, I'd have to take his role and by clan law, I'm not allowed unless I take a wife.

The thought of marrying a Martin makes me sick. Fucking Martins. I've little choice when it comes to marriage, though. The men of The Clan rarely date for sport. A Clan marriage should solidify bonds. They rarely take place because of love. Sometimes we take captives in payment for a crime. Sometimes marriage is an act of retribution, and sometimes we agree to arranged marriage. Often, we're betrothed.

If I decline the Martin girl, what other chance will I have? But more importantly, what will happen to our Clan?

"She's fucking gorgeous," Nolan says to me. We've been given pictures, and I've done a fair bit of social media stalking myself.

"Aye." But what if the girl's looks are only a mask?

"She may be spoiled. Her father's one of the wealthiest in the Martin clan."

Keenan smiles. "You could fix spoiled."

Nolan groans. "I'd fucking love a chance to fix spoiled. Put that little girl right over my knee and teach her the lessons her dad forgot, aye?"

Despite my reservations, I shift on the bar stool. The image of the pretty blonde I've been poring over strewn on my lap tempting as hell. I don't like the more violent line of work we do at times, but I do like what Nolan's introduced me to at the club: deliberate pain laced with raw sexual power.

"Agreed," Keenan says. "Spoiled is an easy fix, and one you'd handle well."

I grunt and take another swig. "Could be a nag." I grimace at the very thought.

Nolan snickers. "Also quickly remedied with a firm hand. Hell, the first thing you ought to teach a woman's to watch a smart mouth."

Keenan rolls his eyes. "For a jovial fuck-up, you're a dominant son-of-a-bitch."

Nolan clinks his drink against Keenan's, smiling. "Why thank you," he says, as if he's just been paid the highest compliment. "And anyway, you should talk. You think I didn't notice the crop and cuffs you nicked from the club, or that slender collar your own wife wears? You might be private, Keenan, but I'm no *eejit*."

Keenan smiles wordlessly as he takes another sip from his pint. He enjoys the finer tastes of domination, but would cut off his own bollox before he brought his wife in the presence of other men. He may have brought her here once or twice, but he's a possessive bastard, and saves his escapades for the privacy of his bedroom.

"You are not," Keenan says. "And Cormac, I agree with Nolan. Both spoiled and nagging are easily remedied."

"Not everything can be fixed with a crop or a firm hand," I tell them, barely tempering the need to roll my eyes.

"No," Keenan agrees. "But you're McCarthy stock. You'll know how to handle her."

"Aye," Nolan says, his bright green eyes widening in earnest. "'Tis easy to train a woman. When she's naughty, you take her across her lap, teach her manners and to watch her mouth. Then you show her just how nice it can be when she obeys you. If you catch the right sort, she might even be wet between the legs after you punish her."

Keenan chuckles. "Aye."

"Then when she's good and well tamed, you reward her for being a good girl. Take care of her, and her heart will be yours."

"You act as if training a woman's as simple as training a feckin' filly."

"Aye, lad," Nolan says sagely. "But it is."

Keenan shakes his head. "Not hardly."

"You ought to talk," I say, shaking my head at him. "You ended up with Caitlin."

His eyes darken, and he places his pint on the table.

"Come again?" The dangerous tone of his voice warns me, but I'm not afraid of Keenan, and I say what I mean.

"Oh come off it, Keenan. All I mean is that she was neither a nag nor spoiled," I tell him. "She was sweet from the day we found her."

"Did you forget she nearly clocked us with a trowel? I had to carry her away, kicking and screaming like a banshee."

"In self-defense," I remind him. "Hardly a banshee."

"No," he admits with a smile, his eyes getting that faraway look when he speaks of his beloved. "Caitlin is a sweet lass."

Sweet lass indeed. He fucking worships her.

"The more pressing question isn't her temperament, lads," Nolan says. "But what our choices are. If you don't marry her, Cormac, she'll have to go to another of the Clan, at the very least. Rejection of a tribute's serious business, a luxury we can't afford. I'd take her myself if you won't, Cormac. It's our duty."

"Aye." Don't I know it. I feel the weight of responsibility to make the right choice. The livelihood of the Clan's on my shoulders. Keenan's wife's heavy with child, ready to burst at any moment, and though he'll have a nanny and help, he'll be occupied for a time. And if we don't take the tribute offered by the Martins, our clans will war. Someone has to marry her.

"Honestly, brother, it isn't hesitation," I admit. "I'll take the Martin girl. I just want to be prepared to deal with her."

Nolan leans forward, a shock of blond hair falling across his forehead. "I've met her, you know."

"Have you?" It's news to me.

"Aye," he says. "Banged one of her roomies."

Keenan's lips thin, but he doesn't speak.

"Course you did. And what'd you find?"

I'm suddenly curious. I need to know everything about the girl I'm to marry.

"I wasn't joking when I said she's gorgeous," Nolan begins, when Keenan's phone rings. He answers, and a few seconds later, drops his pint. It clatters to the floor. Nolan and I look to each other in astonishment. Keenan never loses self-control.

"It's Caitlin," Keenan says. He's on his feet, his eyes wide, hands trembling on the phone he holds.

"She alright?" I ask him.

"Aye. Water's broke. She says her contractions are two minutes apart."

"Christ, man, *go!*" I tell him. "You want me to drive you?"

"No, I'm good," he says, already at the door.

"Good luck, brother!" I shout after him.

He waves, and he's gone.

Nolan and I sit for a moment, stunned. He polishes off his Shandy with a flourish, and slams it on the countertop.

"Brother, it's time we pay a visit to the real part of this club, aye?"

The real part of the club, where women are aplenty, and the air is ripe with the sweet, seductive scent of sex.

"Hell yes."

I pay our tab and head to the back with Nolan. We move past the dimly-lit front room, past the idle chatter and clink of glass, to the thick black door guarded at the back.

"Tell me more," I say to Nolan when we enter the members-only section of the club.

"First," he says with a roll of the eyes, "her name's Aileen, not 'the Martin girl.'"

I punch his shoulder, which only makes him grin while he rubs it out.

Aileen. Have to admit, I love that name.

"Second," he says, smiling and waving to a girl dressed in black latex in the corner of the room. He snaps his fingers and points to the floor. She drops to her knees and begins to crawl toward him, her ready grin revealing this is not a hardship. "She sings like a lark."

He freezes when a man steps toward the little kitten heading his way, lumbering toward her with the grace of a troll. He's masked and wearing all black. He reaches down, blocking the girl's path, and grabs a fistful of her hair. My pulse spikes. I'm used to all manner of manhandling at the club, but the tone of her scream and shocked expression tells me she didn't authorize this.

"Son of a bitch," Nolan growls, and takes off. I groan but follow. If there's a throw-down, I'm his backup. I see Tully and Boner with a few girls nearby, and catch their attention as we go.

By the time we get to the girl, the bastard's got her on the tips of her toes, her hair entwined in his meaty fist. She's beating at his hand, tears streaming down her cheeks. "Flagon!" she screams. *"Flagon!"* It's the goddamn club safe word. He doesn't stop.

Nolan doesn't hesitate but tackles the man full on. The girl topples to the floor, and Tully catches her.

The man's mask falls off, hanging around his neck like an executioner's noose, but he doesn't bother fixing it. His beady black eyes are infuriated. With a savage growl, he lunges at Nolan. They fall to the floor, fists flying. Tully, Boner, and I watch, ready to defend Nolan if we need to, but we let him fight it out, our own bodyguards are about the place as well. No one comes to aid his opponent.

"You fucking asshole," Nolan fumes, landing a solid punch to the guy's nose. We've all been trained in martial arts, and will easily take this guy out. His aim is solid, his fist connecting. Blood spurts everywhere, and the guy covers his face with his hand. In a flash, he reaches to his foot, and the light catches a gleaming silver blade in the light.

"Fuck!" I growl, and in one reflexive motion, kick the blade from his hand. The knife clatters to the floor. Nolan decks him again. He's on his knees, grabbing at his broken nose, when uniformed security guards grab both of them.

"He assaulted her," Nolan says, pointing an irate finger

at the guy, who still looks ready to kill. "She safe-worded and he wouldn't stop."

"She fucking likes it," he growls. He's missing teeth, and his bloodied face is contorted in anger. His thick, heavy eyebrows draw together over black eyes that are too-small for his puffy face, like buttons sewn too tightly on a throw pillow.

"I know what she fucking likes," Nolan fairly spits back.

"He pulled a goddamn blade," I say to security, my voice thick with anger. For half a pound I'd slice the man's throat with his own blade.

He growls and tries to lunge back at Nolan, but the guard holds him back. His shirt rips, revealing pasty white skin and ink I know on sight.

"Shite," I mutter, when I recognize the mark of a Martin.

"Son of a bitch," Boner groans beside me. "Mother of *God*. I know who he is."

I turn to him. "You know him?"

He sighs. "Yeah, brother." He shakes his head. "Meet your future brother-in-law."

Chapter 2

Aileen

I WAKE in the middle of the night to the sound of my parents fighting. I do what I've been doing since I was a child, grab my pillow and pull it over my head. It isn't the fighting I can't stand but my utter helplessness.

I've intervened, all right, but learned quickly that was pointless. I even called the police once when I was a child. They didn't come after I told them the address, and I spent the next fortnight regretting my call. My father has a cruel tongue and a heavy hand, and he wields both with chilling results.

I used to feel badly for my mother. Though she's selfish and shallow, she's still my mother. But over the years, she's lost my sympathy as well.

I hate it here. God, I hate it here.

If I were anyone else, I could leave this place and never

look back. Wouldn't matter where I went, really, as long as I had a place of my own. But the rules of the Clan are iron-clad. Single women, the daughters of the soldiers, do not leave their parents unless they wed or die. In some cases, it's nearly the same thing. My father's a bit of a celebrity, having sired six daughters.

I start when I hear something crash to the floor in the other room. My heart slams in my chest when I hear my father's angry, drunken growls. They're closer to me than they normally are. In my sleepy haze, I wonder if I can find the ear plugs I bought at a concert I snuck into, before I realize they're still at the bottom of my bag somewhere.

I sit up straight in bed, wide awake. Though I can't hear every word, I catch phrases that make my thumping heart come to a stuttering stall.

"Only choice… wed to the McCarthys."

My mother cries, her response barely intelligible. "… gave them all away."

Did she… does she… actually have regrets about what they've done to her daughters?

I close my eyes and ball my hands into fists, pushing them into my eye sockets. I won't cry. *I won't.*

It doesn't matter that my father gave four of my sisters away to one of the men he worked with. Five, technically. Only one escaped, if you can call it that. My sister Emilie. On her wedding night, she took her own life.

It was after Emilie's death that my mother began to protest. Until then, I was convinced she was as complicit as he was. She spent his money with glee. Blood money, I called it, the money they earned from the marriages. I can't imagine the sizable sum Mack Martin, my father's chief, has paid for my sisters. Martin only had one daughter, who supposedly took her own life. Martin needed a ready supply of female virgins, like an ancient priest looking for children to sacrifice to the gods.

I've known since childhood that my future was in my father's hands, not mine.

But he let me go to uni. He let me get my degree. I'm not sure why, if he only planned to sell me off in the end.

I drown out my mother's cries and swing my legs to the side of the bed. I need to find out what's going on. I knew my time was coming, or I should've surmised it anyway.

I should've been paying closer attention.

I throw on a bathrobe and tiptoe to my doorway, my steps soundless on the thick, plush carpet. I open the door. Dermot, one of my guards, stands just outside. I hate him, but he'll prove useful right now. I make a hissing sound to catch his attention, and he looks my way. I crook a finger at him. A large, lumbering, ogreish sort, he moves with the elegance of an elephant and speaks mostly in grunts. I've wondered why my father gives him a gun. He'd be better suited with a club.

I whisper so softly I'm mouthing the words more than speaking them. He cups his ear as if to hear me better.

"What are they arguing about?" I whisper. "Tell me."

He gives me a lewd smile. "I know alright," he says. "But you ain't gettin' it for free."

My stomach coils with repulsion. I frown. "Fine," I hiss. "You know I'll pay up."

He grabs at his crotch, the filthy prick. It isn't money he wants. Bile rises in the back of my throat and I swallow hard, trying to weigh my options. I could find out from him, and pay my dues on my knees, or I could wait and try to find out myself.

I jump when I hear the sound of crashing glass. Frowning, I clutch at the door knob. My parents are reaching a rare level of brawling.

I release the tie at my robe, letting it fall open to reveal my bare shoulder, my breasts barely covered by a thin tank top, and watch as the ogre's eyes go half-lidded. He licks his lips and bends down to me, the smell of stale whiskey and body odor assaulting my senses. For Christ's sake, he's disgusting. I hold my breath and listen as he whispers.

"Supposedly, you're to wed the McCarthy scum."

I stand stock still as ice pulses through my veins. How could this man, who barely knows how to tie his own fucking shoes, know more than I do?

I keep my wits about me and swallow hard, ignoring the way the room sways a little.

"When?" I whisper.

"At the weekend."

It's Wednesday.

No.

I hear my mother sobbing and my father's screams.

Dermot is already unbuttoning his fucking trousers for

me to pay up, but I hardly see him. I see beyond them all, as my pathway's clear as still water.

I have to leave. I can't stay here. I won't allow myself to be given to the "McCarthy scum." I don't think of the repercussions, how I could be caught and how if I am, I'm certain to be severely punished. I don't think of where I'll go or how I'll get there. I've only one thought.

Fly.

I shut and lock the door behind us, ignoring the way his lewd eyes bulge when he drags his gaze down my robe. I fall to my knees on the carpet as he unbuckles his trousers, and his manky cock springs free. I don't care, though. He isn't getting a blow job tonight. Hell, when my father finds out what's happened, Dermot will pay in flesh. I've seen what my father can do to a man, and for once it gives me some consolation.

I pull off my robe and let it fall to the floor, not only to distract him but to make my escape that much easier. My mind churns, going over my options. Wearing nothing but a tank top and shorts won't work. I need to get clothes.

My parents scream on, my mother sobs, my father rails against her. But I drown it out as if it's white noise. They're dead to me. I've never been a daughter to them but a commodity. Even my looks and brains were assets to them.

Dermot, the fucking prick, strokes his cock and groans when I get to my knees. I quickly note what I need. His gun, still fastened in the holster that slumps to the floor, and his wallet, hanging out of his pocket and grazing the carpet.

"Tell me more," I whisper, needing every detail. "Tell me everything you know, and tonight I'll swallow."

He drags the head of his cock to my cheek. My stomach flips with nausea, but I've learned to detach myself, to move my mind beyond my circumstances.

"Will you now, you pretty little slut?" he groans.

I give him what I hope looks like a coy smile. "Not for free," I whisper, wagging my finger at him. "You know better than that."

"Mmm," he groans, stroking himself harder. I want to vomit. "Clan owes them a tribute, you see. Chief'll pay big for a virgin. Temporary truce between clans comes to an end at the weekend. 'Twas only in place to get you through uni."

How generous of them.

"When will they come?"

"Not sure," he says. "But ye won't come back. And Martin's complicated things." He says this last confession with a note of sadness in his voice, not because he'll miss me, but he won't be able to use me anymore.

"What do you mean?"

He shakes his head and doesn't answer. What's complicated?

I close my eyes and think of England, forming my plan while I draw him under a sex-filled spell, and when I've made my decision, I open my eyes. His eyes are closed, his head tipped back, his mouth open like a fish. I've got him right where I want him. I grip his hips and work his cock while I unbutton his holster.

I'm not turning back now. I know what I have to do.

I wait until my father and mother go for round two, and something smashes in the background, before I lift my head back and slam it straight into his hairy bollox.

He falls backward, astonished, his thick, ugly cock bobbing as he grabs for his balls. I bring my fist up and slam him right between the legs again. My aim is perfect.

With a curse and howl, he falls to his knees, but before he's recovered I've got his gun at his temple.

"Shut up," I tell him. I spit the taste of him onto the floor in front of me. He's still gripping his balls, but it's over now. I've got control, and he knows it. "You know I know how to use this gun, and I won't hesitate. Do exactly what I say, and I might let you live."

I couldn't kill a man, even a filthy loser like him, but he knows my father will. His only chance of survival is to do what I tell him. I lift the gun, then slam it to his temple. He crumples to the floor, still half-dressed. My father will find him like this. He won't live to see another sunrise.

I move quickly. I will not cry. *I will not cry.*

I take his wallet and open it. My heart gives a little leap. *Yes.* Must've won a bet or something, he's got a wad of cash, at least a hundred euros. I take the cash and toss the wallet to the side, quickly scurrying to my dresser. I take a bag out of my closet, listening closely to be sure my parents are still at it. By the time I pull the zipper on my bag, they're still going strong.

I take one long, last look at my childhood bedroom before I leave, but I don't feel what I should. No remorse. No sadness. If I'm honest, I'm actually a little relieved.

Dermot was my only guard tonight, so it's easy enough to sneak out of my room. I lock it from the outside. It'll buy me a little time. I creep down the hall, but as soon as I turn the corner, I hear voices.

I flatten myself against the wall, and swallow my breaths.

"Saturday," I hear. I focus, trying to identify the voice. Is it one of my dad's guards? A new one, maybe? I barely recognize it.

"Saturday. My mother can fight all she wants, but the plan's set in stone."

I cringe at the sound of my brother's voice. If he sees me, I'll be taken back to my room, punished, and locked up until the wedding.

"Which is it?"

"Middle brother."

"The big one?"

"Aye, the very same."

"The fat, manky son of a bitch ain't fairly matched to a lass like your sister."

I immediately conjure up an image of an overweight, crass bastard that looks like the man I left in my room with his pants around his knees.

No no no no no.

I won't. They can't make me. I don't care if I have to scavenge for food or clothes or a place to live. I'd rather be destitute than wed to a man I don't love. It's fucking modern-day slavery. I just have to get to England, and then I can easily blend into the masses of people there.

My heart pounds harder when I hear their voices come nearer. How will I explain the bag over my shoulder? The gun in my hand? Why I'm even out of bed in the middle of night like this? It isn't allowed.

They talk about how the wedding will commence, who will facilitate, but I don't care about what they say. They're talking of a wedding that will never happen. All I care about is the direction of their voices.

They come closer. I flatten myself and pray, trembling against the cold white wall. Then at the last second, one of them turns around.

"Son of a bitch," my brother says. "My father texted me. Says the Chief wants a late night meeting of all, here."

No.

That means that any moment, this hall will be filled with Martin soldiers, including my father. I tremble, listening to the sound of their fading voices, and as soon as I feel they're far enough out, I run.

My bag thumps on my leg and slips off my shoulder as I run, the gun pointed at the floor so I don't accidentally shoot someone. Though I know *how* to, I've never actually done it with real people involved.

A door behind me opens, and I hear more voices. The men are coming. They've heard the summons, and they're answering. I get to the end of the hall and head down the narrow staircase that leads to the main floor.

I'll leave by the kitchen exit. It's safest. Thankfully, the men are preoccupied with Martin's summons, for no one's nearby. I run so hard I get a stitch in my side, and I can hardly breathe. I get to the kitchen and yank open the door to the garage.

I come face to face with my brother Blaine.

He takes it all in in seconds, his instincts primed and ready. My startled expression. The gun in my hand. The bag on my shoulder. And just as recognition dawns on him and his gaze darkens, he reaches for me. With a scream, I pull the trigger. He howls and grabs at his shoulder. I'm astonished and nauseated when bright red blood stains the white t-shirt he wears. But I have to get away. I shove past him, run to my car that's thankfully at the very end of the driveway, yank open the door, and toss my bag in as the blare of gunshots ring out. In his anger, he's shooting after me.

My brother stumbles after me, leaving a bloody trail behind him, shouting, but they can't stop me now. The men are on their way to the meeting, so fewer guards are around than usual, and at least one is still hopefully incapacitated and arse-up on the floor of my room.

No one stops me. No one shoots at me. My brother shakes his fist from the garage, and reaches for his phone. My window is short, only inches of runway before me.

I fly.

Chapter 3

Cormac

MY MOTHER STANDS BESIDE ME, straightening my tie, before she pins a white rose on my lapel. She's got more gray in her red hair than she did last year, her eyes a bit sadder. But she's a strong woman, and she's ready to stand by our sides. Dressed in a lovely gown, she's ready to face the day.

"You look so handsome, Cormac," she says, with a wistful smile. "You all do. Your father would be proud."

He would be. I woke today knowing by tonight I'd be a married man. I'm ready to face whatever comes. No matter who she is. No matter how this turns out. I'll be the man of the house, as I've been taught.

"He'd be proud of many things," Keenan says. Normally a humble man, his chest fairly expands with pride as he tucks the wee baby wrapped in his arms, sound asleep and swaddled in a soft blue blanket, to his chest.

"Aye," mam says. "He would." She pats my chest, approving of the finishing touch. "How's Caitlin?"

"Very good," Keenan says. "I wanted to keep her home today, but she insisted she come, so I allowed it."

"Good girl," mam says. "She's a strong one, that woman of yours."

"Aye," Keenan says with a wry smile. "Says *someone* told her it's customary for the women of the Clan to greet the new woman."

"'Tis," mam says. She walks to Keenan and holds her arms out for the baby. She takes wee Seamus in her arms, my dad's namesake, and rocks him, though the lad's already asleep. "Caitlin'll be fine, son. She had a baby, not open heart surgery."

Keenan's gaze darkens. "You say that as if it's nothing."

She smiles. "I wouldn't say *nothing*, but your lass is made of sterner stuff. She'll want to be there, and I bet she'll come looking pretty as can be."

Keenan doesn't let mam butter him up, but only grunts.

"Who's a good little boy," she croons to the sleeping baby. "Who knows his Granny?" The worry lines often knit between Keenan's brows soften a bit, and for the first time since the idea about my wedding came about, I look forward to it.

I'm to take a wife and raise a family. I'm ready for the job.

I scrub a hand across my brow, trying to shake off the night before. Boner and Tully, led by Nolan, came to my room and half-dragged me off to the pub for several rounds. My last night as a bachelor, they said. Keenan joined us.

"She'll be a virgin, ya lucky wanker," Boner said. "Fancy that tight, virgin cunt?" I cuffed him good, but the rest of the men guffawed.

"And she's a pretty lass, to boot," Nolan said.

"She'll be *my* pretty virgin, lads," I told them. "I'll thank you to keep your manky eyes off her."

"The feckin' Martins, though," Tully groaned. "Christ but I hate them."

We sobered at that. I'm not happy the damned Martins will be my in-laws. They're the lowliest of Irish mob life, the bottom dwellers. There isn't a crime they won't commit for money.

Keenan came to my side of the table. "You're doing the right thing," he said. "Though I don't envy you. I want you to know I appreciate it, brother. What you're doing for the good of the Clan. I won't forget it, Cormac."

"Aye, brother," I told him. "It's the right choice."

And it is. Peace between the Clans matters. It fucking matters.

"Are you ready?" he asks.

"Aye." As ready as I can be.

"It'll right in the end."

"It will."

Our father was the old-fashioned sort, and he raised his sons to be the heads of house. We lead an army of criminals, the strongest, most well-respected crime ring in all of Ireland. We don't quail in the face of duty. We do what we must and rule with conviction.

But we take care of our women. Our duty above all is to family, and the women of The Clan never want for anything.

I will learn who my wife is. I will teach her who *I* am. I will take care of her and do my duty by her. No matter what it takes.

Our caravan of sleek, black cars waits in the drive for us. When we arrive home after the ceremony, Keenan arranged for us to occupy the west wing, on the opposite side of the house to him and Caitlin. All week, our staff has been moving my belongings and preparing for my bride.

I bought flowers, and a few other things. Some jewelry. New throw pillows for my furniture. Seemed girly I suppose.

Lube and a riding crop, gifted by my Clan brothers. I shoved them to the back of my dresser.

The Martin estate's a good twenty minute drive from our house overlooking the craggy cliffs of Ballyhock.

"Nervous, lad?" Nolan asks good-naturedly.

"Nah." It's the truth. I've nothing to be nervous about. "Why be nervous? I've a duty to fill, no more, no less."

"You've got a sweet virgin cunt to fill," he says with a wag of his eyebrows.

I can't help but snicker. "That, too. Now skive off. You

say another word about my wife's cunt, and I'll beat the crap out of you," I promise good-naturedly. I mean it, though, and he knows it.

"Aye," Nolan says with a sober nod. "Fair, brother."

But when we pull up to the Martin estate, I can tell something's off. By Nolan's frown, he can, too.

"You boys see what I do?" Keenan says, sitting up straighter.

I stifle a growl. "Aye."

Though there's a white tent set up on the front lawn, there are no decorations, no entertainment prepared to celebrate. No food, or flowers, or *people*. "For fuck's sake, something's rotten in the state of Denmark, isn't it?" Nolan says.

I clench my fists but don't reply. Of the three of us, I'm the one that's slowest to anger, but I feel it now, coiled in my gut like a snake ready to strike. A part of me hopes her brother had something to do with whatever's fucked up. I'd love an excuse to knock his fucking teeth out.

Our car comes to a stop, and I get out first, followed by Nolan and Keenan.

No one comes to greet us.

This is crap. This isn't how things should go. They expected us. Today was the day we were to solidify our connections and move from temporary truce to peace between the Clans.

Did the Martins fool us?

Keenan gives me a tight-lipped smile as he walks

beside me on my left, and Nolan on my right. We step in sync, soldiers come to claim and conquer.

"Mack Martin had one fucking chance to keep this truce," I say. If he doesn't hand me my bride today, our Clans will war.

Men will die.

Keenan growls but doesn't respond. He was the one who allowed this truce, and I wonder if he regrets that now. What have they done in the interim? Have they set us up? He turns to face the guard and Boner, signaling they wait with his hand in the air. He snaps his fingers and gives Tully a nod. He wants them ready if the Martins ambush. Tully lifts his chin to the men opposite him, and the air ripens with men ready to war.

When I walk up the stone steps, the front door opens.

"Welcome, gentleman." Mack Martin stands at the top of the stairs. The rest of our Clan follows behind us. My father may have been older, but he was a man suitable for leading his men into battle: fit, sharp, and astute. Mack Martin's doughy face and heavy jowls speak more to indulgence and laziness than leadership. I don't bother to hide my disdain when I reach the top step. I scowl at him and don't respond to his greeting.

"Martin," Keenan says. The men shake hands, then I offer mine. Martin winces at my firm grip.

Christ.

"Come in, come in," he says, a sheen of perspiration dotting his forehead. His eyes dart around us and behind us, quickly surveying our army of soldiers. They're clad in formal wear, but all are armed and ready to strike at the first order from Keenan, and Martin knows it. The truce is up. He either delivers or he's fucked.

Three large, burly men stand beside Martin and glare at us. By Clan law, they're not allowed to strike. Martin's in the wrong. I don't even bother to look at them.

"Come, boys, come," he says, gesturing for us to follow him to his office. "Have a drink, will you?"

"No." He startles at my response, turning to look at me sharply.

"I didn't come for a drink, Martin," I warn him. "I came for a fucking bride. What are you playing at here?"

He clears his throat and mops a hand across his brow, when one of his men opens his office door and welcomes us in. I sweep his office quickly, noting the large plate-glass windows behind the L-shaped desk, and the ample supply of whiskey and tumblers on a side table. The stale, acrid smell of cigars lingers in the air.

I wait until he turns to face us.

None of us sit. We stand as one to face our rival.

"Answer me, Martin."

"Well, you see," Martin begins, twisting his hands in front of him. "A few nights ago, the girl, well she—" he pauses, as if searching for the right word, then with a sigh, he states the truth. "She left. Escaped, as it were. And we haven't been able to find her."

Nolan curses, his hands fisting by his side. I take a step

toward Martin myself, but Keenan's voice makes me stop. He's the one that will orchestrate what we do next. We need answers.

"A few nights ago?" Keenan asks in a dangerous, cold voice. "And you haven't sent word to us until now?"

Martin shakes his head. "I—well I—you know, she—I was certain we'd find her by now."

"Certain," Keenan repeats.

I take a step forward. "Where is she?"

Martin flinches, but his eyes flash at me like a cornered rodent's. "If I knew, she'd be here, lad, wouldn't she? Hmm?"

I want to grab that tie around his neck and twist it until his face reddens and his eyes bulge.

"You know what this means, Martin," I say in a low voice. Warning.

His lips thin. He winces while he answers, "I do."

"We've our strike force with us," I tell him. But hell, I don't want to war. Both his men and ours will die in battle, and I love my men like brothers.

"I could... I'm going to... well, I can offer another tribute," he says.

Jesus, Mary, and Joseph. Does he have a fucking breeding ground?

"Just listen, boys," he pleads.

He has the fucking gall to call us *boys* as if he's a smarmy headmaster and he's called us into his office to pat our heads?

"Yes?" Keenan asks. I turn to face him. Martin knew about my bride's absence for four fucking days. How are we to trust him?

She left. The girl *left*. Does she know what she did by leaving? How she's brought death and destruction to both her family and mine? Does she know what's at stake if we don't solidify our truce?

"Yes," Martin repeats, his eyes widening. "A bit younger, though."

A knock at his door interrupts us, and before he can answer, the door swings open. My stomach tightens when I recognize the man who walks through, with his puffy face and beady, cruel eyes. The very same one who pulled a knife on my brother, the fucking bastard. He doesn't look at us, his gaze steady on Martin. I note his reddened nose when he swipes his hand across it. His hand shakes. Fucking coke.

"I found her. I brought her back."

I tighten, holding myself back with effort. I saw how he touched that woman at the club. I witnessed his cruelty. If he touched one goddamn hair on my future wife's head, fuck the goddamn truce. I'll break every finger in his hands.

Martin sighs in relief. I watch as he takes a step forward and his eyes narrow, flashing with a maniacal glee, as if he can't wait to get his hands on her himself . "Good work, good work, Blaine. Where is she now?"

"She's in holding. But I'm warning you, if you let her go through with this wedding—"

My body tightens. The fucking audacity of him.

"Enough." Martin's eyes are wide with fury, his nostrils flaring. "Not another word of warning from you. I told you why I've made this choice and I didn't ask your opinion."

Keenan and I share a curious look but say nothing.

Blaine fumes. "Fine. You'll bring wrath upon our entire clan." He twitches, his face contorting. He's high as a fucking kite.

What the hell's he going on about? *Not* marrying will bring wrath upon his clan.

He drags his eyes to me, his gaze boring into mine with raw hatred. "Yer the feckin' groom, aren't you? Let's make this clear. I won't have her bringing war to the fucking clans. She'll be punished for this before she's presented to you." He spits out *you* like it's distasteful. "Could be the only way to stop what will happen."

I take an involuntary step toward him, but stop when Keenan grabs my arm.

"She will," Martin says, his nostrils flaring. "Severely. She can't put everything at risk without consequence. We have to make an example of her."

His placating demeanor vanishes, and for the first time since we came here, I see the mask of the ruthless leader, the man who'd kill you as soon as he'd look at you. "I'll see to it."

The fuck they will.

They're well within their rights, by Clan law, to punish her before she marries me, to show both their allegiance to us and their adherence to Clan law. But the very thought of this man, or any of them, touching my future wife, sends savage, wild fury ripping through me.

I make my decision, and as soon as I do, I know it's the right one. Keenan will back me up.

"Aye," I say. I don't even recognize my own voice, as if someone else has taken over my body and held back the demon that wants to spill the blood of the Martins.

Keenan and Nolan look at me. It's my call now. I'm the one who's to wed her. "She ought to be punished," I agree. And I mean it. Keenan nods in agreement.

"She brought us to the brink of war." I shake my head. Silence hangs in the room while they listen. "But I'll forgive your transgression against us on one condition, Martin."

He raises an eyebrow. Unblinking. Nolan and Keenan tense.

"*I'm* the one who'll punish her."

Martin sputters, but he seems at a loss for words. Nolan's lips quirk up, likely seeing the promise in this plan, and Keenan nods approvingly. "It's fair, Martin," he says.

I don't want their filthy hands on her. She belongs to me now, and soon she'll bear my name and ring.

If she's mine to take, she's mine to punish.

Martin looks relieved, not even hesitating when he issues his command.

"Show him where she is."

Chapter 4

Aileen

"Let me go, you arsehole!" I kick my legs and manage to wriggle myself out of the grasp of the fucking henchman holding me. He curses when my heel kicks him in the crotch, but as soon as I'm free, another one grabs me.

"You bitch," he says through clenched teeth. "If you were any other fucking wench I'd split your lip open."

"Come at me, then," I say. "Fucking do it. Make me as ugly as you can before you drag me before my future husband. I'm sure he'll be grateful."

His eyes narrow from his crouched position, but he doesn't respond. The man holding me does, though. His grip slackens. They know I've struck a chord. If they deliver me to my future husband as spoiled goods, they'll regret it. I think I've finally gained some traction, when a cold, hard voice sounds behind me.

"Selfish and arrogant, just like the rest of them. Don't even know the fucking trouble you've caused."

I close my eyes as cold fear sweeps through me. I'd know Blaine's voice anywhere.

The rest of them. My other sisters.

Granted privileges from birth, Blaine was taught that women are substandard, that men are the ones in power. He mimics the disrespect shown my mother and sisters by my father, and when he came of age, he pleased my father by leaving a long line of abused women in his wake.

I turn to face him. When he smiles, the black spaces where he's missing teeth give him an appearance of a ghoul, something macabre and terrifying. He inherited my father's thick, heavy eyebrows and tiny eyes, deeply embedded in his heavy face. I try to be brave, but this is the man who once kicked a puppy to death for stealing his dinner. That's all I am to him. Another animal who's threatened his belly.

He stalks toward me, and I glance quickly behind him. Will my father come, too? Will they punish me together? For the first time, real fear claws at my insides, and I feel as if I'm going to be sick.

"You haven't won, you spoiled brat," my brother says with a sickening grin. "We've brought you here for your punishment, and when we're finished with you, you're marrying the bastard McCarthy."

I look quickly about me for a means to escape, the need to flee an instinct I can't quench. But there's nowhere to go. We're in a windowless room, the walls thick and impenetrable. The floor's cold, charcoal-gray concrete. There's a small, plain wooden table in the center of the room and two chairs. They're both sturdy and thick, but the one closest to me sends a shudder through me when I see the metal handcuffs attached to it. In the opposite corner of the room stands a pole with sturdy rings above it. I shake, my mind easily conjuring up a prisoner strung up to be punished.

Like me.

I've never been to this room before, but I can imagine it's the setting for wicked, torturous things.

I can't escape, but I can delay.

"Will you, then? So brave of you, half a dozen armed men against one defenseless woman. How noble."

"Shut it," Blaine snaps. I don't, of course. I have no weapon, but I have my tongue.

"I bet the little sluts you fuck think you're quite the knight in shining armor, don't they?"

"*Shut it.*"

But I won't. I don't want him in control. I want to unnerve him, unsettle him.

"No. Fuck you. You're a bully, that's what you are. No more than a—"

I know I've struck a nerve when he flinches, he rears back, and before I can turn from him, his fist connects with my cheekbone. Pain explodes across my face, and too late I lift my hands to defend myself. He grabs my arms, knees me in the stomach, and shoves me to the ground. He leaves me wheezing, gasping for air.

"Fuck," he growls. "He's coming. Lift her up!"

Who's coming? I'm in a pain-filled daze as they drag me to my feet, the sound of hefty footsteps fall just outside the door. Foreboding gathers in my belly. If it's my father, I'm going to be sick.

The thick door swings open. I don't want to look at him so I look to the floor. Thick heavy black boots enter the room.

This is not my father. He's much bigger, and broader, though he's masked and wearing all black. I try to decipher who he is, but there's none in my father's company so tall, with such wide shoulders.. He's got the body of a boxer, muscled and powerful, but he doesn't remind me of anyone I've met before, and I've met all in my father's company. I was raised among these men. Have they brought in a stranger to punish me?

This man could lift me up with one hand. I can almost picture it, being held in the air while I dangle from his fist like a helpless kitten. I swallow hard when he stands in the doorway, his hands on his hips. I can't see his eyes because of the mask, but I imagine he's glaring.

"Leave us," he thunders, in a deep, rugged voice I don't recognize.

When no one moves at first, he grows impatient. "*Now!*"

As they flee like scattering ants, he points one large, masculine finger my way. "Except you. You stay *right. There.*"

Great. I'm to be left alone with a huge, powerful, masked stranger. I'm not sure this option is much better than being left in the hands of my father. Then I remember what my brother said.

This is the man who's come to punish me.

My stomach drops, my heart racing. I don't realize I'm backing away from him until my back hits the cold, hard wall behind me. I gulp in air, panic rising in my chest when he shuts and locks the heavy door. He carries a black bag in his hand I didn't notice when I first saw him. He drops it onto the table.

Turning to face me, he crosses his arms on his chest. The overhead light casts an eerie glow on him. Though he's masked, I get a brief glimpse of his eyes through the holes. His eyes are green. Unblinking. Flinty.

I turn my face away from him, hidden in shadow. His eyes roam over my body. I must look a sight. My clothing is torn and ragged, my hair tangled and matted. When I escaped just a few days ago, I hid like a vagabond. I couldn't risk them finding me. But I should've known better. The Irish mob has eyes in every pub, every city, every hiding place in Ireland. I never even made it to the border.

He breaks the silence with his steely, hard voice. "Do you know what you've done?"

"Other than botch up my escape? No."

He holds my gaze another minute. "You've brought the clans to the brink of war. Do you know what that means?"

"War? Yes. Sheltered though I've been, I've read a bit of history."

The green eyes narrow. His muscles flex.

"Tell me."

I clear my throat. "It means that... people will... fight," I say, feeling like a child before a jury, woefully inept and silly.

He nods. "That's right. People will fight. People will kill." His voice lowers. "People will die."

"Right." I swallow hard. "If you've come to punish me, I would appreciate it if you could just... get it over with and spare me the lecture."

"Get it over with?" he repeats in his husky voice. "Are you that blasé about being punished?"

I wish he wasn't masked. I'd like to read his expression right now.

Swallowing hard, I don't answer. I'm suddenly dizzy with nerves.

I can handle pain. I've withstood it many times. But I hate the anticipation of something terrible. I'd rather face it already.

He unfolds his arms, crooks one large finger at me, his voice a low, dangerous purr.

"Come here."

I don't have a choice, do I? I walk to him on wobbly legs, shaking as he watches every step. When I reach him, the light reflects in his green eyes. Still stern. Still immovable. But there's something more in those depths now. Curiosity?

"It would go well for you if you do exactly what I say."

I nod. "You're about twice my size and have a bag of

weapons. It would be rather foolish of me to try anything else."

"It was rather foolish of you to run away."

I clench my jaw and don't answer. He has a point, goddammit.

Wordlessly, he reaches for my wrists and shackles them in his strong fingers. Holding me in his tight grip, he looks to the post with the rings above it, then to the table and shakes his head, as if dismissing the notion. Not the post, then. If he weren't so strong, I might feel relieved. I'm sure that thing's a whipping post.

"Right, then," he mutters. "You'll lay over the table."

I balk, my mouth slackening as I stare at him.

"Excuse me?" I whisper. It hadn't occurred to me he could violate me in this room. Bent over the table, he could rape me easily.

"You have thirty seconds," he says. "Or I'll do it for you."

"My future husband will not be pleased with this, you know," I say, my words tight with anger. "I'm to be married after I'm punished." A lump forms in my throat at the prospect of my impending humiliation.

"I'm not going to fuck you. I'm going to flog you."

I shudder.

He glances at his watch. "Twenty more seconds."

I don't bother to wipe the tears that stream down my cheeks. I'm not trying to appease or persuade him. If I grin and bear it, as the saying goes, he doesn't win. He might beat me, but he won't take my pride.

I stalk to the table, flop my body down on it, and close my eyes. Embracing my anger. If I wear it like a cloak, he can't hurt me. Nothing lasting, anyway.

I'm shaking, my body trembling against the cool table, splayed out like this... like an offering. I listen for the sound of something, the tug of the zipper on his bag, something at all that will indicate how he's to punish me. But all I hear is his voice.

"You've earned this for what you've done. Your reckless, thoughtless decision endangered the lives of countless. What do you have to say for yourself?"

Must he lecture so?

Anger is my weapon and friend.

"Fuck. *You*."

Crack.

The blistering pain sears me.

"Silence now."

I grit my teeth. Did he strike me with his... hand?

"If you want me to be silent, don't ask me questions."

Crack. He lands another blow, then another, until he's given me so many hard, blistering swats, I lose count. I whimper, biting my tongue. I'm an idiot to mouth off to a man his size, who's got everything from power and strength to weapons on his side.

I gasp when his rough, toughened hand caresses my inflamed backside, and he leans his heavy, muscled body against me so he can whisper in my ear. His rumbling voice makes me shiver.

"I've been sent in here to punish you before I deliver you to your future husband. I won't mark you. I won't deliver damaged goods. But I want this to make a good impression. You're to obey your future husband. Consider this your first lesson."

I still. It's an odd thing for someone sent by Martin to punish me to say.

Did the rival Clan send him to me, then?

A terrible, alarming thought resurfaces.

Will he rape me as punishment?

But no... no, he can't. My future husband expects a virgin. We were never allowed even unsupervised dates as teens, and my father was adamant: his daughters would stay untouched until they married. It wasn't until he married off my oldest sister that I knew why.

My new husband will have to take my virginity... Still, I'm not safe here.

Why did he send the others away? Does he mean to violate me?

And then I hear it, the sound I've been dreading, the whirr of a zipper. Oh, God, he's going to fuck me.

"If you rape me, my future husband will kill you."

He doesn't respond.

I look to the side and breathe out in relief. It wasn't his zipper but the bag's.

My relief is short-lived when I hear the clink of metal. I

grip the table and grit my teeth, preparing myself mentally for what's going to happen. I've withstood worse. I likely may still. I can do this. And then pain explodes and my mind erases with the first excruciating crack of something against my skin.

I cry out in pain, but I can't get away. I twist and writhe, but his firm hand on my lower back holds me in place, delivering one wicked blow after another. I can't think beyond the pain, and even my breath seems frozen in space and time as I drown in pain. He's lecturing, the fucker, prattling on and on about orders and rules and war and blah blah blah, but I can't process a thing he says. My world is agony.

He strikes me over, and over, but never in the same place, whatever he's using to punish me is thin and supple, because it's on my legs, it's on my arse, he's dragging it across my throbbing skin. I gasp for air when he pauses. Has he given me momentary reprieve?

"Why are you being punished?"

Goddamn it, the lecture again.

"I left," I gasp. I lay still. I'm in too much pain for a snarky reply now.

His hand comes to my lower back. "Very good. And why must you never do such a thing again?"

"Because I'm..." I can't speak, my throat suddenly clogged with unexpected emotion. I swallow hard. I don't mean to defy him. It would be foolish to do so on purpose, not when I'm vulnerable like this. He asked a question and expects an answer. So I push myself to speak through tears. "Because I have no choice in this."

Unbidden tears splash on the table.

"That's right," he says, and I don't know if it's my imagination, but is that sympathy I hear? A softening to his tone?

"Easy for you to say," I say, angry tears rolling down my cheeks. But to my surprise, he doesn't strike me again but pauses.

"Oh? Is it? You know nothing about me, and yet you believe it's easy for me to say?"

"You're a woman with no freedom?" I ask, turning my head to look over my shoulder at him. He stands behind me, holding some sort of wicked-looking black rod in his huge hand.

He scowls at me. I continue.

"You're to be married to a monster?" For the second time, I wish he didn't have a mask, that I could see his reaction.

"Quiet," he snaps. "This is punishment, not negotiation." And holding my eyes with his, he lifts his arm back, before swinging the whistling tool through the air. I cringe and yelp. God, but it fucking hurts. I'm a fool to snap at him when he wields a weapon against me, but sometimes I can't shut my mouth.

There's no more talking, then, and at least I'm grateful he's stopped the damn lecture. He holds me in place and whips me again, until nothing in my world is in focus but blistering, heated pain.

I'm not sure when he stops. I'm not conscious of the

moment the pain ceases. I'm panting, sliding on the table now wet with tears and perspiration.

His voice is hard and sharp when he addresses me. "Have you learned your lesson?"

"Yes," I say through clenched teeth.

"Very well, then. I'll tell Martin you've been thoroughly punished."

I lay where I am, prepared for him to take a picture or take some such mortifying record of my humiliation, but he doesn't.

It's over. The brutality of it is over, anyway.

"Come here."

Again, the order. I push myself off the table, my body throbbing in pain and discomfort, as I turn to look at him.

His eyes narrow when he looks at me, before he reaches a hand to my face. His fingers are large and rough but his touch gentler than I expect. Cupping my chin, he stares and rubs a thumb lightly over my cheek. On instinct, I flinch, which makes him growl.

"Who did this to you?" he asks.

"What? Who did what?" I don't know what he's talking about. Does he wonder who's made me balk at the touch of a man who just punished me?

"*This*," he says through gritted teeth, pointing to my eye.

I lift my hand gingerly upward and feel the swollen, tender skin.

Oh.

"I'm assuming I'm bruised?"

"Aye," he growls. "Got a fucking black eye." Does he fear my future husband will think he's done this to me?

"I'll... I'll tell the man I'm to marry you weren't the one who did this."

Why do I feel the need to defend him? Why?

He glares at me. My response didn't placate him at all, apparently.

"*Who did this?*" he repeats.

It's almost as if... he's angry I'm hurt? Why would that anger him, when he's just whipped me, humiliated me, and my body still throbs in pain?

I don't respond.

"Your father?" He asks. I shake my head.

"Mack Martin?"

I shake my head again.

He tenses. "Your brother?" When I don't respond, he curses. "Fucking Blaine." He mutters something under his breath I don't catch.

He knows him, then. Of course he does.

"Let's go," he says, his gaze still implacable, his tone still granite.

He takes out his cell phone.

"The lass has paid her dues," he says. "We move on as planned."

I look at him strangely. Something is odd about this. Something is off.

Who is this mysterious stranger? I don't know enough about the Clan to know who they send as executioner or punisher, who their strike force may be. It's unnerving.

The men left, though. They weren't surprised by his presence at all. And the men of the Clan, especially my brother, would not have left unless ordered to do so.

"Who are you?" I ask him. I need to know. I imagine my future husband sent someone out to do his dirty work for him. Will this be someone I'll share residence with? A mate of his? Maybe he'll think it fun sport to share me with his brothers. I cringe to think of what awaits me next.

I expect he'll ignore me, but he doesn't. Instead, says in a low voice, "You'll see soon enough. Come with me."

Chapter 5

Cormac

I WANT to marry this woman now. I want to take her with me, make her mine, carry her away to my home in Ballyhock. Away from the men who hold her prisoner. Away from Martin and his filthy, conniving band of manky sons of bitches.

If her brother shows his motherfucking face, I'll make him lose the few teeth he has remaining before I slit his thick, meaty throat. Happily.

She's learned her lesson, I've no doubt. I reckon she'll remember the way she squirmed under the cane I wielded. Christ knows I won't forget it. For the first time since we've started all this, I'm grateful for the fucking duty I have to fulfill. I'm eager to claim the beautiful, innocent girl for my own.

And she is a fucking girl, her virginal body untouched. It's a requirement for any arranged marriage between

Clans, of course. But now that I've seen her, now that I've glimpsed her luscious curves and milky white skin, I long to take her beneath me, to fully claim the lass as mine.

She's nine years my junior. The first time I took a man's life, she was still in fucking grade school. But it's no matter. Age is just a number for anybody. It's even truer in families like ours, when social norms and expectations are shite.

I can imagine her smooth, soft skin beneath my palm, covered by thin fabric when I braced my hand on her lower back, when I wielded the cane on her upturned arse. I can still hear her soft cries, still feel her flinch in pain when the rod connected.

I whipped her soundly, and I'd do it again if I had to. And now something deep inside me wants to make it better. To wipe her tears and soothe the pain.

I wonder how she'll react when she realizes who her punisher is.

I take her hand and lead her to where my men wait in silence. I've got to give her credit. She holds her head high, unblinking, though she winces a bit when she walks.

"Where are we going?" she asks.

"To meet your future husband, lass. You're to be married now. Thought you knew that."

"Like *this*?"

She gestures to her mangled clothing with her one free hand, the other pinned firmly in my grasp on her wrist.

I shrug. "That's not part of my job. Though I reckon someone'll fix you up first."

We walk in silence for another moment before she asks another question.

"Do you know my husband?"

"Aye."

She swallows hard. "You work with him, then."

I don't respond.

"Is he... is he an evil man?"

Christ, the way she feigns bravery but can't mask her shaky voice raises my ire. What have the fucking Martins told her about me? But I want to see what she's made of.

"They're all evil, aren't they?" I say truthfully. "You're talking fucking mafia."

She swallows hard. "I know, but..." her voice trails off as if she's trying to collect her thoughts. "I thought... it's just that... well, some are more evil than others."

She isn't wrong.

We both grow silent as we go up a flight of stairs. I was told to bring her to the library when we were finished. At the very top, we're greeted by two of Martin's brainless, beefy henchmen. They wear suits, their weapons drawn, both parked at either side awaiting us. They don't acknowledge us at all but stand stock still.

"You don't recognize them," she says. "They didn't greet you. You're with the McCarthys, then."

She doesn't miss much. Very observant.

Martin greets us when we enter the hall, his voice tight and controlled. "She's been punished, then?" he asks, his voice laced with utter disdain, as if he wishes he could have hurt her himself. Fucking bastard.

"Thoroughly."

A muscle clenches in his jaw. He sweeps his eyes over to her. "Good," he says. He looks at her as if she's distasteful, pursing his lips and grimacing. "She ought to remember her place now."

"Aye," I growl.

I look over Martin's shoulder to see Keenan standing, his eyes narrowed on Martin. "Hand her to me. I'll see to it she's brought to the ceremony and waits for her betrothed."

I push her toward him, I'm that eager to get him away from Martin. She stumbles, and I take a step toward her to steady her. I right her. Martin's narrowed, beady eyes watch my every move.

"I'll be sure she—" Martin begins, but Keenan already has her, chastely holding her elbow and taking her toward the exit. He's the one in charge now. Not Martin.

"Your husband will be arriving shortly," Keenan says. "You'll be cleaned up before you're presented to him."

Aileen still holds her head high. She doesn't make eye contact with Keenan, or Martin, or any of the other soldiers who stand and witness her being handed off, but keeps her gaze transfixed, her eyes on something in the distance. I tear myself away, turning back to a changing room on the main floor where I've left my clothing.

Though I stepped in to be sure that none of *them* touched her, she'll know I was the man who whipped her. And part of me is pleased at that.

After I dress, I go to the large room where both my men and the Martins are assembled. A small area's been prepared for us to take our vows. My mother waits at the front, standing beside Caitlin, but she doesn't meet my eyes. Not yet. I wonder if she knows what I did today.

Minutes pass. No Aileen. Though logically I know she's likely being prettied up by her mother or other clan women, I won't rest easy until I see her again. Until I cart her home and make her mine. Until I get her off this godforsaken property and onto mine.

I find Keenan at the front, beside Father Finn, our parish priest and today's presider. My father's younger brother, he's aged in recent months, his gray hair thinner, his eyes lined with wrinkles.

Keenan nods to me. "She's a brave one, Cormac," Keenan says. "I'll give her that."

"She headstrong and wily as well."

His lips twitch. "Aye. You'd do well not to lose that cane."

I snort, grateful for a chance to laugh. Today's been bullshite. "Aye."

"Lucky bastard," Nolan says out of the side of his mouth, standing beside Keenan.

I grunt at him, silencing him. "The girl's to be my wife in minutes. Shut yer fucking gob."

His eyes twinkle, but he obliges by shutting his fucking gob.

I tap my foot and check my watch. Five minutes. Ten minutes.

Fifteen fucking minutes.

Martin's getting restless, pacing near the cluster of chairs opposite the podium where Father Finn waits.

"Where the fuck is she?" I ask out of the side of my mouth.

"They're gettin' her pretty's all," Keenan says, but the grooves on his forehead furrow.

"Who'd you give her to?" I ask.

"Her mam," Keenan says. "Relax."

One of Martin's men suddenly turns, yanks the handle of the door, and leaves. I look to Keenan, then Nolan. What the fuck is that about?

When we've waited twenty-five minutes, I've had enough.

"Bring her, Martin." He jumps at the sound of my voice and swivels to look at me from his pacing. "I don't fucking care if she's ready or not."

"She's coming," he says. "Stay patient."

"I'm fresh out of patience."

Several of his men stiffen, and one has the nerve to touch the butt of his pistol.

"Keep your goddamn knickers on," I tell them. "I'm not going to kill him. Not yet, anyway. But I came here for a reason, and I've no more patience. If you don't—"

The door swings open. The room falls into silence. An older woman appears in the doorway. I wonder if this can be Aileen's mam. She looks older than Aileen, of course, her blonde hair silvery gray at the temples. And like her daughter, she sports a fucking bruise I can see even beneath her makeup.

Goddamn motherfucking Martins. We're ruthless men, and I won't deny that. We're not above disciplining a lass in our charge. Clearly. But goddamn it, my father would've castrated a man who abused a woman in our company, and Keenan would do the same. We were taught to respect our mam, to respect women, to provide for and take care of them.

Never, *never* to abuse them.

"We're ready," she says, turning to face me. "You're her betrothed, are you?"

I don't trust this woman. There's something about her that's slippery, like she's donned this demeanor just for me.

"Aye."

She takes in a deep breath, then releases it, when a voice I recognize comes from behind her.

"Can we skip the formalities and get this over with?"

For one brief moment, so brief I almost miss it, the woman's eyes turn snakelike, her lips thin, and her nostrils flair. "Of course, dear," she says. "Come in."

I stop thinking for a moment. I can't reason or speak.

Aileen's entered the room, and she's fucking stunning. Clad in a dress with lace and pearls, it hugs her svelte figure, accentuating her curves and beauty. Her golden hair's tucked up onto her head in little ringlets, a few fetching curls gracing her forehead, and a small veil of sorts is pinned to her curls.

This is no radiant bride, though. Her jaw's clenched, her eyes are narrowed, and her cheeks are bright pink with anger. She clutches a cluster of white flowers between her hands so tightly, they're bruised and broken. She's here begrudgingly. She'd likely rather be literally anywhere else on the planet.

I stand up taller and look toward her, unblinking. It doesn't matter. None of this does. She will be my wife by law. She will learn to follow the rules.

Moving her blazing gaze from Martin to his men, she swivels her eyes on me.

It's almost comical, how she tips her head to the side with curiosity, the anger vanishing as she stares at me.

What is she thinking? What does she see?

Does she recognize me from the room? Soon enough, she'll know I was the man who meted out her punishment. I'd rather her know sooner than later. If she's to be my wife, I want her to fear me. I want her to know what to expect if she misbehaves. I want her to know her place.

But my patience is gone. I'm not playing a nice guy, and I want to leave.

I snap my fingers and point to the ground in front of me. "I've waited long enough. Come here."

She purses her lips and glares at me. Does the little vixen plan on defying me? In front of a room full of men, like this?

She'll regret that decision.

But she isn't given a choice, as her mother grabs her arm and half-drags her toward me.

"So sorry to keep you waiting, Mr. McCarthy," she says in a sickeningly sweet voice. "Had to pretty her up, you see. Isn't she lovely?"

"Lovely," I repeat through clenched teeth. "Let her go."

She releases her as if she's on fire, fairly pushing her my way. Aileen stumbles in front of me, but I quickly grab her arms and right her, dragging her in front of me, my fingers so tight on her arms she winces.

"Look in my eyes," she hisses. "Hold my gaze."

I don't take orders from her, so I look toward Father Finn. He knows the way of the Clan. He doesn't flinch at the roughness in my tone or firmness of my grasp, but pulls out his book and begins the ceremony.

"Look at me," she repeats. While Father recites the opening prayer, I hiss out of the side of my mouth.

"Don't order me again."

"It's your voice. It *is*. It's *you*."

She's caught on quicker than I expected.

"You were the one who took me in that room," she says. "You have the nerve to—"

My grip tightens. "Be quiet, woman."

She fumes in silent fury until it's time to state her

vows. She mutters her way through them, and I mutter my way through mine. I don't even hear the applause that surrounds us, as blood thunders in my ears. I'm only dimly aware of people standing and cheering around us.

"Home," I order. *"Now."*

It's time I made the acquaintance of my wife beyond what I've already done.

"The car's waiting," Keenan says.

Her mother's greedy eyes light up with excitement, and her father gives me a grim smile. For all he knows, he just sold his daughter to the devil, and all he cares about is how much money Martin pays.

Despicable.

I gather her up, satin and lace and pearls and all, and lift her in my arms. I don't want to fight with her. I've claimed this woman. I've done what I came here to do. Now I want to leave with her and never look back.

"Put me down," she says, but it's likely only a protest she feels she needs to make or can't help, because she's bright enough to know that isn't happening.

My men begin to disperse, heading to their vehicles. I'm grateful now there will be no reception. No celebration. This was a business meeting. No more, no less.

I'm heading to the door when I feel someone grab my arm. I turn in surprise to see my mother. Her usually-gentle gray eyes look flinty, and her grip on my arm is firmer than necessary.

"Cormac." She spits the words out, her tone one I

haven't heard since I was a lad. She's pissed at me. I'm pissed that she's pissed. For Christ's sake.

I grunt in reply, still holding my tight-lipped, stunningly beautiful wife, who might as well be an ice queen.

"Put her down."

"No." The time for my mother to instruct me has long since gone.

"A *word* with you, son."

"Aye, but you'll speak to me in front of my wife, or not at all." A part of me's afraid if I put her down, she'll run.

Keenan grunts behind me, reminding me to watch my tone.

"She's a slight thing but no feather, mam," I tell her. My wife curses in protest, kicking her legs, and tries to get down, but I don't allow it.

"Be gentle," my mother chides me. "Please, son. Just because she's yours, doesn't mean that—"

"Mam." I shake my head at her when she opens her mouth to protest. Does she really not know me well enough to know this? "Just trust me."

"I don't trust him!" Aileen shouts over her shoulder, and mam opens her mouth to speak again, but I don't stay to listen.

I'm carrying this woman home.

I'm consummating our marriage.

I'm teaching my wife what her role is now.

Chapter 6

Aileen

I'M SO angry with him I could spit.

"Put me *down*," I say, slapping at his wide, massive chest.

He doesn't even flinch, just walks down the stairs and toward the exit. I don't bother to look to see who's witnessing my humiliation.

The jerk probably thought I wouldn't know who he was, what he did. And to think, I'm doomed to spend the rest of my life with this *arsehole*.

"I would've thought your punishment before your wedding would've subdued you," he says almost thoughtfully. "Instead, it seems I've only raised your ire."

"I—you—we—argh!" I'm so angry, I'm at a loss for words.

The jerk fixes me with a stern look, one brow arched with authority.

"Noted."

Noted?

What did he note?

"I am *fully* capable of *walking* by myself like an adult!"

"Certainly," he says in the same infuriating, calm tone.

"Then why don't you put me down?"

He shrugs. "I need the exercise."

The hell he does. He's nothing but raw muscle because *of course*.

"Oh, you're funny."

His jaw clenches. Where are we going?

"And you're a brat."

"Am not."

"Oh, sweetheart," he says, this time giving me a smile that doesn't reach his eyes. "I won't tolerate backtalk, either."

My throat tightens and my nose tingles with the utter helplessness of the situation.

"Of course you don't," I say, and to my horror, my voice wavers, and a lone tear falls down my cheek. "Reckon you're fully prepared to beat me again, aren't you?"

For some reason, that seems to strike a nerve with him. His grip on me tightens, and his jaw firms, but he doesn't speak.

We walk outside and down the small flight of steps to where a fleet of sleek black cars await. My stomach twists with nerves. These cars speak of opulence and power. Prestige. Money. The Martins don't have cars like this. It doesn't give me hope, though, but serves as a stark reminder that my future is a wide open expanse of unknowns.

"Ready, sir?" Someone in a uniform stands beside the car. If he's surprised to see my ogre of a husband carrying me, he doesn't show it.

"Yes. Straight back to Ballyhock," he says. Still, he doesn't put me down but bends at the waist, and places me in the waiting car.

Cormac. His name is Cormac. We've had no introduction, but I know that's his name. And he's my husband now. My husband, the man I just took tight-lipped, furious vows to.

The lump in my throat grows. I won't cry in front of him. *I won't.*

I'm relieved when he releases me, but the relief is short-lived, because after spouting off a variety of instructions to the driver, he joins me in the car.

I turn from him, looking out the window and cross my arms on my chest.

He slams the door and clears his throat. I suppose that's some sort of barbaric bossy man signal to look his way, but I don't bother.

Make me, I think.

"Aileen."

He spits out my name as if it's the bitter dregs of a cup of tea.

I don't respond.

"So this is how we're going to play things, then?"

That gets my attention. "Play things?" I repeat, still staring out the window, which is fruitless since they're tinted and there's nothing to see anyway, but I'm stubborn enough not to look at him. "I'm not *playing* at anything."

I can see his reflection in the window, though. He shrugs out of his suit coat and tosses it beside him, then reaches for a glass and decanter.

"You wondered if I'd beat you," he says, pouring himself a shot of whiskey.

"*Again*," I correct. I finally cave and turn to face him. I want to read his body language now.

He swings his drink down in one gulp, sighs, then looks at me, his jade green eyes flashing. "What sort of man do you think I am?"

"Think?" I repeat. "I know. You were the one who humiliated me."

"Would you have preferred punishment at the hands of Martin's lackeys? Did you miss the bloodstains on the floor by their whipping post?"

My stomach flips. *Gross.*

It's as if he thinks he did me a sort of kindness.

I glare at him. "I would've preferred not to be punished at all."

"I see. Unfortunately, you left me no choice."

"Oh, *really?*" Does he think I'm stupid?

In the same calm, placid voice, he responds. "Really. You weren't mine yet. You were subject to be punished at their hands. I've seen what they're capable of, and something tells me you have, too."

I have. Still, I refuse to grant him any sort of pardon, if that's what he's looking for.

"You humiliated me."

He nods. "You put the lives of my men and your father's at risk."

I look out the window in silence. I don't want to talk about this anymore. What's done is done, and my body still aches in remembrance.

He doesn't say anything else for long moments, sipping the drink in his hand. I continue looking out the tinted window.

He finally breaks the silence. "What do you know of me?"

I shrug. "Not much."

"Nothing at all?"

I swivel my head to look at him, anger taking over once more. "My brother said you were a fat, manky son of a bitch." It gives me some pleasure to repeat it.

"Fat, manky son of a bitch," he repeats, his eyes darkening. He holds my gaze thoughtfully, then places his glass down.

He begins to unbutton his shirt. I watch as the buttons

give way, the fabric revealing a crisp white t-shirt underneath. When he unbuttons the last button by his waist, he tugs the bottom of the shirt up, and takes it off. I let my gaze roam over him, while he sits in front of me in nothing but trousers and a t-shirt. I swallow.

He's sturdy and muscular, and... *definitely* not fat.

Definitely not manky.

The scent of his cologne fills the small interior of the car as he grabs the bottom of his t-shirt in his fist and yanks it up, over his head, and whips it to the side.

"Do I look fat to you?"

I swallow hard. "No." He's nothing but muscles and chiseled planes, his chest sprinkled with dark hair. Something unbidden stirs low in my belly, and my throat feels tight.

His eyes narrow. "Manky?"

I shake my head, unable to speak. He's raw alpha male, in every sense of the word, the type of man women lose their knickers over. Too bad he's a twat.

"I suppose time will tell if I'm a *son of a bitch*."

"Suppose," I manage to croak out.

He holds my gaze for another minute, as the car bumps and rolls before he crooks a finger at me.

"Come here, Aileen."

He likes this particular command, apparently.

"Come... where?"

He pats his knee. "Here."

My heart hammers, instinctive remembrance of having been punished once already at his hands. I know I've pushed this far enough. I don't dare disobey him. Not after what he's done, what I know he's capable of doing again.

"I can't... I can't stand in this car, I'll—"

"Do it."

The command reignites my anger. He's used to being obeyed and has demonstrated what he'll do if I don't obey him.

Not bothering to disguise my hatred, I make my way over to him. When I reach him, he wraps a hand around my waist and yanks me onto his lap. I wince. I'm still sore from the punishment he inflicted.

His large hand travels to my arse, and he gives me a squeeze straight through the miles of fabric.

I hiss in protest, but he doesn't stop.

His voice is low and dangerous when he speaks, commanding, though I can tell he is at least trying not to frighten me this time. "Do you know what has to happen tonight?"

I close my eyes as if that'll somehow stop me from facing what has to happen, what we must do.

"Yes," I say with resignation. I do know. Tonight, we consummate our marriage. If we don't, our vows are considered null and void, and we're right back where we started from. I might not want to be married to this jerk, but going back to my childhood home is not an option. I'd run away and become a penniless beggar before I'd allow that. And I know I'm fighting this, but

I'm not stupid either. If I don't stay with him and make our marriage valid, our Clans will war.

He loops his arm around me casually, holding me to him. "Say it."

"You have to... we need to..." why is it so hard to say aloud? Why is he even making me?

He squeezes my arse again.

"Sex!" I gasp. "We need to consummate our union."

His lips thin and he gives me a tight, angry nod. "Right. No matter what. Whether you want me to or not. Whether you hate me or not. Whether you agree, spread your legs and let me fuck you..." he pauses before he finishes. "Or not."

I'm no fool. I hear the implication. "So you'll rape me, then?"

"I'd like to avoid that particular option."

He doesn't deny it. Cold fear spikes through me. I shiver and look away, but his large, strong fingers grasp my chin and drag my eyes to his.

"I'm guessing that makes two of us, then. So think carefully about how you want this night to go."

I don't understand. "It isn't up to me, though. It's up to you."

His hand still on my chin, his deep green eyes bore into mine. "You have far more choices in this than you think you do."

Before I can respond, the car cruises to a stop. I hear voices outside, doors shutting.

We're at his home. I know what has to happen next. I'm faint with nausea.

I've been through many ordeals, including the punishment he gave me earlier today. I've been beaten and abused at the hands of my brother and my father. I've been manipulated by my mother and put up with her harassment and control. But somehow, knowing he's going to fuck me tonight makes me quiver in fear, a violation I haven't yet known. How will I recover?

He releases me, pushing me onto the seat beside him, and dresses back in his shirt before we exit.

"You'll be meeting your in-laws and servants who'll wait on you shortly," he begins. "I expect your behavior to be polite and dignified. Understood? I'll have none of that surly attitude from you, lass."

I huff out in indignation, when I feel his hand on my arm.

"I said, do you understand me?"

I think he somehow instilled fear in me with the punishment he gave me, for my heart does a quick beat in my chest at the memory, of him holding me down and wielding his palm and weapon on me.

"Yes. I understand." I'd rather be on good terms with them anyway.

"Good."

And then we're exiting the car, and I'm trying not to look at anyone. There are so many. Uniformed servants and men in suits, some that attended the service today and some that didn't. Right before me stands a beautiful, black-haired woman holding a baby in her arms, and beside her a shorter woman with the McCarthy family green eyes and dark brown, wavy hair, full pink lips, and a ready smile.

The black-haired woman smiles at me, an almost other-worldly look about her. I wonder where she fits in here. The woman beside her gives me a tentative wave.

"Welcome," the woman holding the baby says. "You're Aileen?" Her voice is pretty, almost musical. How can she look so normal and cheerful when she's witnessing this travesty?

A squeeze of my neck reminds me he's watching, goddamn it. "Yes," I say, then look away. I'm embarrassed to be here in front of the others.

"I'm Caitlin," she says. "Your sister-in-law. I'm married to Cormac's brother Keenan, Clan Chief. And this is little Seamus, your nephew. And meet Megan. She's cousin to your husband."

My husband. My stomach flips.

Still, these two seem decent enough.

"Thank you."

Her eyes soften in sympathy. "Poor thing," Caitlin says. "She's tired, Cormac."

"She's fine."

Megan adds her opinion as well.

"Cormac, really, perhaps she—"

But he's whisking me away before she can finish.

"Taking her upstairs?" It's the man who stood beside

him at the wedding. Caitlin's husband Keenan, then? He eyes me curiously, his lips pursed like Cormac's. He doesn't trust me either.

"Aye," Cormac growls.

Keenan speaks to the men around us, and everyone disperses, even Caitlin and little Seamus. This is no cheerful welcome home, no honeymoon. I'm goods he's acquired, no more, no less. It's what I expected.

"Welcome home, Mrs. McCarthy," Cormac says with a grim smile. My stomach tightens. I don't like how he says that. He waves his hand at the estate, and despite my anger and apprehension, I have to admit, this place is beautiful. The large mansion overlooks the gray, craggy cliffs of Ballyhock, the Irish Sea churning just outside the front windows. Blue-green and gorgeous, endless miles of ocean extend as far as the eye can see.

A beautiful garden surrounds the front of the house. I don't have time to take in all the details, but quickly note stone benches, an archway laced with greenery, and beautiful flowers in full bloom. The beauty that surrounds contrasts so much with the cold, sterile home I grew up in. There were no beautiful views, no gorgeous flowers or greenery. The grounds were well kept but more reminiscent of a prison than a home.

But there's more. I can't quite put my finger on it, not now, when I'm being pulled along toward the steps that lead inside. There's something else that makes this place very different from what I'm used to.

We enter the house, people greeting us on all sides. I smile tightly and nod, but don't have time to make real introductions. I suppose there will be time for that later. Cormac wants me away from everyone, and makes that clear with his curt replies and rapid steps.

The house smells warm and welcoming, like warmed vanilla and cinnamon. Someone's baking, the scent reminding me it's been a long time since I've eaten a proper meal. Every surface gleams, and bright light filters in through large, diamond-shaped windows in the entry hall. The staircase that leads upstairs is majestic, narrower at the top and wider at the bottom, swooping gracefully downward like the swells of a lady's gown. Above us, the tall ceilings are graced with crystal chandeliers.

I might not like my husband, but perhaps he'll be busy most of the time. I most certainly like this new home.

We walk up the carpeted stairs, and when we reach the top, he tugs me to the left. "We're on the third floor," he growls. "Caitlin and Keenan are opposite us. My mother lives here, as does my brother Nolan. The others live nearby."

"Excellent." I don't like the detached, cold tone of my voice, but I can't seem to help it. He's a prick. It doesn't bring out the best in me.

Nolan... I know that name. I can't place it, though. Have I met him?

After we go up the small staircase to the third floor, we walk down long, carpeted hallways, the sounds of voices dying. My heart begins to beat faster. We're secluded up here. And when we're finally alone...

I can do this, I coach myself. *I must do this.*

We walk down the hallway and I note a small table holds a potted plant, green and vibrant, and on another table, a large bouquet of blooming white flowers fills the bowl. The fragrant scent wafts toward us as we hasten by. If I didn't know better, I'd think this was a home for upstanding citizens.

"Why are you in such a hurry?" I ask. He doesn't reply.

We pass doorway after doorway, my heart sinking the further we go away from the others. We're so isolated here, so far from the others, we might as well be in our own country. No one will come to rescue me. No one will hear me if I scream.

He's planned it this way.

Finally, he comes to a stop outside a large door. He releases my hand, and without looking at me, orders, "Stay right there." I watch as he opens the door, before he reaches for my elbow and yanks me in again.

"I can walk myself," I tell him. "For goodness sakes, stop yanking me around like I'm—"

My words die on my lips. I look around me in wonder.

This entire room is like the inside of a botanical garden, teeming with flowers and vases. Tulips and daisies, roses and asters, a myriad of the most gorgeous flowers I've ever seen welcomes me home.

"Oh my," I whisper.

"For Christ's sake." He rolls his eyes heavenward as he slams the door, then throws the deadbolt in place. "Leave it to Caitlin to plant a fucking garden."

"Caitlin? The pretty, black-haired woman with the baby?"

"Aye."

"You asked her to set up flowers?"

"Well, no," he says, shrugging out of his suit coat and tossing it on a hook by the door. "I asked her to make it look presentable in here. Less...manly."

"Well," I say, reaching my fingers out to touch the silky petal of a crimson rose. "It certainly is."

"This is our flat here," he says, waving his hand around, and though he's still being gruff, there's a note of unmistakable pride in his voice. "You'll see no kitchen, though. We eat our meals downstairs with my brothers."

"I see."

"But there's a kettle." A small dining area stands to the left, and behind it, a large, carpeted living room, shelves lined with books, a leather armchair, and comfortable-looking furniture. The black leather and dark wood accents give it a decidedly masculine air, but the flowers soften it.

"Your bags have been brought up," he says. "But you'll only be allowed very few garments." He's loosening the buttons at his neck as he leads me to the bedroom. "Come along."

I look at him sharply. "Excuse me? What am I to do, walk around naked like a little sex kitten?"

He turns to me. "I like the fucking sound of *that*."

I choke. "What?"

He snorts. "Relax. I only meant I don't want you to wear the clothes you wore in the Martin clan. You'll have new clothes here. I'll pick them out."

"Will you?"

"Aye." If he notes the icy tone of my question, he doesn't show it.

"For fuck's *sake*."

He's pushed open the door to the bedroom, and this room is much like the entryway, laden with flowers.

"She changed the fucking duvet?" He looks with disgust at a floral and ivory coverlet on the huge bed.

"That's the biggest bed I've ever seen in my life," I say, before I can stop myself. "It's like a cruise ship."

"You may have noticed I'm a large man."

The way he says it makes my heart make a sudden leap in my chest. Is he... is he a large man in *every* way? Will he hurt me?

"Cormac, I—" I freeze. It's the first time I've ever said his name aloud. He turns to face me. Sunlight filters in from the window, illuminating his handsome face. He raises his eyebrows questioningly.

"I like the sound of that, too," he says, his tone the softest I've heard from him yet.

I swallow hard. I'm not sure what to say to him, how to respond. My throat feels tight and my nerves are shot. I'm shaking. "Of what?" I finally whisper.

"When you say my name. I imagine you've called me all sorts of things in your head."

Am I that transparent?

"But it's the first time you've called me by name."

I swallow again. "Aye. Wish I could say the same about

your saying my name." As soon as I say it, I wish I could take it back. "I—I'm sorry. My mouth has a way of getting ahead of my brain sometimes."

His eyes harden, and I wonder if I imagined any softness. "I've noticed." He unfastens the shirt again, like he did in the car ride here. "I want to take a shower. You're to stay here in this room while I do. You may get out of that dress and wear the robe you'll find in your closet. Rest, explore, I don't much care what you do."

I nod. But the question of our consummation looms. I want to know.

"Cormac?"

"Yes?" He's taking off his t-shirt, revealing again his muscled torso. I couldn't put my arms around him if I tried. His arms are as large as small trees, his hands could span my waist. He's got several tattoos, but the only one I recognize is the Dara knot. Is it a McCarthy one, then?

I realize I'm staring.

"Did you have a question, lass?" he asks, his fingers coming to his waist.

"The... our... our consummation," I say in a strangled sort of voice. I don't know how to ask this, so I just say let the words fall from my lips unchecked. "When? How?"

"After I shower. We've not time to waste." He looks at his wristwatch.

My heart thunders in my chest. "So soon?" I ask. "Why?"

"Your brother will want proof. And I want the basta off my arse as soon as possible."

Oh, God. Oh *God*.

Proof that he's taken my virginity. My legs give way and I sit heavily on the bed while he shuts the door to the bathroom.

Chapter 7

Cormac

WHEN I ENTER THE BATHROOM, I make up my mind. That was the last fucking time I'm asking Caitlin to do anything hospitable. Even the bathroom's strewn with flowers like a goddamn greenhouse. The scent is nearly cloying, but at least Aileen seems to like them. And I suppose that matters.

God, but the lass pisses me off. She's got a smart mouth she'll learn to tame, but a quick wit I hope she doesn't. I like that about her. She's a clever lass.

I wonder if she thinks she's been given some freedom in here, but soon she'll see she hasn't. My men stand guard outside the door, and the windows are barred with thick metal. Though the purpose is to protect us from intruders, it goes both ways. If she's foolish enough to try to escape again, she'll have no luck.

I strip off the rest of my clothes. My rock hard cock springs free. I grip it and groan.

I know this is a job. I know she's afraid. But damn if I'm not at least a little eager to fuck that pretty, virgin cunt of hers. I stroke my cock, momentarily contemplating the thought of stroking one off so I'm not so eager to take her. So I can have some fucking self-control when I finally do.

Christ.

But I decide against it. I need evidence of our consummation, and soon. I quickly lather up, welcoming the steaming hot stream of water that cleanses the Martin filth from my pores. I stand under the billows of steam and water and think of what's happened today. How I punished her. How we took our vows. Our terse talk in the car on the way here. The way her eyes lit up when she saw the garden, the view of the ocean from the front door, the flowers in the room. She hasn't even seen the full estate, the greenhouse we built last year, or the woodshed behind it where we store wood for winter's hearths.

The Martin scum live in near squalor, the manky bastards. At any rate, I can offer her a better home, and happily. Reckon it'll help me tame the lass.

I shut off the shower, and reach for a towel, cursing when I knock over a fucking vase on the floor. The glass shatters, pink tulips splayed on the floor like lily pads in a pond. I grunt, step over them and onto the small bath mat, and towel dry off. I'll have to have someone clean those up.

I open the bathroom door to find Aileen in the doorway. She's white as a ghost, and her eyes are wide and fear filled. My pulse spikes.

"What happened? Are you alright?"

The poor girl looks a fright. Her long, blonde hair has come loose from the pins that held it, damp strands clinging to her forehead. Her makeup's running, black eyeliner or whatever the fuck giving her the look of a raccoon.

I'm out of patience. "I asked you a question, lass."

"I heard the glass break," she whispers, her fingers coming to her throat as if in self-preservation. "I—I fancied you were angry about what you had to do and you—you broke it on purpose."

Anger spirals in my belly. What sort of fucking *bastards* were the Martins that she acts like this? When I get my hands on her brother, I'm going to enjoy pummeling the living hell out of him. Her father, too.

"No," I say, shaking my head. "Caitlin's filled the feckin' bathroom with all sorts. Flowers and greens and vases like a goddamn garden."

She blinks.

"Knocked it over by accident is all."

"Oh." Now that her fear's been put to rest, it seems she realizes I'm wearing nothing but a towel. Her eyes roam over my body, and her fingers on her throat splay.

Her words come out in a rushed whisper. "You're a very large man, Cormac McCarthy."

"Aye." I can't help but give her a wry smile. "Serves me well in this trade."

"What's your role?"

I don't hesitate. Our roles are fluid, changing with the seasons and time, but Keenan's needed muscle he can trust. "Bonebreaker. Clan Captain, having taken his role when he took the throne, I'm second in line as Chief." That makes me his confidante as well.

"Aren't you all, though?"

I look at her with curiosity before I respond. "Are we all bonebreakers?"

"Aye."

"Well, no. We have different roles in our Clan. I'm the larger one, trained *ealaíona comhraic*." As an Irish girl, she'll know what I mean, as many of us are trained in martial arts. "Trained at St. Albert's. Captain."

"Oh, that's right," she says. "My dad said y'all were posh. Had a finishing school."

I definitely don't like her father.

"Aye." We all attended St. Albert's, the finishing school for our Clan, and learned everything from reading and writing to boxing, wrestling, and stick fighting.

"So you're the strike force, then?"

"Aye. When we need to strike, I'm called. I'm also second in command."

"Keenan's first?"

"Aye."

She takes it all in with a serious nod.

"And if you're second in command, that means you prepare for the possibility that one day you'll be first in command."

"I do. Keenan's a fair leader, and he likes my counsel as well."

She nods again, her words coming fast and furious now. I wonder if she's stalling. "Will you introduce me to all of them? Tell me their roles?"

"Aye, in time, lass."

She takes a step back from me, and her back hits the doorway. She conks her head and winces. Christ, but the girl's bravado has failed her. She's scared.

We're not prolonging this anymore.

"Come here, Aileen."

"You say that a lot."

"What?"

"Come here."

"Eventually you'll learn to come without me telling you," I say, crooking a finger at her. "Now come."

She holds my gaze across the room, a little bit of the vixen returning. "Now that we're married, will you punish me if I disobey you?"

"Especially now that we're married."

She doesn't like that. Her brows furrow and she purses her lips. "Excuse me?"

"Enough talking, lass. I said come here, and I mean it."

She takes in a deep breath, squares her slender shoulders, and walks to me. When she's a foot away, she stops, lacing her fingers behind her back primly.

I reach for her, grip the back of her neck and squeeze. Not hard. Not soft. Just enough to remind her who I am. Who she is.

"Why, Cormac?" she whispers. "Why do you want me?"

I bend my mouth to her ear and whisper. "Because it's time, lass."

"I—what if I want a shower first?"

"No."

"But you took one. It isn't fair that I—"

My grip on her neck tightens. "I said no."

After I've fucked her, after we've consummated our union, I'll take her to the bathroom and clean her myself, with my own hands. But for now, I want her as she is, disheveled and vulnerable.

I want in her.

Now.

"Will you always be so—"

I silence her backtalk with a kiss before she earns a good spanking. It will happen, I've no doubt, as the only discipline I've administered was under the guise of another man. She hasn't yet learned to obey her husband. She will.

Her eyes flutter closed and her head bends back as I explore her sweet, sensual mouth. She tastes like peaches and cream, sweet and rich, and the more I taste, the hungrier I get. I don't want to break this kiss, not when we're just beginning. So I lift her in my arms and walk her to the bed, our lips still joined.

I lower her, then kneel beside her, bracing my arm above her head, effectively caging her in, before I heighten the kiss.

Has she kissed a man before?

I'm no virgin, but in that moment, when her beautiful mouth yields to mine, it feels like this could be the first time I've ever kissed a woman. I groan as I slip her robe off her shoulder, massaging her sweet, soft skin. She moans, and I've only just touched her shoulder. My cock strains against the towel.

If she's this responsive to a kiss and chaste touch, how will she respond when I really begin to work her body? When I suckle her nipples and fondle her breasts? When I finger her secret folds? When I eat her sweet pussy and she comes on my tongue?

I pull my mouth off hers with reluctance, only long enough so I can issue a command. "Robe off," I say, helping her do it by slipping the white fabric off her other shoulder, while she unties the belt at her waist.

She places both her hands on my shoulders, her eyes wide and fearful like they were just moments ago in the doorway. "Cormac."

"Aye?"

"How will you... what will they..." her cheeks heat pink. "How will they know you've taken my virginity?"

It's a fair question, but she should know this. Should've been schooled by her mam.

Fucking Martins.

"Did your mother not explain this?"

She gives a derisive laugh. "My mother? Hell no. I found out about my period from my nanny."

How much does she know? "Do you know... how much about sex do you know?" I'm bracing myself above her on one arm, but my cock's pressed up to the soft swell of her belly.

She swallows, and her cheeks turn a deeper shade of pink. "I have friends and the internet, you know."

"Answer the question."

"Plenty. I know plenty."

It's a moot point. She'll know soon enough.

"Some women bleed when they lose their virginity," I tell her. "And we can present sheets. If not, we'll have our doctor examine you."

Her eyes fill with horror and her mouth parts open. "No," she breathes. "No!"

"Aye, lass. 'Tis the only way."

"It's hard enough being fucked by a man I hardly know," she says, and the girl with the iron will's returned, though there's a thin thread of fear in her voice she can't mask. "I won't consent to be violated by a doctor."

"He wouldn't violate you, lass," I try to say gently, but she'll hear none of it.

"*No,*" she says. Then she grits her teeth and meets my gaze unblinking. "Make me bleed."

Make me bleed. Christ, this woman.

"You may not, though."

Her hands wrap around the back of my neck, and though her voice shakes, she doesn't blink. "Do your best."

I wonder why she balks at the thought of a doctor but not at being fucked to the point of bleeding? Still, I've a duty to do. And hell if I'll start our marriage off with the memory of painful, bloody fucking.

"You'll enjoy this," I insist. I'll be sure she does. To my surprise, she actually laughs.

"Is that a sign of your manhood or something?"

I slap her thigh, and she laughs again. "Or something. Spread your legs, lass."

Her amusement flees. Her eyes still fixed on me, she obeys. I take the rumpled robe and yank the tie from it before I toss it to the floor. She eyes the tie with fear. I take her wrists and lift them above her head, marveling at the way her gorgeous, pert breasts are on display. I yank the tie and wrap it around her wrists.

She blinks. "Oh, God."

I smile. "I hope you'll be screaming my name and not his when you come, but honestly, either will do."

She whimpers.

I spread her legs, and eye her pretty, bare pussy.

"Good girl," I approve. "I like you shaved like this."

She flushes pink again, but doesn't respond.

"If your pussy tastes as sweet as your mouth, I may

never resurface," I groan, lowering myself to the sweet vee between her thighs.

"Oh, God," she repeats, and her eyes flutter closed, as if she has to block out the intensity of this moment. Hell, maybe she does. Not me. I want to revel in this.

If I eat her out and make her come, it'll go easier on her when I fuck her. It should, anyway.

My cock's a steel rod when I spread her legs and breathe her in. The sweet, feminine musk of her arousal makes me groan. I fall to the floor and bring her to the edge of the bed, draping her legs over my shoulders.

"Cormac," she protests, trying to lift her hands to stop me, but she isn't able.

"Aye?"

"This is too... no, I can't... please don't."

She's scared, the wee thing. She ought to be, and I can't shield her from what we have to do. We don't know each other. She's never been fucked. And hell, I'm no boy when it comes to fucking. I'm going to take her, firmly, and present the evidence. But Christ, she can enjoy this part.

"You asked me to make you bleed, sweetheart. That will hurt. Let me prepare you."

"By—by doing *that?*" her tear-filled eyes break me a little. She has no idea how enjoyable *that* can be.

"Have you ever had your pussy licked?" My words come out in a growl I don't intend.

She'd better answer no.

"Oh God *no*. Of course not."

I smile, before I kiss her inner thigh. She jumps like I just pulled the trigger on a gun. Christ, the woman's so strung up she's about to snap. It's time I took control.

"Close your eyes, Aileen." My voice hardens, issuing a command, and it has the desired effect. She closes her eyes.

"Good girl. Just like that. Now breathe, sweetheart."

Obediently, she draws in a deep breath, then lets it out again.

"Good girl. Do it again."

She does.

I get up from my kneeling position and return to her breasts, weighing one in my left hand, while I drag my tongue along the hardened bud of her second breast. I work her nipples, suckling and tugging, then laving again before I go to the second, until she's writhing beneath me and the scent of her arousal permeates the air.

Still suckling her nipple, I bring my hand to her bare pussy and part her folds. I glide a finger in and out, pleased to find she's so wet. I relish the sounds of her soft breathing, the little mewls and purrs. I suckle her nipple and fondle her until her hips rise and her breathing becomes ragged. She's on the cusp of climax.

I kiss my way down her body, from her jaw to her neck then lower still, down the valley between her breasts to her belly. I drag my tongue through her navel, relishing the salty sweet taste of her naked skin, then lower still, to her sweet pussy I'm eager to taste.

This time, she lets her legs fall open.

"Good girl," I approve. "Just like that, sweetheart."

I position myself in front of her, drape her legs over my shoulders, and lower my mouth to her pussy. I kiss her there, inhaling her intoxicating scent. Her pelvis rises and she groans. She wants more. She's eager.

I kiss her again, pressing my lips to her swollen folds, then licking the creases on either side of her pussy. I want her dying for my tongue, ready to fly. I part her with the tip of my tongue, my cock straining. She gasps, holding her breath. I let the heat of my mouth pervade her, until she's panting before I've even licked her.

"Beg me before you come."

"May I? Please?" I can't help but chuckle. She's that ready? I begin with slow, lazy, deliberate strokes of my tongue through her seam.

"Oh God!" she knifes up, yanking on her restraints, but they hold fast. I hold her thighs down and lap again. And again. *And again.*

Within seconds, she's panting and heaving.

"Cormac," she whispers.

"Beg me."

"Please, Cormac, oh God. Please. I'll do anything you want. Anything. Let me come, Cormac, *please*," she begs, her voice trembling along with her hips, rising to meet my tongue.

I don't answer, working her even closer to climax.

I wait until her sweet body trembles against my tongue, before I lift my mouth. "Come, sweetheart."

She lifts her bound hands, as if she wants to bury her hands in my hair to support herself, and I almost wish I hadn't tied her. My lips tip up in a grin when she moans. I grip her hips, hold her pussy to my lips, and lazily lap again until her voice pitches off into a ragged scream.

She comes against my mouth with abandon, my lust-filled groans and her mewls filling the room. I feast myself on her pussy, until her hips fall back to the bed, then I join her, crawling back up the bed to straddle her.

"Absolutely fucking gorgeous," I tell her, the sweet taste of her juices still on my lips while I drag my hand across my mouth and smile at her. Her wide, beautiful blue eyes go half-lidded, and she bites her lip.

"Thank you," she whispers.

Christ, I'd do that morning and night to hear those words in her beautiful, lilting voice.

"My fucking pleasure."

That makes her laugh, and for just one moment, we're on the same team, the two of us. We're married, though we hardly know each other, but right then, we can laugh together. And hell, I love that.

I can't waste any time, though. She'll be nice and wet, still high from climaxing. It's time I claimed her.

"We've a duty to do." Her lust-filled eyes widen a little. She swallows and nods.

Brave girl.

I yank the knotted towel at my waist and toss it to the floor. Her eyes travel to my stiff cock, and she licks her lips.

She licks her fucking lips.

My cock aches with the need for friction with her.

"Let me... you could let me return the favor," she suggests.

"Come again?"

"You could... I could do to *you* what you just did to *me*."

She wants to blow me?

Fucking hell.

Her offer gives me pause, though. Why would a virgin make such an offer?

I can't hide the impatience and anger in my voice when I demand, "Have you done that before?"

She doesn't respond, but the way her eyes slice away guiltily is answer enough. I don't realize I'm growling until her eyes widen in fear.

"Who?" I demand.

"Doesn't matter," she says, her eyes narrowing on me. "I was trying to be nice, and you're ruining it."

"Thought you were a virgin."

"I *am*," she snaps.

"A virgin who's had dick between her lips?"

She turns her face away from me with a haughty *hmph*. "I take it back, then. Offer's off the table."

Oh hell *no*. Jealous possession sweeps through me before I can stop it. I lean over her and grab a fistful of her hair, yanking her eyes back to mine.

"What's on and off the table's *my* fucking call." She winces when I yank her hair. "The thought of you with any other man, in *any* way, makes me want to knife the fucking bastard and spill his blood."

"Cormac." Her words are soft, a plea.

"I don't ever want to hear of you with another man. Any man who touched you before now broke code and will pay with his life."

She opens her mouth to respond, then closes it. Her eyes wide and fear-filled, she nods.

"Now spread your fucking legs."

This isn't how I planned it, it isn't what I wanted. But I'm so angry right now, I can see nothing before me but an end goal: take her virginity and fucking prove it, before our union is threatened.

Claim her. Fuck her.

She spreads her legs like she's a goddamn brasser at a whorehouse. Glaring at me. I ignore the look of betrayal she gives me. I took this woman from the filthiest Clan in all of Ireland on the grounds she was a virgin. If any of the men in her Clan were the ones to touch her, I'll find them. They'll pay for what they've done.

I position myself above her, my fist closing in around her bound wrists. Holding her in place. And though her eyes flash at me, she can't hide the fear. It only spurs me on, only makes me want to take her harder. Faster. Lay claim to the woman who now bears my name, and some day my children.

Mine.

She stares at me unblinking, silently daring me to do what I have to through my haze of anger. I line my cock up at her entrance and drag it through her sopping folds. I groan, my cock throbbing.

"Fuck me, then, Cormac McCarthy," she says through gritted teeth. "What are you fucking waiting for? Go at it. Do it."

I hear her sweet, fearful voice in my mind again as I hover above her.

Make me bleed.

I slap her thigh. "Quiet."

Her eyes water, but the pink flush of her cheek tells me it's from anger, not pain. She asked for this, I tell myself, she wanted this. Bracing myself above her, her thin wrists still held in my hands, I don't take my time. I don't ease myself in. With one firm push, I slam my hips into hers and break through her barrier. She gasps, but I thrust again before she's recovered. I want to bring her pain. I want to make her cry. I want to punish her for her cheek, her goddamn insolence, for being so fucking vulnerable.

My groans fill the room, my anger momentarily forgotten. Her pussy clenches around me, so tight, so hot, my eyes flutter closed and I utter an oath. She may have been touched by another man, but she's still a fucking virgin.

"Mother of *fucking* God." I don't move within her, not yet, but relish the feel of her pussy squeezing my cock.

She tries to hide her wince of pain, but I see it, even through my haze of anger.

Her voice wavers. "*Fuck* me. What are you fucking waiting for?"

I bend my head to hers, our foreheads nearly touching. "Careful, Aileen." I warn her. "Don't bait me, lass. It's too easy for me to hurt you."

Though she's putting on a brave front, I don't miss the way she swallows hard, or the dots of perspiration across her brow. And it almost softens me.

Almost.

"You're an arsehole, Cormac McCarthy," she says. "And I fucking *hate* you."

I thrust, to punish her, to silence her.

She winces, then whispers, "Is that all you've got?" But her voice is weaker this time.

"Don't try me," I say in a dangerous whisper, my hold on my anger tenuous, like gossamer thread. "Do you reckon I can't hurt you?" I lift my hips and thrust again. The tight walls of her pussy hug my swollen cock. My balls tighten and my cock throbs inside her. It feels so fucking good I want to lose myself in this, fuck her hard and fast until I chase my release and fill her with my seed. But I won't.

"You're mine, Aileen McCarthy," I whisper in her ear, reminding her she now bears my name. I weave my fingers through her mass of hair and pull. Her head tips back and her lips part on a moan as I thrust again. Hard. Vicious. She told me to make her bleed.

I have to.

I want her to know this, to feel this. "As mine, you belong to me. All of you. Your mouth. Your body. Your sweet, virgin cunt."

I lift my hips and slam into her again, and again, until a tear rolls down her cheek and she winces, but a moment later her lips are parted in pleasure.

"I know," she says, her voice tight and controlled. "I fucking know."

She closes her eyes and more tears roll down her cheeks, but I can tell a part of her likes this, because her hips rise to meet my thrusts and she bites her lip, caught somewhere between pain and bliss.

I thrust again, unable to stop my need to fuck her, my need to come in her. Holding her wrists in my hand, I rock my hips. I slam my cock into her, thrusting in and out, and though her slick juices make it easy, and she rocks her hips with mine, she can't help a little whimper.

My need to claim her spurs me on, until I'm on the edge of release. She turns her face away from me. I hold her wrists with one hand, but take my free hand and grab her chin. I yank her eyes to mine.

"Watch me," I order. "Hold my eyes as I take you."

She closes her eyes, the brat. I slam my palm against her thigh on instinct. Her eyes snap open. She looks at me with nothing short of fury as I thrust one last time. Our heated, furious gazes lock as boiling, blistering ecstasy washes through me. Even furious, she can't help the way her body reacts. Moaning, writhing beneath me, she comes as my seed lashes into her. And still she holds my gaze, utter hatred in her eyes. I spill every last drop of my come in her.

Spent. Sated. I pull my cock out of her and roll to the side of the bed.

Make me bleed.

Her thighs are smeared with blood when I pull out, bearing witness that I took her.

Chapter 8

Aileen

I WANT to hide myself underneath these blankets and weep. I want to ball up in the corner of this massive bed and sob out my pain. I knew my first night with my future husband wouldn't be glamorous, that it wouldn't be the stuff of dreams. I've known that since I became a woman.

I witnessed how my mother and sisters were treated, how my oldest sister left our house young and full of promise, and how every time I saw her, she'd grown thinner and more despondent. We didn't talk of this. I didn't want to ask questions. But I knew, a part of her died being wed to the man she was forced to marry.

And the others weren't much better. One isn't allowed contact with us, and another lives far off in the Middle East now.

But still... a part of me hoped. Dreamed. Longed for a

man who would truly love me, who would treat me better than if I were a whore. But no. Not this man. Cormac McCarthy might've been a good man once, but he's caved to the pressure of his clan. Any man who'd whip me, tear me away from my family, then fuck me the way he just did doesn't have an ounce of tenderness in him.

My body aches. I can still feel where he lashed me earlier, the skin tender and bruised.

Like an idiot, I told him to make me bleed. And he did.

"Come here," he says, his voice tight with anger. I don't move, even though I know he'll punish me if I disobey him. He grabs my shoulder and rolls me over. I don't bother to hide my tears. I'm so angry I want to hurt him, but so tired I don't know how.

He takes the crisp white sheets, as pristine as fallen snow, and swipes over my legs. Bright red blood stains them. Not much. I hardly gushed. But it's enough to give evidence of what we've done.

Some girls hope they aren't the type to bleed when they lose their virginity. Not me. While it's hard to be fucked by a man I don't love, I will not subject myself to the invasion of a doctor's intrusion. That happened to me once, against my will. Mack Martin, clan leader, ordered me inspected by the Clan doctor before he promised me to the McCarthys. Bastard.

It was painful and humiliating. So even though Cormac's fucking me right now hurt, I'm almost grateful. I told him to make me bleed for a reason. And he did.

I only wish I hadn't climaxed. I don't like that he had

that control over me, that I didn't have that control over myself. But he's hot, the damn prick. Muscled and powerful, his body sculpted as if from an artist's hand. And when he licked my pussy, I had no more control over coming than I do over my heartbeat.

I watch as he wipes every drop of blood from my thighs, my pussy, and his cock. My stomach coils with nausea, and I turn away, but he won't let me hide. He yanks the flat, bloodstained sheet to the side, crumples it into a ball, and tosses it to the floor.

I close my eyes. I want to sleep. I want to forget this ever happened. But my eyes flutter open when I feel him step toward me. He's dressed himself in boxers. What is he doing? His lips set in a thin line of determination, he bends to me and lifts me in his arms. Wordlessly, he carries me to the bathroom.

"I'm tired," I tell him. "I want to sleep."

It surprises me that when he speaks, his voice is softer now, tender. "You'll be able to sleep shortly, lass. They'll change the sheets while you wash."

Still holding me in his arms, he leans into the large shower and cranks the handle. In seconds, hot clouds of steam fill the room.

"In you go."

Does he think I need a shower? A pang hits my chest. He thinks I... I don't know, smell or something? Why does he think I need to shower? Is he that disgusted with me?

To my surprise, he strips his boxers off and joins me.

"Earlier it felt good to wash the Martin filth off me," he says. "I want the same for you."

I laugh without mirth, the sound hollow and troubling. "It doesn't matter how hot your water is, how powerful your soap. You'll never wash the Martin filth from me. Don't you know that?"

"Hush." His voice is so low it's almost a suggestion. But by now, I know better. I hush.

He's reaching for my hair, tugging it back, and I have to admit it does feel good when the warm water massages my scalp. He lathers my hair in a fragrant, lavender-scented soap, then rinses me off. Foaming up a washcloth, he rubs it over my back, my tender arse, between my legs. I let him.

"Good girl," he says approvingly, when I turn to let the water wash me. "You did well, lass."

It's almost like this is an apology. A silent act of service that means *I'm sorry*.

I stand and let him do this. He shuts the water off, steps out of the shower, and grabs another towel before he reaches for me.

"Come here," he says.

"Again, *come here*," I say with a sigh, but I'm tired and there's little bite in my tone. "Why don't you snap your fingers."

Nonplussed, he nods. "We'll get there."

The hell we will.

He towels me off and wraps me up, then lifts me up and over the broken glass on the floor. There's a glass of wine on the bedside table I didn't notice before, the bed's made, and there's a little nightie waiting on one side of the bed.

"That's to be your side," he says.

"Oh? Why?"

"It's furthest from the door. I sleep on the side nearest the door."

"Really? Why?"

He gives me an exasperated look, as if the answer's obvious.

"In case of intruders, lass. Don't tell me your brother and father didn't teach you that?"

"Teach me what?"

"That *your husband* sleeps by the door. That if we go out, my position will be in view of an entrance. That when we walk on a sidewalk, I'll be the one facing the street. The very basics."

I look away from him while I process this. I shake my head. "Well, no. They didn't. But they weren't... the protective sort."

"Bloody hell."

I turn to face him. "Why would someone who wants to protect me give me away to the enemy? Hmm?"

"Duty," he says.

I shake my head and change the subject.

"Did you call someone?" I ask, while I tug on the nightie. It's short but soft, and comfortable.

"Aye. They brought us drinks, and made the bed. I'll clean up the bathroom, as well. Now drink," he orders. "Then sleep."

I sit down on the edge of the bed and swig the wine. It's cool, fruity, and sweet, and warms my insides like a hot toddy. I drink until the glass is empty.

"Aren't you going to drink as well?"

He shakes his head. "No. I've got work to do."

I push the wine glass back on the table and lay down in the bed.

"Now?" I yawn. Is he talking about cleaning up the broken glass? Seems odd to refer to that as "work to do." My entire body sinks into the mattress. I'm so tired. So bloody tired.

I listen for his response, my eyelids already closing.

He doesn't answer my question. "I'll be back in a few hours."

And then I remember. The sheets.

"You want to deliver the sheets yourself," I say on a yawn.

"Aye. I want to deliver a *few* things."

I wonder what he means.

I ask my questions, my eyes still closed. "Aren't you... are you going to join me?" Isn't that his job as a married man? A part of me is sad this is how my wedding night's going to end. Alone. In pain.

"Later," he says. I open my eyes a little, and from the

corner of my eye, I see him open a drawer and remove a pair of jeans.

"When will you be back?"

He doesn't respond. I close my eyes, so tired I can't keep them open anymore, and he flicks the light off on the bedside table. He bends down and whispers in my ear. "You're safe here, now, Aileen."

But I'm not, and he knows it. I'm not safe from *him*.

My eyes are closed, and sleep beckons.

Why did I bait him? I yawn, when I feel the sheets and blankets tucked in around me. I hear a rustling and want to open my eyes, but they seem too heavy. Maybe Cormac does have a tender side.

I drift off to sleep, assaulted by memories of what happened today. But the wine mutes my memories, and soon I'm in a dreamless sleep.

I wake what must be hours later to the sound of movement in the other room. Moonlight illuminates the room from the window, the shade not yet drawn. The door to the bedroom opens, and he enters. He tiptoes into the room as if not to wake me. If he wasn't an arsehole, it'd be cute.

"You're back?"

"Do I look like a ghost?"

"Absolutely not." I roll over to watch him undress. It's a fair good sight.

"You should get some sleep."

"Aye." I don't, though. I just watch. It's too dark in

here to see his eyes, and I may be imagining it, but I swear I see his lips twitch.

He shrugs out of his jacket and hangs it on a peg by the door. He's tidy, I'll give him that. Next comes his shoes, and then his t-shirt, each neatly put away. Soon he's standing in front of me in nothing but his boxers. He stalks over to the bed, lifts a corner of the blanket, and slides in. I roll over toward him.

"Now can I ask where you went?" I ask, folding my hands under my cheek.

"You can ask me anything you want," he replies. He fluffs the pillow, then lays his head back. "Doesn't mean I'll answer. Hell, most of the time I won't."

"For my own good," I say, unable to keep the bitter tone out of my response.

If he hears the sarcasm, he doesn't react. "Aye."

A beat of silence passes.

"So where did you go, then? Did you take the sheets to my father?"

"Aye. Your brother was kind enough to take them," he says, his voice dripping with sarcasm.

My stomach clenches. God, I hate my brother.

"Oh?"

He opens one eye and looks at me. "Oh. I knew where your brother would be tonight. I met him there."

"It took you that long just to hand him sheets?"

He shakes his head and turns back away from me,

facing the ceiling before closing his eyes. "No. I told you I had more than one thing to deliver."

"Aye? What was the other thing?"

"Thorough beating to your brother," he says with a satisfied nod. "Owed him a black eye."

I sit up in bed. "Wait, *what*? You gave my brother a black eye?"

He yawns again. "Two of 'em."

"But *why*?"

"He hit my wife. Bastard's lucky I let him live."

"But he... but you... he hit me before we were married. I wasn't your wife then."

I might fall in love with a man who defends me.

"Doesn't matter."

Again, another beat of silence passes while I process what he's just told me. "Did you... Cormac, please look at me?"

He obliges. "Yes?"

"Did you... defend my *honor*?"

He smiles for real this time. Hell, I wish he'd do it more. His eyes light up like jade-flecked crystal, and up close like this, I note a dimple in his cheek I didn't notice before.

"Course I did." He leans over and tweaks my nose.

"Hey!" My cheeks flush.

"Hey what?"

"Don't pinch my nose like I'm a cute little girl."

"Ah, but you *are* a cute little girl. And sweetheart, have you forgotten I'll do whatever I like?"

How could I forget?

I *hmph* in indignation, but know better than to fight this.

"Well. Thank you," I finally say.

"For what?" he asks, yawning again.

"For beating up my brother. I hope you gave it to him good. He's a class-A arsehole."

He chuckles, the sound so sexy my heart beats a little faster.

"He absolutely is, and I absolutely did. Now sleep, Aileen."

I close my eyes, but sleep doesn't come right away.

My brother is hardly one to take a beating without recourse.

I go over what happened today. What happened tonight. My husband is a demanding man, but he's a protective one. He's jealous, too.

"Cormac?"

"Mmm?"

"Will there be blowback? Will he retaliate?"

"He could, but I think I made it clear that would be a mistake."

I lay in silence, wondering what he means by that. Wondering what magic he possesses.

"I can almost hear your brain spinning," he says. "I said sleep. Now do you need me to force the issue?"

I yawn. "How would you do that? You can't exactly spank someone to sleep."

"You can try."

I surprise even myself by laughing, then shaking my head and rolling over onto my side, away from him. He moves closer to me, slaps my arse teasingly over the thick blankets, and drapes one of his heavy arms over me. It feels nice, somehow. Soothing. I close my eyes, and for the second time that night, fall asleep.

My dreams are dark and troubled. In one, I'm being held prisoner by my father, locked in my room with no windows or light. I wrestle through it, only to find the harder I fight, the tighter the restraints. I wake in a cold sweat, panting. Cormac's arm's still tight around me.

"Y'alright?" he asks from behind me.

"Aye. Just a bad dream."

He holds me tighter, and I finally drift back to sleep. I almost wish he wasn't like this, that he wouldn't hold me and do things like defend my honor. It's hard to hate someone who treats you with momentary kindness. But hell, if I'm to be married to this man, I might as well make the most of it.

I wake the next morning to the sound of running water in the bathroom. I open my eyes, and look about the room, and feel a bit lighter this time. Seems I slept off some of the heaviness of the night before.

He was mean yesterday. Hell, he was even cruel at

times. Then he dragged himself out to punish my brother on my behalf... to avenge me, like the knights of old. And maybe somehow, as I slept, my subconscious worked that one out.

I look about the large room, past the massive bed. The walls are bare save one small framed print near the closet, but I can't see what it says. I yawn widely. Looks like it might be the knot tattooed on Cormac's arm, or some seal or something.

There's a table and chairs, but the furniture in here is otherwise sparse. Still, it's dust-free and clean, and I can see faint trail marks in the carpet that indicate someone took a Hoover to it the day before. The fragrance of the flowers still permeates the air. I take in a deep breath, then let it out again.

I wonder how much freedom my new husband will give me. Just outside this window, I can see the edge of a beautiful garden in front of the house. Around the bend is the front of the house, with the stunning trellis and greenery, the blooming flowers, and roughly-hewn bench.

Will he let me roam these grounds? Will he let me go to the kitchen, or to the library? Will I be allowed the freedom to shop? To have a job? I look around the room, wondering where my phone is. Will I be allowed to call my friends? To see them again?

Thankfully, he opens the door and steps into the room. I want to ask him these questions.

"Will I be given any freedom?"

I look straight in his eyes when I ask the question, then realize he's wearing a towel slung around his waist, and *Mother of God*, even though he angers me, the man's a walking god.

"Well, good morning to you, too," he says, walking over to the chest of drawers nearest the bathroom.

"Good morning," I say impatiently, waving aside his greeting. "I have questions, Cormac."

His back's to me now, as he takes folded clothing out of his drawers, and my, what a back it is. Broad. Muscled. Dotted with tats in intricate swirls, knots, and tribal markings. I bet they have meanings. I long to know them.

"And lucky for you, lass, I have answers. Now, you want to know how much freedom you'll have?"

He lets his towel drop to the floor and I get a full view of his magnificent arse. I stop lamenting the fact that my husband's so built. Being married to an arsehole who let his body go to seed would be infinitely worse.

"The answer is, you'll have some freedom, but you're under my protection now. So you won't be allowed to do things that will endanger you."

My heart sinks. "Like what?" I'm aware my voice sounds like a petulant child's.

"Shopping, for instance. I'll allow it, in moderation, and money isn't the concern. You'll be given a credit card, cash, whatever it is you need. But you won't be traipsing around the shops with your mates, and putting yourself in harm's way."

I frown. "Then how will I shop?"

"I'll clear the stores and give you leave or go with you myself." He grimaces, as if the very thought is painful.

I blink. "You'll... clear the stores?"

"If I can't go myself, aye."

He turns to face me as he yanks a clean white t-shirt over his chest. For the first time, I notice he's got a cut across his chin and nose, and a bruise on his cheek.

"You're hurt! Did my brother hit you?"

He looks puzzled at first, then raises a hand to his cheek, as if just remembering the cuts and bruises. "Ah. He did, before I throttled him."

"I'd have paid to see that," I muse. And I would have. Watching my brother get his arse kicked by Cormac would've been worth it. "Now back to the shops. What were you saying?"

"We'll set it up ahead of time. You'll have the shops to yourself, and you'll have either me with you or my men."

Is he that much more powerful than my father that he'll give me a private shopping day? It's hard to imagine.

"Well. Okay, then. What about these grounds?"

"You live here, now, Aileen," he says, his green eyes holding my gaze. "You're my wife. That grants you freedom and privileges unlike most here, save Caitlin. She's wife to the Chief. But you'll like her, lass. Behave yourself and you might get along."

I huff out in indignation. "I typically *behave* myself," I tell him. "For goodness sakes, I'm not a child."

"You only play one on the telly?" His eyes twinkle, but I'm not amused.

"Oh, shut it."

He wags a finger in my direction. "Careful, lass. Watch that smart mouth."

"Or what?" I throw back. I know damn well *or what* but I feel like pushing him. I want to make him say it. Maybe if he says it out loud he'll realize what an overbearing ogre he is.

"Really, now," he says. He lifts his leather belt from the dresser, but doesn't thread it through the loops on his trousers quite yet. He forms a loop with it, tugs the folded end, and snaps it. "Do you need me to say?"

I swallow hard and sigh. "Yes."

He smiles, but it's condescending, not amused. "If you mouth off to me, sweetheart, your arse meets my palm. Or my belt, as it were. As mine, you'll do as I say and show respect. And in time, you'll learn what's expected of you."

I don't like this one bit, but I suppose it's fruitless arguing the point.

"Does Caitlin have the same rules, or is it just me because I'm new?"

"It doesn't interest me what rules my brother has for his wife, but I'll tell you this. *All* the men of The Clan are heads of their own houses. It's how things have always been and always will be."

"That's *backwards*."

He shrugs. "Call it what you will, it's part of our code. We protect and care for our own. And in turn, we ask you grant us that privilege."

Well, that's fucked up. I'm wise enough to keep that to myself, though.

"Am I allowed my cell phone?"

"Yes, but there's tracking on it so I know where you are." I expected as much. "And we'll meet with my men shortly, to go over expectations. As a member of our Clan, you're never to discuss business matters with those outside The Clan."

"More rules?"

"Aye. But you're a smart girl. You'll catch on."

"Lovely." If he notes my sarcasm, he doesn't show it.

"You're welcome to walk about the grounds. We have beautiful gardens, and our home overlooks the Irish Sea. As long as you're careful, you keep your guards with you at all times, and you do what I say, you'll have a good deal of freedom."

I don't respond. It's hard for me to reconcile my bear of a husband with the man who's talking to me now. Perhaps it's part of his seduction plan.

A knock sounds at the door, and I jump.

"Relax, lass," he says, his brows drawn together. "You're jumpy as a wee rabbit. It's only breakfast."

"Thought you said we'd dine downstairs?"

He walks to the door and speaks over his shoulder. "Thought we'd eat up here, but we can go down if you'd like."

I do. I want to see Caitlin and his mother, and I've other reasons as well.

"I would. Please, can we eat with the others today?"

His brows draw together as he thinks on it. He opens the door, says something to whoever's waiting on the other side, then turns back to me. "Aileen. Can you tell me why you wish to go downstairs?"

So maybe he *will* actually listen to me once in a while.

"Aye." I explain my reasoning. "I'd like to see Caitlin and your mum, but I also don't want anyone to think that I'm too shy to see them or too weak to face them after my claiming last night. I want to show a brave face. Make a good first impression."

I may've fucked that up with my husband, but I won't with my in-laws.

He scratches his beard. "Well, I must confess that surprises me. But yes, I'll allow it. It'd be easier for me to talk to my brothers as well."

I'm getting out of bed while I talk, eager to get dressed and go downstairs.

"How many brothers do you have?"

"Two blood brothers, and several dozen adopted."

I turn to face him in shock. "*What*? Your parents adopted dozens?"

But he isn't laughing or even paying attention to what I'm saying.

"Jesus, you're gorgeous," he says, taking a step toward me. My heart beats faster.

"Thank you." I look down at the little nightie I still wear. It's rumpled from sleep, clinging to me with static, so it does little to protect me and leaves *nothing* to the imagination. "I'll give you this, you don't hold back on the compliments."

His lips twitch. "Lucky for you I've got to meet my brothers," he says. "Or I'd have to fuck you again before breakfast."

It makes me a little nervous. "There will be plenty of time for *that*, Mr. McCarthy."

That gets me a full-on smile. Something flutters in my chest.

"And you didn't answer my question about the brothers. How do you have so many?"

His brows furrow in confusion. "My mates in the Clan, lass. Don't tell me your father and brother don't call their men brothers as well?"

Again, his code is so different from theirs it startles me.

"They don't," I say. "Never."

"Bloody hell."

"Can we please just go downstairs and eat now?" My stomach gnaws with hunger, but I want to leave for a different reason. I don't like talking about my brother and father.

"Aye. Get dressed, and we'll go."

He gestures to the dresser adjacent his. I open the top drawer, and find it filled with socks, nighties, bras, and knickers. Some are mine, but most are new. I look through every drawer, marveling at the quality of clothing.

Maybe I *will* like it here after all.

Chapter 9

Cormac

MOTHER OF GOD, I knew the Martins were a manky Clan, but really? Do they have any code at all? They don't protect their women but sell them like cheap French whores. They don't even call each other brother. Is there no fellowship between them?

Last night, when I met Blaine at the club, I delivered the bloodied sheets. He tossed them in the trunk of his car and didn't even have the decency to acknowledge me, just turned his back and walked toward the club, the fucking twat.

I didn't let him go, though. I wanted him to pay for his treatment of Aileen, and I didn't want to spill his blood inside.

He paid. I sent him home with two black eyes, broken ribs, and a warning he'd better fucking heed. I would've preferred spending the night with my new wife, but I had a duty to perform. And her thanks and appreciation were payment enough. I want her to know that arsehole will never come near her again.

I don't miss the way Aileen's eyes light up when she looks at the folded clothes in her drawer. I had my staff put some of her own clothing in here, but I had quite a bit bought new. A new life. A new start.

"Let's go," I tell her. "You can give me a fashion show later. There are more clothes in the closet." I gesture to the large walk-in closet in the corner of the room.

"Are you *kidding* me?" Her surprise is adorable.

"No. But I'm starving, too, and I get impatient when I'm starving."

"So that's the ticket, is it?" she asks, stepping into a tiny pair of lacy knickers. I swallow hard, my cock thickening as I watch her dress. Christ, but she's gorgeous, that full, heart-shaped arse begging to be kissed, spanked, and bitten. I swallow.

"The ticket to what?" My voice is hoarse like a horny teen's.

"Keeping you well fed keeps you happy. Feed your belly?"

She's got a smart mouth, but fuck, I love it.

I have to touch her. I need to be close to her again, to inhale her seductive scent and touch her silky skin. I cross the room and reach for her from behind, anchoring my hands on her hips. She stills when I bring my mouth to her ear. Her body's warm against mine, and my cock strains against my zipper.

"Good girl," I whisper in her ear. "That's right, lass.

Satisfy all my appetites, and you'll find I'm much easier to get along with."

She closes her eyes and moans when I nibble her lobe before licking the shell of her ear. Christ, but the girl's responsive, eager. I splay my hand on her belly, my fingers grazing the lacy edge of her knickers. She pushes her arse against me. My cock throbs.

"I'll let you heal before I fuck you again," I whisper in her ear, tracing her ear with my tongue. "But that doesn't mean I'll keep my hands to myself."

I slide my fingers past the elastic band on her knickers. I love the way she trembles and pants before I even touch her.

"Did you like it when I made you come last night, lass?"

"Oh, God," she says in a strangled whisper. "Are you joking? I fucking loved it."

"Good girl. Tell me, sweetheart. Do you touch yourself?"

She grabs my arm, holding on so she doesn't sway. She nods, then swallows hard when I cup her bare, hot pussy.

"Do you make yourself come?"

She bites her lip but nods again. "Aye."

"Tell me what you think of when you come." I take one finger and part her folds. Waiting.

She whimpers a bit.

"Tell me," I repeat.

"I... I sometimes think about... being dominated."

Christ. I mentally fist bump in victory.

I reward her with one stroke of my finger. She gasps, and parts her legs, silently begging me for more.

"Do you? How so?"

"I... I've imagined being handcuffed and used," she whispers. Again, another rewarding stroke of my fingers, but this time I enter her core. Gently probing. The sweet, seductive scent of her arousal makes my mouth go dry.

"Go on."

"I've imagined what it's like to be spanked or whipped, but I—" She opens her eyes and gives me a reproachful look. "It's *nothing* like what you did to me."

"Aye," I say with a smile, fingering her again so that the look of reproach vanishes. "It rarely is."

"What?"

"Fantasy versus reality. But have you thought of your whipping since I gave it to you?" I stroke her harder. Faster. Her clit pulses against my finger, and she whimpers but doesn't answer.

I freeze.

Aileen's a quick study, and she understands that if she answers me, I reward her, and if she doesn't, I don't.

"Yes," she admits in a choked whisper. "I... I have."

"Good girl. That's a good answer." I stroke her again. "What else do you think about?"

"I think of... being taken from behind."

I chuckle at that. "Is that right, sweet girl? On your hands and knees?"

"Yes," she breathes. "I imagine that's... that I'd feel dominated then."

"You would." I'd see to *that*.

"I fantasize about several men, sometimes," she whispers. She continues without prompting, lifting her hips to meet my hand as I stroke faster. The way she's panting and gripping me for support, I know she's getting closer to climax. "One fucking me while the other... oh *God*... one eating me out while the other licked my nipples, or one fucking me from behind while the other worked my clit."

I will never share my wife with another soul. But I have other methods that will push her to the brink, make her feel various sensations while she climaxes over, and over, and over again.

"You're a dirty little girl." I cluck my tongue. "I'll have to punish you for that." I circle the edge of her tight hole gently before returning to her clit.

"No punishment," she breathes.

"You'll learn to beg for that, too."

"Please, Cormac."

"Please what?"

"Let me come."

I fondle her breast while I stroke her pussy, then whisper in her ear, "Come, Aileen. Do it. Let yourself go." I tweak her nipple, then bite her neck. She throws her head back and moans. If I weren't holding her up, I reckon she'd fall, she's that overtaken by the bliss that races through her. She moans and pants, rocking her hips as I stroke her to completion until she slumps against me. Spent.

"Good girl." I kiss her cheek and spin her around to face me. On instinct, I draw her near and embrace her. "I love to make you come."

She drops her head to my chest and holds onto me but doesn't speak. I give her just a moment to recover.

"Let's get you dressed now. I have to meet my brothers."

"What about…" her voice trails off.

"Yes?"

She places her hand on my hip. "What about you?" Her cheeks flush pink when she asks me that.

"I'll get mine later," I promise with a wink that makes her giggle. Just when I think I can't take her sass, or her feistiness, her temper or her mouth, she does something cute.

By the time we get downstairs, many of my brothers have assembled in the dining room.

Boner sees me first and sends up a loud, raucous cheer. "Welcome to the newlywed couple!" He bobs on his feet like an overexcited puppy, nearly spilling his tea.

Nolan, standing by the buffet pouring himself a cup of coffee, grins at me. Caitlin and Keenan, sitting at the large dining room table, clap, and Tully, buttering a scone at the very end of the table, hoots. Aileen smiles shyly.

I pull out a chair beside Caitlin and gesture for her to sit.

"Tell me what you want and I'll get it for you."

"I can get my own food," she says, but I shake my head.

She looks a little pink around the ears but doesn't balk. She looks at the table laden with food. We often have a buffet-style meal in the morning, so that our men can eat on their own time. "*Wow*, that's quite a spread. Okay… two scones, with butter, some clotted cream, a couple of fried eggs with some sausage, and some berries, please."

I nod while she pours herself a cup of tea, then pile the food on her plate.

"Girls' got an appetite," Boner says approvingly in my ear.

"Aye." I'm glad that she does. I like a girl that can eat.

"Hope she's got another appetite as well," he says with a wink.

"Shut it, Boner," I say, but can't help but smile at him.

He guffaws. "For Christ's sake, would ya look at you, the feckin' cat that caught the canary."

"Cat? Fuckin' lion," Nolan corrects with a snort.

"*Shut* it." There's no avoiding talk of sex, but I don't want Aileen to be embarrassed. I look back to where she sits. She's busy in conversation with Caitlin.

"Heard you brought evidence of yer claimin' to the club, eh?" Nolan asks.

"Aye. Had to."

"Also heard you busted her brother's nose and gave him two black eyes."

"He's fuckin' lucky I let him live."

"Feckin' wanker," Boner says. "I hate the plonker."

"Same," Nolan says on my right. His eyes twinkle at me. "Lucky for you, she wasn't the one got hit with the ugly stick, aye?"

I snort. "Ah, no."

"Told ya she was gorgeous," Nolan says.

I give him a warning look. "You did, but that's the last fucking time you'll speak of my wife's looks."

Nolan sobers. "Aye, brother. Just pleased for you's all. Hope to God she's got more sisters."

But he's joking. We've done our duty and will have no more unions with the Martins.

We walk to the table, and I slide Aileen's food in front of her. "Thank you," she says with a small smile.

I sit beside her and grab a napkin.

"Cup of tea, Cormac?"

"Please. Thank you, lass."

Keenan watches our exchange with interest.

My mother enters the room, her gaze coming straight to me and Aileen. She smiles, but her eyes look tired.

"Is mam alright, Keenan?" I ask him while she goes to fix herself a plate.

Keenan sighs and scrubs a hand across his brow. "Dunno," he admits. "She's been troubled lately. Worries about us, you know."

"I'm telling you," Caitlin says. "Let your mam watch over the baby. We don't need that nanny. I don't like her anyway. Always going on about educational opportunities and fine motor skills, when all the baby needs when so young is love and affection."

I don't miss the way Aileen's eyes cloud for a moment, before she turns back to her food and tucks in.

"She got the best ratings, Cait," Keenan says.

"Aye," Caitlin agrees. "But from whom? College professors or real life mothers?"

Aileen snorts. "Good question," she says. "The mothers will give it to you straight, won't they?"

The girls talk about nannies and children and babies, and Keenan looks my way. He speaks in a low voice, so the girls don't overhear.

"Heard you paid a visit to The Craic last night."

"Aye."

His gaze swings to Aileen. "Fulfilled your duty, then."

I nod. Mam comes to the table and sits across from the girls. She pours cream in her tea, then sips it thoughtfully with an appreciative sigh.

"Mornin', son."

I nod. "Mam."

"Will you be needin' any of my help today? To show Aileen around the estate, maybe?"

"Aye, thank you." I'll have her do that while we have our morning meeting.

She nods and joins in conversation with the girls.

Keenan takes the opportunity and leans in to me, lowering his voice to a whisper.

"Cormac, a word." He stands and gestures for me to follow him. We walk back to the buffet. I know what's coming.

Keenan crosses his arms and fixes me with a serious look. "Don't blame you for lettin' him have it, brother. But next time, do me a favor and ask me first."

I nod. I reckon he's worried about blowback. "He won't retaliate," I tell him. "Made it clear it would be the last thing he did."

"Just the same, the Martins don't play fair and never will. Don't forget the only reason you have Aileen is because they paid tribute to us. Without your marriage, we'd be at war with the bastards. And they'll do anything to save their own arses and pockets. *Anything.*"

He's right.

"Aye," I say with a nod. "You're right."

He grins. "Tell me you made him wet his trousers."

"Made him feckin' shite 'em." He nods with approval, and we go back to the table.

Mam's talking in her quiet voice to the girls, while Keenan and I tuck in. Nolan's telling a crazy story, waving his hands around like a madman, and the men around him are laughing so hard they're wiping tears from their eyes. Boner slaps his back and catches my eye, giving me a wink. Tully sprays tea all over the place when Nolan catches him off guard and he busts a gut laughing.

These are my brothers. My family. My home. I grew up with these men. I knew that though we beat the tar out of each other and fought like dogs some days, that they'd have my back, and they do still. Mam oversaw the gentler side of our education, and Dad saw to the sterner side. We were raised to be ruthless, but we were raised to be loyal.

What was Aileen's upbringing like? She's already revealed much. Shock that I'd protect her. Awe at our house. Surprise that I call the men of The Clan my brothers. How did they treat her?

Aileen talks easily to mam and Caitlin, in between large bites of food.

"Do you tend the garden?" she asks mam.

"Some," she says, with a bashful smile. "I've got help, but the flowers are all mine." Though we have gardeners and staff that tend to our land, mam takes special pleasure in tending to the flowers.

"Could you show me?" she asks.

Mam looks to me, likely wondering if Aileen's allowed. She knows how we work, and though she's already asked if she can give her a tour of the estate, she needs my approval.

I nod. "She can go after breakfast if the guard is with you."

The women are free to roam our grounds and often

only have a guard with them if they leave. I want Aileen to get used to being watched, though. She's too new here.

"I'm done," Aileen says with a smile. She points to her empty plate.

Mam finishes her scone and stands. "Let's go then. The baby's with his nanny, then, Cait?"

Caitlin nods. I watch as the three of them walk toward the exit toward the garden.

"Good," Keenan says, as the girls leave. "I want a word with you boys." He gestures for Nolan, Boner, and Tully to join us as well.

We crowd the dining table, and listen to what he has to say.

"Yesterday, we made alliance with the Martins, as you men know," Keenan says. "Aileen was delivered to Keenan, after they'd found her, and he punished her. But she bore a black eye from her brother. Damaged." I hate how he puts it, like she's property. I know Clan code, I know what he means, but I clench my fist to keep my temper in check just the same.

His gaze swivels to mine. "And we have your word she was untouched? A virgin?"

"Aye." It's important she was a virgin when I took her.

"And you proved to the clan she came from she's no longer a virgin, your consummation's complete."

We won't call the Martins "her clan," but "the clan she came from." She's McCarthy clan now.

"I did."

Nolan slaps my back. "Well done, brother. Christ but I'm jealous. Bet she was—"

"Finish that sentence, it'll be your last," I say. He shuts his trap.

Keenan goes on. "Now that we've settled with the Martins, I want as little to do with them as possible."

"Hear, hear," I mutter. "Thank *Christ*."

"Why's that?" Boner asks.

"Manky sons of bitches," Keenan says. "Underhanded. Conniving. Don't trust 'em far as I can throw 'em."

We may be mafia. We may be feared in all of Ireland, and for good reason. But there's a decided difference between mobs that bully and mobs that rule. Even as mafia, we see to the needs of Ballyhock with generous contributions to the church and a promise of protection. The residents of Ballyhock know who we are and turn a blind eye to what we do, and for good reason, while the Martins' locals cower in fear.

"Same," I say. "I don't trust them either. What little my wife's told me of her family confirms this. They'd just as soon kill their own as they would another clan."

Nolan shakes his head. "And her brother's a right twat."

"Acts the maggot on the regular," Boner says, his lips pursed. "Damn near scuttered at the weekend, took a girl against her will. Club couldn't do nothin' about it. Some of the boys did, but he won't see justice."

"Raped a lass at the club?" Keenan asks with deadly calm.

"Aye," Boner growls.

"Glad you busted his arse," Keenan says to me.

"We afraid of blowback?" Tully asks. "Fuckin' hope the motherfucker comes at us. I'd like a chance to break his nose myself."

"I say we catch him, string him up, and take turns like a piñata at a fucking birthday party," Nolan says, and though his lips tip up his eyes promise vengeance.

The men laugh, but a moment later a woman's high-pitched scream rents the air. We're on our feet, weapons drawn, before the echo of her scream dies.

"Garden," Keenan says. I'm the first though the door. I race toward the garden, but don't see the girls or mam.

"Aileen!" I shout, looking to my brothers for help.

"Christ almighty, they're by the greenhouse," Keenan says.

"Where's the fucking guard?"

"Calling them now," Nolan says.

I'm not prepared for what we see.

Thick black smoke pours out of the greenhouse, flames licking at the sky.

"Help!" a voice screams from ahead of us.

"It's Aileen," I say to Keenan.

We race to the greenhouse and Nolan calls for backup. We reach them in record time.

What the bloody hell is this? The doors are locked, and it's going up in *smoke*. They're fucking barricaded.

I step back before I lunge at it, trying to knock it down, but it's no use. They scream louder, while the flames get bigger, hotter. Someone locked them in here and set it to fire, goddamn it.

I take the butt of my gun and slam it against the glass, but it's no use. The glass is solid. It won't budge. I look around me for something, anything at all I can use to break the door down.

"Open it!" I scream. "Unfasten the lock!"

"I can't!" It's Aileen. "It's broken. Won't open!"

"Get the ax!" Keenan shouts. Behind the greenhouse is the woodshed our groundskeeper uses to chop wood for fires in the dead of winter. Nolan's there before I am. He runs back with it and I take it from him.

"Get the guard," I growl to Nolan. "Find the fucking guard."

My men stand and wait, prepared to save them, but this is my job.

"Stand back! I'm going to break it!"

I lift the ax and slam it against the glass. It shatters into a million shards that clatter to the ground like a hailstorm of diamonds. I swing the ax again, and again, until the wood frame splinters and we can get them out. But the flames are too thick, and I can't see them.

I launch myself into the thick of it. Smoke immediately chokes me, but I pay it no heed. I need to get to Aileen, to Caitlin, to my mother.

"I've got Cait!" Keenan shouts somewhere behind me.

"And mam!" Nolan says. There's a jumble of confusion, blinded by smoke and flames.

Aileen is still there. She screams again, when I hear the sickening sound of the roof collapsing. I see her just in time. She's huddled on the floor, covering her head.

"Aileen!" I scream. I reach for her when the roof begins to cave. I throw my body over hers, caging her beneath me. Something strikes the back of my head. The world goes black.

Chapter 10

Aileen

THEY'RE SPEAKING BESIDE ME. Voices I don't recognize, though some are vaguely familiar. At first they sound distant, like they're in a tunnel. Or I am.

Where am I?

"She could've died," one deep, rumbling voice says.

"Severe head trauma," says a pragmatic, scholarly voice in reply.

"Would've died if he hadn't shielded her. Will she wake?" The last voice is decidedly feminine.

"If she doesn't, I'll fucking kill them." The deep one again. This last voice is somehow vaguely… very vaguely… familiar. I can't recall how I know it, though.

"Who? We don't know who did it."

"We can guess," the rumbling voice responds. "Said

something about Martin ruining everything. He brought the wrath of someone on us…"

It's as if the words are being spoken in a foreign language. Without context or understanding, they're meaningless to me.

I lie still. It's odd being surrounded by voices I don't know. Something soft's on my body, and beneath my head are piles of pillows. I'm in a bed, but it isn't my bed. It's nothing at all like anything I've felt before. It's too comfortable. The only bed I've ever slept in was the small, cramped bed… somewhere.

Where am I?

What happened?

Who am I?

My eyes flutter open, and the chatter around me dies. I don't move except to swing my gaze nervously about the room. I try to swallow, but my throat's too tight. I don't speak. I could be a prisoner for all I know. Everything around me is foreign.

There are three people in this room altogether: two men and one woman. One of the men looks like he could be a doctor, with a telltale stethoscope around his neck.

The woman's the oldest, I think. She's got soft red hair graying at the temples, and kind, gentle eyes that have seen many things. I can tell by the aged, wise look she gives me, when she gently nudges a large, younger man sitting beside her.

"The lass is waking, son."

She's his mother, then. Whoever he is. His head snaps

up, and bright green eyes meet mine with recognition. My belly stirs with discomfort, though. Why is he looking at me as if he knows me, when I don't have the foggiest idea who he is?

I swallow several times, trying to figure out what to say, but settle on nothing. It's unnerving not knowing what to say.

He gets to his feet. His clothes are rumpled, his hair untidy, as if he's slept in his clothes for days, but he's incredibly handsome, with his dark curly hair and strong, muscled body. Everything about him is ruggedly masculine.

I wish I knew who he was.

"Aileen," he says, coming to my bedside. I look to the woman. Is she Aileen? But they're all looking at me. Who's Aileen?

"She's just a bit disoriented," says the man with the stethoscope.

"Where am I?"

He reaches for my hand. I flinch, and pull my hand away. I don't like strangers touching me.

"Don't touch me," I whisper. "I don't know who you are."

The entire room stills. No one speaks for long minutes, the tension palpable.

Did I say something wrong?

The taller, thin man I guess is the doctor walks over and places his hand on his shoulder. "Cormac, remember what I told you."

His name's Cormac. The name's familiar, like a long-distant memory from my childhood. I don't know it, though. He has no place in my catalog of thoughts.

I sit up, and I reckon my own face mimics the stricken face on the man before me. He's white and pale, his eyes wide in disbelief. I know how he feels.

"What's my name?" I say. My voice cracks, and tears well in my eyes. "Where am I?"

I try to get out of bed, but the man called Cormac shakes his head. "Stay in bed," he says. His voice brooks no argument, as if there's no question about obeying him. "No getting out of bed without assistance."

Why should I listen to him, though? What harm is there in sitting up? I ignore him, shoving the blankets aside, but he grabs my wrist and pulls me back to sitting.

"I said stay, Aileen."

So *I'm* Aileen. My name's Aileen. His scent washes over me, raw and masculine and virile. He's an attractive man, whoever he is.

"My name's Aileen," I say, shaking my head. "How come I couldn't remember that?"

"Aileen, my name's Sebastian. I'm the clan doctor, and I've come to help you," says the man beside Cormac.

I don't reply at first. The pretty, older woman with the graying red hair comes to my side, too, and tentatively reaches for my hand, then pulls away. "We're here to help you, love," she says in a clear, compassionate voice.

She's here to help me. If Cormac and this woman are on my side, it's going to be okay. "My name's Maeve."

Maeve. It rings another vague bell, but too soon the clanging of the memory fades.

She opens her mouth to speak, but Sebastian shakes his head and holds up a palm to her. "Not too much Maeve. It'll overwhelm her."

"I want my sister," I whisper. Do I have a mother? I don't remember. I do know that I had a sister, and she was kind to me. I know that much. My sister is the one who helps me. Who listens. She'll help me understand.

"Which one, sweet girl?" Maeve asks, stroking her thumb along the top of my hand.

Oh God. I have more than one?

I blink, and a tear rolls down my cheek. I don't know. I can't remember her name.

"We could ask her family for help," Maeve says to Cormac.

He glares at her. "Are you out of your mind? For all we know, her family's responsible for—" He pauses, and looks at me. "*No*. I don't trust them. No fucking way."

He's fierce, this man. Fierce and protective. Am I supposed to like him?

"Who are you?" I ask. He looks to Sebastian before he answers me.

Sebastian nods. "It helps if we spoon-feed information, specifically things that might trigger a memory recall."

Cormac looks to me and swallows before answering.

His eyes are a beautiful green, vivid and intelligent. "I'm your husband, Aileen."

Cold realization leaks through my limbs. I must look stricken, for the doctor mutters, "*Spoon* feed, not drown her."

I blink, trying to understand.

I'm married to a stranger.

"No," I whisper. "I have no husband. I can't. You're not my husband." My voice raises to a shriek, as a full panic attack consumes me. "No! You people aren't my family. I don't know you. Bring me home!"

Even as I say it, I know I don't want to go home. I don't like home. It's nicer here. But I'm scared, and I want to be back in a place that's familiar.

Cormac looks saddened, and his face drops, but he's determined.

"You aren't going to let me go home, are you?" I whisper.

"No, lass."

The door opens and we all look to see another man enter the room. He looks from me to Cormac, then back again. He resembles Cormac, but he's a little thinner, and a little older, I think. His brother, maybe?

"She's awake, then. Thank Christ," he says. But the somber response to his statement makes him pause mid-step. "What is it?"

"Amnesia." Sebastian says.

Amnesia.

I don't know who I am. I don't know where I am. I'm married to a stranger. You don't know how terrifying the lack of memory is until it happens. No context for what they say, or who they are. No recollection of what my place is in this world. How do I even function if I don't know who I am?

"Family meeting," the man says. "Assemble the men. We have to talk about what happened, and how we help Aileen. Mam, you stay here."

Keenan looks to me, and his stern eyes soften with kindness. "Aileen, do you know me?"

I shake my head in silence.

His eyes soften. "My name is Keenan. I'm your brother-in-law, Cormac's older brother and Clan Chief."

I nod.

"Before you had a head injury, you met my wife, Caitlin. Would you like to see her now?"

I shake my head. "No. No, thank you. I'm tired. I don't want to see anyone."

"Understood," Keenan says. He gestures for the men to join him, but Cormac shakes his head.

"I'm not leaving her side, brother."

"We need you, Cormac."

Cormac shakes his head with vehemence. "*No*. Fucking phone me in if you have to. I'm staying with her. Anything you tell the Clan you can relay to me. I'll do my duty, but my first duty is to Aileen. As her husband."

I don't know the man, but I like that he's loyal to me, that he prioritizes staying by my side. Is being protective in his nature, or does he feel responsible for what happened to me? So many questions.

Keenan's lips press together. He finally nods. "Aye. It is." He smiles at me. "Your husband is a good man, Aileen. I hope when your memory comes back to you, you remember that."

I swallow. I'm not going to lie. "I hope so, too."

I don't believe any of them right now. I don't know who they are or how they've treated me. I hate that I don't have any recollection, any foresight at all into how I should act with them.

"Leave us," Cormac says to the room. "I want a word alone with my wife."

So patience isn't his strong suit.

Maeve takes her leave, as does everyone else.

"I'd like to see your mother later?" Even though I don't remember her, I know I have an ally in her.

"Aye," Cormac says. "You will."

When we're alone, I turn to face my pillow. I'm honestly scared. I don't know him at all. What if he *isn't* a good man, as his brother says? Would my instincts know? All I can tell right now is that he's definitely someone who commands authority, and he's capable of doing dangerous things. He's here with me... and by the look on his face, he looks as if he's been here a while. Does that mean he cares about me, then? How would I know?

"Aileen, look at me." Cormac sits beside me.

I look at him. I'm suddenly filled with a strong, irrational sense of longing, to be held by him. I'm scared. You don't know how your memory brings you comfort until you lose it. It's terrifying not knowing who I am or how I got here. Even though I don't know him, and didn't want him to touch me, he looks strong. I bet it would be nice to be held by him. I bet it would feel comforting.

"Why don't we start by answering your questions."

"It isn't possible," I whisper. Tears well in my eyes. I swipe them away, angry at how emotional I've become. "I've too many questions to ask you."

"Aye," he says. "I imagine you do. But why don't you try?"

"Okay," I agree with a nod. "You look as if you haven't slept in days," I say to him. "Why is that?"

His eyes quickly widen before he schools his features. I don't think he expected that question.

"I'm your husband," he says. " And it's my duty to care for you. You've been unconscious for a number of days. I couldn't leave your side. I've been worried, so no. I haven't really slept. But I'm fine."

I feel my jaw drop. I don't speak at first, processing this. I've been unconscious for days?

"Why?" I whisper. "Why was I unconscious? Why did this happen to me?"

"I don't quite know why," he says, and if I'm not mistaken, the flash in his eyes indicates temper. Did something I say anger him? "I'm not sure who attacked us, but you, my mother, and Caitlin were attacked a few days ago."

"Attacked? How?"

"Someone ambushed our guard and set fire to the greenhouse you were in."

I gasp. "Did everyone escape?"

"Aye," he says. "Only before you and I did, the ceiling collapsed and you suffered serious head trauma."

"My God," I whisper. "Did you get injured as well?"

His jaw firms. "I did, but I'm larger. I sustained the injuries more easily. Concussion. We were afraid you experienced brain damage."

I feel as if I'm going to throw up. "Did I?"

"You've suffered amnesia. Just means you've forgotten a few things. But Sebastian says they'll come back."

I let the words settle as I process them. "How? How will they come back?"

He reaches for my hand, and this time I let him take it. "I'll help you remember. I have to talk to Sebastian, the doctor. The man who just left. We weren't entirely sure how you'd respond when you eventually woke, so we aren't totally prepared."

I nod. "So with… time and… whatever it is that Sebastian tells you to do… will my memory come back?"

"Aye," he says with confidence. "Absolutely. I'm sure of it. This is only temporary. And you're a strong lass. You'll weather this, I know it."

"Am I?" I ask. "A strong lass?" I don't feel very strong

right now. I'm lying in bed, grasping fruitlessly at memories.

He runs his thumb along the top of my hand. "Aye. One of the bravest." His hand feels warm and rough holding mine, and my need to be held, to be comforted, grows.

I look about the room. I'm in a massive bed, so large I'm dwarfed by it, like a child playing house. There's a bathroom to my left and to the right, a doorway that leads to another room. I see the door to a closet, and a few pieces of well-made, sturdy furniture. It's neat and clean in here.

"I'm not in a hospital."

"No, this is our bedroom. We're in our wing in the family mansion that overlooks the Irish Sea in Ballyhock. Home of the McCarthy Clan, of which you're a member."

Okay. Alright. I can understand that much at least. I'm grateful for his clear explanation of facts.

"How long have we been married?"

"Only a few days."

I blink. Days?

"Days," I repeat. "How did we meet? Have we known each other long?"

He shakes his head. "No. Our marriage was arranged by our Clans."

Clans. I know that word. I can't define it, but I know it means something like family.

"So I've only known you for a short time, then?"

"Aye."

For some reason, that brings me relief. A moment later, I realize why.

"So we *are* strangers, then. Still getting to know each other?" I can pick up where I left off, I guess.

He smiles. Oh, wow, his green eyes are gorgeous, and there's a dimple in his cheek. It's hot. *He's* hot. And he's my husband. My heart flutters a little.

"Aye."

"Do I have a family?" I whisper. "Are there people... somewhere else... that love me?" I can remember a sister, but that's it.

His eyes darken, and his nostrils flare. I've made him angry. What did I say?

"Your family is here, now, Aileen."

"Are you just saying that because you want me here, or do I really have no family?"

A muscle ticks in his jaw before he responds. "You have a father who gave you to me and a mother who enabled him. They are not good people, and I don't wish you to have contact with them again."

My nose tingles, and my throat tightens. I'm overcome with emotion about all of this. This is terrible. That's harsh. I don't know enough about this to even contradict him, so I leave it for now.

Your family is here, now.

I swallow the lump in my throat. "Cormac, another question, please."

He nods.

He's my husband. I need this. I'm going to ask him.

"Will you... will you sit with me for a little while?"

It might be my imagination, but for one tiny sliver of time, I imagine his own eyes water. The next second, he blinks and he's sober again, so stern and formidable I wonder what made me think that, and furthermore, what made me think being held by him would be nice.

He doesn't speak, but stands, kicks off his shoes, and climbs into the bed beside me. I'm surrounded by piles of pillows and blankets. He moves them aside and comes closer to me, folding the blankets down and sliding beneath them. He leans back in the bed against the pile of pillows and lifts his arm.

"Come here, lass," he says in a soft, gentle voice that makes my eyes prick with tears. Why am I so emotional? Is it foreign to me to be treated with kindness?

"I don't like being like this," I tell him.

"Like what?"

"All... emotional. It feels weak."

"When people are under trauma, they sometimes need a little help is all," he says. "Doesn't make you weak."

"Something tells me if *you* got conked in the head and knocked out and woke up not remembering who you were or how you got there, you wouldn't go all teary-eyed. You'd probably come up with your fists raised."

He chuckles. "Aye."

I slide under his arm and lay my head on his chest. My

eyes flutter closed, and I breathe in deeply, before I let my breath out again. I like his strong, masculine scent. The coolness of his t-shirt against my cheek. The firm expanse of his chest. The way his arms encircle me and he holds me tight.

I listen to the steady beat of his heart in the stillness. *Thump. Thump. Thump.*

The lump in my throat dissolves, and I feel warm, wet tears leak onto his shirt.

"I don't know why I'm crying," I say. I hate that I am. "I don't want to. I want to be the strong lass you say I am."

"Hush, sweetheart," he says. "Crying doesn't weaken you. Sebastian said this might happen."

"Did he?"

"Aye. Says amnesia and trauma sometimes trigger emotions. But don't fear that, Aileen. Just let it out, lass. I don't think any less of you for havin' emotions. Cry it out, if you must. Might even make things a bit better."

Is he just pretending to be sweet? Am I supposed to like him? Because I do, and I'm not sure if I should.

I don't try to check the tears, but let them flow freely. I want to know who I am. Who he is. Where we go from here. I hate that I have a family that doesn't like me, but I'm grateful I have a home here. And I'll remember who I am. I will.

After a few minutes, there comes a sort of peace. He doesn't speak, but just holds me in the silence. I push myself up, one hand on his chest to look into his eyes.

He reaches out and brushes a tear off my cheek with the pad of his thumb, then laces his fingers through my hair to the back of my head.

"I'll help you remember. But we need to get you out of this bed, washed up, and fed."

"We do," I whisper, ridiculously enamored by how hot he is. Did I know this before I lost my memory? Or did who he is color my perception? I don't trust myself or my feelings.

Still holding my gaze, he reaches for his phone on the bedside table, and sends out a text before putting it back down. He holds me the entire time.

And then he's kissing me through salty tears, his mouth meeting mine with purpose, gently at first, then firmer, a gentle stroke of his tongue against mine.

It triggers something in me, some sort of memory, and a flare of arousal licks at my core.

He's good at this. He knows how to pleasure me.

With one hand still at the back of my head, he holds me with the other, kissing me until I shiver with need. Soft, sensual lips, a stroke of his tongue on mine, a sharp, sensual flare of pain when he bites my lip then kisses me again.

He releases me and holds the back of my head. "Do you remember anything, lass?"

I do. *I do.*

I nod. "I know that we've... that we've made love before, haven't we?"

His body stills. "We've had sex," he says with brutal

honestly. "Haven't quite made love yet, but I *have* made you come a few times, and I'm damn proud of that."

I laugh. "Well, then. Seems you take your husbandly duties seriously."

He gives me a playful slap to the arse. "Aye."

A flare of arousal licks at me at that. "Um. What was that?"

"What?"

"You just spanked me."

"Aye, I swatted your arse. Wasn't quite a spanking."

I furrow my brow at him and pull away. "Do you spank me?"

And better yet, does it turn me on like it just did?

He snorts. "I have. And will still if the situation calls for it."

My heart beats a little faster. "Oh? How so?"

There's a twinkle in his eyes, though he speaks with firm conviction. "I'm your husband, and head of this house. I expect you to obey, and if you don't, I'll punish you." He frowns a bit. "Seems it's something else I need to remind you of, hmm?"

I huff and push away from him. "Not so sure about *that*."

Reaching over, he pulls me back over to him, and to my shock, he reaches for me, and lazily arranges me over his lap.

"Not so sure about that, is it?"

"What are you doing?" I ask, squirming over his lap, knowing exactly what he's doing.

"Sebastian said to help you remember." He pats my arse over the cotton pajamas. "I'm following doctor's orders."

"Cormac!"

"Aileen?"

"This seems wildly inappropriate."

"If this seems wildly inappropriate, I can't wait to show you what else I have in store for you."

He rubs his large palm over my arse, up and down the swell of it. To my shock, the very feel of his skin on mine sends frissons of awareness through my body. I moan a little, and he continues, massaging my naked skin.

"You may not remember, but I do."

"What?" I gasp.

"What you told me."

Oh, God. "What did I tell you?"

"What you fantasized about."

"Now, Cormac. That was another woman. That wasn't me. I'm an entirely different—ow!"

His palm slaps my arse. It isn't very painful, but it's hardly a love tap.

"Nonsense," he says. "It's my job to help you remember, and I take my job very seriously. Spread your legs, lass."

When I do, I remember, just a little, the vaguest of memories, how he masters my body and commands me to climax. Now this I could get used to.

I open my mouth to protest but forget what I'm protesting when he strokes a finger toward my clit. Even over clothing, it feels so good my breath hitches. I groan as he works me harder and faster, until a knock at the door outside this room interrupts us. I whimper at the loss of his touch.

"Motherfucker," he mutters. "We'll come back to that."

I scramble off his lap and pull the blankets up over me. Did anyone hear him? I will *die* if anyone heard him. But the entryway door is quite a distance from here. I can't even hear what they're saying though the door's open.

"Hope you're hungry," he says. My stomach growls as if on cue.

"Starving."

He places the tray on a little table against the wall. I throw the blankets off and try to stand, but my legs are weak. It's shocking to me how many things I can't do right away.

He's by my side, holding my elbow. "Easy, now. Take it slow. One step at a time."

"I think I've just been in bed too long," I say with chagrin.

"Aye, lass, but you're in good shape. You'll bounce right back, watch and see."

"If you say so."

He chuckles. "I do say so."

"And something tells me what you says goes, hmm?"

"Aye. See how quickly you're remembering everything? Well done, you."

He pulls a chair out and gestures for me to sit. My stomach rumbles with hunger when I smell the fragrant scent of freshly-baked bread.

"What time of day is it, anyway?"

"Evening," he says. "On the third day after your attack."

He lifts the lid on a large tray. My mouth waters. Two small bowls of stew sit beside thick, crusty bread and a crock of golden butter. The main course looks like creamy fish pie topped with mashed potatoes, roasted carrots on the side, and two generous helpings of apple cake topped with icing. *Yum.*

"Okay, wow, this looks good."

"Remember," he says with a teasing smile. "You're a voracious eater."

"I don't need you to tell me *that*," I say, tucking in. I could eat this entire tray and leave none for him.

We eat in silence until I lean back with a satisfied smile.

"Delicious."

"Finish your veggies," he says, pointing his fork at the carrots I left on my plate.

I frown at him. "What if I don't want them?"

He chews then swallows. "Didn't ask you if you

wanted them. I gave you a reasonable portion. Sebastian says your medication without food will make you nauseous, and good, healthy food will help you heal more quickly."

The highhanded instruction makes me angry. "Fuck Sebastian."

"Aileen." There's warning in his voice.

"No, fuck him," I say, pushing the plate away from me. "I may not remember everything, but I do know I wasn't a pushover."

He crosses his arms on his chest and gives me a look that makes me quake despite my bravado. "Perhaps I need to remind you, neither am *I*."

Chapter 11

Cormac

MY PHONE RINGS. I watch Aileen eating her food with a petulant look that would give a grade school brat a run for her money. She's lucky I'm giving her a little space. She's been through quite a fucking ordeal and I don't want to be *too* overbearing, but at the same time, the quicker we establish our roles, the easier it'll go.

I answer the phone and nod in approval. She rolls her eyes. My palm twitches.

It's Keenan. "How's Aileen?"

I grunt. "She's good, I suppose. Bit of a brat at the moment."

"Hey!" she protests.

Keenan chuckles. "Aye, but you know how to handle a brat."

I look pointedly at her and say loud and clear, "I absolutely know how to handle a brat." She pouts, and she's fucking adorable.

"Sebastian says it's good if she's out of bed and getting some exercise. You didn't marry a wallflower, so her returning to the natural state of things might be a good thing."

"True." I don't tell him how I'm torn, though. I want to remind her who she is, but we're still learning, still getting to know each other.

When I woke in the hospital wing and saw her beside me, hooked up to IV's and beeping machines, her face pale and wan, it destroyed me. I wasn't as badly injured as she was. I failed to protect her.

Sebastian was confident she'd wake up, but wasn't sure of the extent of the damage to her brain. And now... Christ, now, I'm not so sure how to proceed.

Some women need a firm hand, and Aileen is one of them.

Keenan continues. "We aren't sure who instigated the attack," he says slowly, as if anticipating my response.

"How can we not fucking know? Had to be the Martins." I'm so angry I want to hurl this phone across the room. Aileen watches me with interest, and it might be my imagination, but I think a shimmer of remembrance passes over her when I say *the Martins*.

"No, it doesn't have to be the Martins," Keenan says. "We called Mack Martin, and he was shocked to hear of the attack. Said her family wanted to know how she was doing."

"Right," I say with a derisive snort.

"Cormac," Keenan says. "The Martins gave us the girl to keep order. Do you think they'd willingly jeopardize the peace we just established by attacking us not two days later?"

"And not hours after I whipped her brother's arse?"

Keenan is silent for a moment. "You told me you didn't think he'd retaliate."

"I didn't. But Christ, Keenan. Who else would?"

He sighs. "Lots of others. You know this. Listen, it's been a long few days, and you—"

"Don't fucking placate me." Fuck his condescension.

His voice is tight and angry. "I might be your brother but I'm still your fucking Chief, and I'll thank you to remember that."

Christ, but he's right. I sigh. "Sorry. I'm sorry, Keenan."

"Now listen," he continues. "We've a list of who it could be."

Aileen gets up from her chair and stretches. The little cotton top she wears rises, revealing the sweet curve of her lower back. The image of bending her over while I lick that secret spot and finger her pussy distracts me. I don't hear a goddamn word he says.

"…and we can't forget the O'Gregors."

The O'Gregors are rivals to the Martins. We're all separate Clans but irrevocably tied to one another in various ways.

"Anyone inspect the latest trade?" The arms trade is our largest, most profitable business we run.

"Aye. And all looks good there. But Father Finn says there's an increase in the drug trade, and we suspect the O'Gregors are behind it."

"We have nothing to do with that."

"Don't we? We've got half a dozen cops on our payroll. My sources tell me they've got none."

I grunt. Alright, then. The O'Gregors are on the list.

I start when I hear the shower turning on. Is she trying to shower herself? She'll still be wobbly from the head injury.

"I have to go, Keenan, Aileen needs me."

"Aye. Come see me tonight, and I'll run by the rest of the suspects."

I hang up the phone and head to the bathroom.

Who's behind this? I want to know. I need to know who's responsible for the devastation they brought to my wife. For nearly killing her. I'll find out who's responsible, and they'll fucking pay.

But first, I'll see to my wife.

I hear her singing when I approach the shower and pause. I forgot the lass could sing. It's a stark reminder of how little I do know about her, how far we have to go still.

I don't want her showering alone. Sebastian said she could be dizzy from her head injury. I don't want her tripping or falling. I go to open the door, to go help her, when I find it locked.

Mother of God, the lass is pushing my buttons.

I pound on the door. "Open this door!"

She continues to sing, belting out an old Irish ditty warning about the wiles of mermaids.

"Aileen. Open the door!" I pound it harder. Her singing stops.

"Who is it?"

Who is it? Is she pulling my chain?

"It's Cormac!"

"I'm occupied, Cormac. Taking a shower."

I take in a deep breath to steady my nerves. "Open. The. Door."

"In a minute."

"Fucking *now!*"

Her footsteps approach the door, and I hear a click of locks, before the door swings open. She's dripping water all onto the floor, a towel pulled haphazardly about her. Her long, blonde hair hangs in unruly, damp waves.

"Well, you don't have to shout."

I step in the room. "Seems I do. Knocking *politely* hardly helped."

"What do you have your knickers all in a wad over?"

I growl, prowling toward her, and she quickly drops her towel and hops back into the stream of hot water.

"Cormac, you don't have to—eek! My goodness, you still have your clothes on!"

I don't bother to strip, but step straight into the shower with her.

"Doctor said you could be dizzy," I tell her. "Said to be sure you don't shower without help."

"I'm *fine*."

I slap her wet arse. "You're not fine until I tell you you are."

"My God, I married a Neanderthal," she laments to the ceiling.

"Damn right you did. Now give that here." I gesture for the bar of soap beside her. Frowning, she obeys. I lather her up, and as much as I want to be pragmatic about this, I can't help it. My dick hardens against my sodden jeans, while arousal coils in my belly.

I rinse her back and between her legs. Only days ago, I did this for the first time. But then, it was different. I knew who I was. I thought I was at least beginning to know who *she* was.

When I lather between her legs, she parts them and moans. God, I want to eat her out right here, right now. Sebastian says to do things that trigger memories. I'd be happy to try *that*.

I hold myself back, mustering all my self-control. I have to ease back into things with her.

"Ok, out you go, lass," I say, stepping out of the shower. I towel her off, then have her sit on the toilet while I strip my own soaking wet clothes off. When I toss them to the hamper, she shakes her head.

"I did *not* remember how fucking *hot* you were," she says. "Must admit *that*."

I give her a smile. She's still the same girl, adorable and witty. I drape a towel around my waist and lead her to bed.

"Cormac?" she asks. For a moment, the subdued little girl who woke earlier returns.

"Mm?"

"Did we... if I'm your wife, do we... do we like having sex? Do we have it often?" She's pink to the tip of her nose.

Christ. She doesn't remember. She can't recall the way I fucked her on our wedding night. How she asked me to make her bleed. How I fucking did.

I have another chance.

"Of course." I towel off and don't meet her eyes.

"Was it... was it good?" I turn to face her, stepping into a pair of boxers. She's eyeing me warily, then her eyes dip to my cock. She purses her lips.

"Of course it was good," I say. "You think I'm going to let you take a stab at my manliness?"

She laughs.

"Honestly, though," I tell her. "It was your first time. I took your virginity."

Her eyes wide. "Ohhh." Then she bites her lip and her eyes roam over my damp body. "Want to help me remember what it's like?"

Christ, do I want to. So badly, my dick aches to be inside her.

"Tonight, we take it easy, lass."

She frowns but finally nods. "Alright, then."

I lead her to bed and lay beside her. My mind churns with questions that need answers, but she has questions of her own as well. I answer her questions until she tires of them. I give her her phone and show her how to watch TV. It seems to quiet her a little, to have something mindless to do, while I answer my emails and get some work done.

When I come back to her, the sun's set low and she's fallen asleep. Her phone has fallen to the bed, her head tipped to the side. I take her phone and slide it onto the bedside table, then plug it into a charger. I lift the blanket and tuck it in around her, but she opens her eyes and blinks up at me.

With a big yawn, she whispers, "I fell asleep. Seems it takes a lot out of you lying in bed and eating food, hmm?"

I climb in beside her. "Aye. You're still recovering, lass."

She closes her eyes and rolls over on her side. I lie beside her, and pull my body up against hers. Her arse nestles easily against my crotch, as if she were meant to lie just like this, right here against me. I wrap my arm around her, holding her to me, and she sighs. Christ, she's gorgeous, all curves and feminine allure, the scent from her shower wafting over me like magic. I breathe her in, the soft golden waves of her hair tickling my cheek. She's little, but fierce. She'll overcome this.

It takes me a moment to realize she's breathing heavily. She hasn't fallen asleep. It seems my wife isn't immune to the power of sexual attraction. My cock stiffens and my balls tighten. I press my erection against her arse, and she pushes back. Encouraging me.

Wordlessly, I move my hand to her breast. Her breath hitches when I cup the weight of it, letting my thumb drag over her nipple. I tease her right over the thin fabric, until she's panting and trembling. Slowly, so slowly I swear she holds her breath, I lift the top and splay my hand across the soft, naked skin of her belly. I let my thumb graze the swell of her breast a few times before roaming upward. I pinch one hardened nipple between my thumb and finger and she gasps.

I tease her nipple for long minutes, kneading and pulling, first one breast, then the other. The heady scent of her arousal is intoxicating. I imagine her riding me, full breasts on display and those gorgeous eyes of hers half-lidded with arousal and need.

I swallow hard, release her breast, and slowly drag my hand down the length of her belly to her hips. She trembles when I shove the elastic band of her pajamas aside, and slide my fingers downward. Wordlessly, she parts her legs, welcoming me to finger her. I push my hips against her arse, my erection throbbing for release, but I want to ease her back. I want her to trust me. I want to bury the memory of our first night together and replace those memories with good ones.

I kiss her shoulder when I reach for her pussy. She moans. Holding her against me, I stroke my fingers through her slick, swollen folds. She sighs with deep contentment, moving her hips in time with my fingers. In silence, I stroke her pussy, gliding my finger in circles over the little bundle of nerves. Her gasps and moans spur me on. I glide my fingers toward her center. I circle her core before I plunge my fingers in deeper. She gasps when I finger fuck her, her hips writhing. I release her core and return to her clit.

"Come, Aileen," I breathe in her ear. I stroke harder, faster. She likes to be dominated, so I plant the seed. "Unless you need me to punish you. Do you need to be punished, sweetheart? Should I take my belt to you? Hmm?"

I feel her tremble beneath me, turned on by the thought of being dominated.

"Do I need to tie your wrists, bend you over, and cane your pussy?"

"Oh God," she whispers, just as she lifts her hips and moans.

"Are you coming for me, sweetheart?"

"Yesssss!"

I stroke her pussy with gentler touches while her hips writhe against my hand and she pants through her release, until she collapses beside me and groans.

"Oh God, that felt so nice," she whispers, her voice exhausted. "So nice."

My bollox ache, and there's a yawning need in me I can't ignore. I'll wake with fucking blue balls between my legs, but I'll deal. I don't want to ruin this, to push too hard or fast.

She falls asleep, her pretty lips parted, holding my arm to her like I'm a stuffed animal or something.

"Really, Aileen?" I mutter, watching her cozy up to my arm. She only sighs in her sleep. I smile to myself. I hate that she was injured, and I honestly fear how she'll be when she remembers. But for now, I'm grateful we have a second chance.

I don't want to wake her. I won't fuck her, not now. Not like this. I'll ease her into that.

Maybe I'm too gentle, I don't know, but we go on like this for days. I return to work, and Aileen tours the grounds with Caitlin and mam. She loves little Seamus, and I frequently find her bouncing the baby on her knee, or holding him in a swaddled blanket, singing one of her Irish ditties again.

"It's good to keep her busy, Cormac," Sebastian says. "Keep her singing. When she remembers the lyrics of her childhood songs, it'll help trigger more memories."

It's triggering memories I'm afraid of, though. But she needs this.

Every day, she remembers a little something more, it seems, but she remembers little about us. Makes sense, I suppose. There wasn't much to remember.

Keenan would normally send me on a few jobs, but I insist I won't be far from Aileen. I stay here for now, nearby in case she needs me. Our guard let me down once. I won't give them a second chance.

I know I'm treating her with kid gloves, but I can't seem to help it. I could've lost her. I don't want to risk that again.

I find her on the third day after she's woken, sitting in the garden on a beautiful spring day. She's got the baby in her arms, and Caitlin's braiding her hair.

"Aileen, a word."

"Just a minute," she says.

I've given her slack these past few days, even after my reminder of who I am and who she is. I've teased her with promises of punishment only to arouse her, but in our interactions I let her get away with murder.

Every day, she's been pushing her limits with her back talk and mouth. Before her injury, I wouldn't have tolerated that, but now I can't help but give her some leeway.

"Aileen."

"I'm right in the middle of something. Not now."

Caitlin looks at me with wide eyes. She isn't allowed to speak rudely to Keenan. I know it as well as she does. We're an old-fashioned clan. We protect and care for our women, but there's a hierarchy of authority even between the men, and everyone knows their place. She's forgotten hers.

"Not in a minute," I tell her. "*Now.*"

Caitlin finishes plaiting her hair and fastens it with a rubber band.

"There you go," she says. "Your hair is lovely. Can't wait to play with it again." She comes in front of Aileen and takes the baby. "Now, go with Cormac before he gets all angry. You know these McCarthy brothers have no patience."

She gives me a small smile and a wink. I grunt in return.

Aileen stands up, and to my shock, doesn't come toward me, but turns and marches away. I look at

Caitlin in confusion, but she only shrugs. I stalk after Aileen.

"Where do you think you're going?" I ask her.

"Away from *you*."

What the hell is this?

"Excuse me?" I reach her and grab her arm, spinning her around to look at me. "What the bloody hell are you talking about?"

Her lips purse together. "Not sure why you even want my attention. Don't you think it best you go on with your men? Hmm?"

"What are you yapping on about?" I say with a frown. "Why do you have a hair across your arse?"

"Hair across my arse?" she says, her pretty eyes flashing at me.

"Watch it, woman," I warn. "I've let you get away with much, but I've had it with your smart mouth."

"Have you?" she says. "You wouldn't know it, Cormac."

We reach the bench under the trellis, and the shadows hide her features.

"Sit *down*, Aileen." I don't give her a chance to disobey, but yank her hand until she sits beside me. "Now tell me what's going on."

"Fine," she fumes, her cheeks pink with indignation. "You've touched me a few times, but you haven't done any more than that. I suppose someone barely over being an invalid doesn't appeal to you, hmm?"

"What?"

"We don't make love. You don't talk to me. You do your job and leave me alone, like I'm going to come apart at the seams if you breathe the wrong way."

"Excuse me?"

"I'm stuck in that room or the grounds and I have nothing. No knowledge of who I am. No memory of what I liked, save the little songs that come to me in bits and pieces and drabs of memory, and those memories *suck*."

Ahhh.

"Go on."

She's going stir crazy. I've handled her too gently, and it isn't helping at all. I've given her space and time to heal, and it seems it's done the opposite.

I vowed I'd give her leniency, and instead she's lost respect for me.

I kept her on the grounds when she wants to spread her wings a little.

It was a mistake.

Her face colors a little deeper. "And I don't like being treated like I'm a fragile little creature. That first night… that first night when I woke, you…" she swallows hard, clearly embarrassed, but determined to speak her mind. "You showed yourself as a real man, one I could depend on even if he pissed me off, not this—"

Real man? Now I've had it.

"Enough." She freezes.

"Go back to the room," I tell her. "And get yourself ready. I'm taking you into town. We'll go to the shops and get something to eat, and perhaps it'll help you. When we come home, I have *other* plans for you."

Her bright eyes and soft smile tell me I may be on the right track.

I've slept beside her for days, so eager to fuck her it's killing me. She's right. I've treated her like an invalid but Christ, I missed my mark. My girl needs so much more. She's young and healthy, so her recovery was quick. Physically, anyway.

I stand and take her hand, lifting her to her feet. "Go. And be quick about it."

I send her off with a sharp crack to her ass that has her squealing, but I swear she leaves with a smile on her face. I dial Keenan.

Chapter 12

Aileen

I'M NOT EXACTLY sure what happened down in the garden. Sometimes I wonder if I'm right in the head.

I've enjoyed my time with Maeve and Caitlin, and we've all spent time with Maeve's niece and Cormac's cousin, Megan, a beautiful, brass girl who's instantly friendly and kind. I like them all. And they answer questions honestly when I ask them, not shielding me from the truth. It's pretty clear that I've not known them for long, so fortunately it seems that we're nearly starting fresh.

I love baby Seamus, and I love the garden. The library holds untold hours of entertainment. They've even, in fairly recent months, set up an actual movie theater *in their home*. Complete with a surround sound stereo system, padded seats, and a large screen with an overhead projector.

But I don't like being home all the time. And it's most unsettling because I still don't know exactly who I am.

The first night I came to, Cormac was dominant to the point of being domineering, bossing me around and promising that I'd learn to obey. And it turned me on. It fucking made me wet. He's made me climax, and he's really damn good at it.

But he hasn't fucked me.

He's likely bangin' one off in the shower when he's able. What's wrong with me? Is he afraid he'll break my delicate bones?

Jesus, Mary, and Joseph.

I know I acted the brat in the garden, and I didn't quite mean to. I absolutely didn't. But God, the tender, gentle distance he holds between the two of us pisses me off. If he's supposed to be my husband, he can grow a pair already, and not treat me like I'm going to dissolve into dust at the merest breath.

I walk up the stairs to the house, and I swear I feel for a moment as if someone's watching me. I pause, and turn around, but all I see is the garden behind me, the well-kept lawn that surrounds me, and far off in the distant, the blueish green of the Irish Sea. Birds twitter in the air, and I even hear some of the guard just beyond the entrance to the home. They're a burly, gruff bunch, that follow us around, ready to swat a damn fly if it comes too close.

I frown, looking around me for evidence to support my gut feeling, but there's no one. Nothing. It must be in my head.

I turn back to the house, and my stomach suddenly

rolls. My mouth waters with nausea. I shake my head, dismissing it. What fresh hell is this? Head injuries are complicated, Sebastian says. I blame it for the nausea and ignore it. Cormac says he's taking me into town, and I don't want to miss it.

I enter the house to see several of the men in the entryway. Keenan and Nolan are among them.

"Y'alright, Aileen?" Nolan asks. I nod.

"I'm good, thanks."

"Have you seen Cormac?"

"Aye, he's just in the garden. Sent me up here to get ready to go to town."

Keenan gives me a curious look. "Town?"

"Aye."

He pulls his phone out of his pocket and mutters to himself. "Missed his call." He calls him back.

Nolan smiles. "Gettin' a little stir crazy, are ya?"

I smile at him. Nolan's my favorite. "Aye, you could say that."

"Go on, then, if he's waiting," Keenan says, his phone still to his ear.

I walk up the stairs toward our bedroom, but hear their voices behind me.

"Could've set something up in the garden, no? Need to see if we're tapped."

A flash of memory hits me so quickly, it's nearly physical. I grab the rail to steady myself, allowing the memory to wash over me all at once.

My mother... it's my mother, I know it... standing in the window of our living room, peeking from beneath a slit in the blinds to the street below our window. "He kissed her. He kissed her, right there on the street where anyone could see."

"Bloody hell." My father sits in the corner of the room with a tumbler of whiskey. Who is the "her" they're talking about? It isn't me. I'm just a child.

"She isn't allowed out with him again," my father says. "Never should've let her out to begin with."

"Aye. And the boy?"

"My men will deal with him."

I CLOSE my eyes to steady my nerves. My older sister. I have several sisters. There were many of us. My memories flood back to me in bits and pieces. My older sister snuck behind their backs and met a boy she crushed on. She was punished for that, grounded to her room and disallowed anything socially for months on end.

Nausea rolls in my belly again.

I remember. God, I do.

She was punished by watching on screen the way my father's men tortured and beat her friend to teach him a lesson.

The chilling memory makes the nausea return.

She married the year after that. A different man, of course, one she'd never met. I remember. God, why do I have to remember *that*? Why can't I remember something good?

Do I even have any good memories? I must.

The door downstairs opens and closes, and Cormac enters. He talks to his brothers and looks up to me.

"Aileen," he says, his brows drawing together. "Y'alright, lass?"

I must look a sight, gripping the bannister and standing here frozen like I've been turned into stone.

"Fine," I lie. Even my voice wants to betray me, wobbling like I've been gargling with stones.

He holds my gaze, then finally nods. "I'll be up in a minute."

I turn back to the stairs, and keep walking up them. One foot in front of the other. One at a time. I finally get to the landing and head to the room.

I have few memories of this house, but Cormac says it's because I haven't been here long.

What would happen if I were to go back to my childhood home?

Would I remember what it was like to live under that roof? I shudder to think of it. Cormac told me I'm not allowed contact with them. At first I wondered if it was Clan law, then I wondered if it was his own doing, and he's a control freak. Now I suppose he feels he has good reason.

But how will I remember who I am if I don't? How will any of it come back to me? Maybe I need to find a way to go back home, safely, without him finding out and losing his mind. I'm scared of what I'll remember, but it scares me worse to be assaulted with memories as I just was now.

I could ask him to take me back. To protect me while he did. But he won't. And then he'll know I'm planning to go back. But he won't.

I go to my room and nausea swirls in my belly again. I haven't eaten in hours, so I figure I'm hungry. There's a platter left from breakfast on the table, some soda bread and butter still waiting to be picked up. I slather some butter on a slice and eat it, and my nausea abates for a bit.

I pick out some nice clothes, dark colored jeans and a cropped light blue top that matches my eyes. None of these clothes are familiar to me, but I'm okay with that. He provides well for my needs, and I sort of like having new clothes, even if they're only new because I can't remember them.

I dress quickly. I want to get into town, to go see the shops. And he's promised me tonight he has other plans for me as well.

I still hardly know the man, so it's almost like a date. Almost. We share a bed, a last name, and vows that bind us. I brush my hair, quickly apply some makeup, and slide lip gloss on my lips, when the feeling I'm being watched returns. It's disconcerting. I wonder if it's because my memory's coming back. Do I only *feel* as if I'm being watched? How could I be, anyway, in a room like this, with bars on the window and guards at the door?

Is this how it feels when memory resurfaces? I look at myself in the mirror. My eyes are bright and my cheeks light pink. My hair shines glossy and golden, cast beneath the glow of sunlight that filters through the window.

My face is round and full, and is it my imagination, or does it look a little softer somehow? I open my mouth and close it again. I wonder if doing some jaw exercises or something would firm up my face a little. I turn to the side and open and close my mouth with wide, exaggerated poses, when I hear Cormac's voice.

"Aimin' to catch some fish, lass? What the bloody hell are you doing?"

I feel my cheeks flush a bit, but I keep at it, nonplussed.

"I need to firm up my jaw," I say, stroking my chin. "I'm getting older or something, because my face looks... *fleshy.*"

"My God, it doesn't," he says. He steps into the bathroom and stands behind me, his hands on my hips. A little tingle races through me when he touches me.

"Are you out of your mind? *Fleshy?* Mack Martin's got a heavy-jowled, fleshy face. Your face is perfect."

"And look at my eyebrows," I say, arching my brows up and down. "They need a good pluck."

He blinks and doesn't respond right away. "They look fine to me," he mutters.

"Pluck," I say stubbornly. My eyes drop to my breasts. "And my breasts look bigger, no?" I squeeze them, wincing in pain. "Aye, they're tender. Must be gettin' my monthly soon."

"Mad," he says under his breath. "And I've no objection if your breasts are bigger." He gives me a wink.

I elbow him. "My breasts aren't good enough? You need bigger, is it?"

He laughs out loud, releases my hips, and gives me a teasing smack to the arse. "Go on with you," he says. "Let's get to the shops before they close."

"Hey!" I ignore the way my stomach flips with nausea. I'm not going to miss a chance to get out of here, to actually do something. But he's already nearly at the door.

I take one of the bags hanging up in the closet and slide my phone in a pocket. I've got a wallet, with cash, and a credit card he's gotten for me.

"Cormac?"

"Hmm?"

"Are we going alone?"

"Course not. We'll have a few men with us as well."

I frown. "Is that *always* the way?"

"Aye. Naturally."

"Was it that way with the Martins?" I ask. I don't remember having a guard on me. Did I?

"I know you had a guard of some sort, but I can't say how or when or where." He frowns. "Wouldn't be surprised if it was hardly a guard at all."

"Why not?"

He purses his lips, pausing before he responds. "The Martins aren't the protective sort."

I blink, and a memory surfaces again.

I'm in a small room, decorated in whites and yellows with a girlish duvet and thin pillows. It isn't posh, like this room, but small and utilitarian. Was it my childhood home, then? And there was a man standing out front. Watching guard. I don't have a fond recollection of him, but a sick feeling of dread twists in my belly when I think of him.

It comes back to me in a rush. He'd give me information or help if I asked in exchange for sexual favors. He took advantage of my situation.

His name was Dermot. Blaine said they killed him for letting me go.

"Aileen? Y'alright? You look stricken."

I blink, shoving the memory away, the bitter taste of it still on my lips. I shake my head.

"I'm fine."

He gives me a curious look, frowning. "You sure?"

I sigh. "Yes. I'm sure. It's just that some of my memories are coming back to me, and so far none of them are pleasant."

His eyes widen so slightly, it's barely noticeable, before he hardens his face again. He nods. "I see. Perhaps we need to speak with Sebastian. See what it is that you can expect, or if you—"

"No." I shake my head, resolute.

"No?" he asks, quirking a brow at me. My heart pitter pats a bit quicker.

"No," I repeat. "You said you're taking me into town, and I mean to do just that."

He raises his brows and leans his hip against the doorway. "That right?"

I feel somehow smaller with the way he looks at me. In the garden, like an idiot, I challenged him. Perhaps that was a strategic error.

I decide it likely smart I rephrase my request. Just to be safe. "I mean… please. Can we please still go into town? Maybe just call Sebastian on the phone or something?"

Another wave of nausea hits.

He stares at me for long seconds, before nodding, his lips pursed. "Right then. Off we go. But if I say it's time to go home, you'll obey without giving me that smart mouth of yours. Understood?"

"Yes," I breathe, barely tempering my desire to bounce up on the balls of my feet and clap my hands like a child. *"Yes!"*

"And when I ask you to recount the memories you do have, you'll tell me."

I pause, mulling this over. Not as easy to say *yes* to. I hesitate, but after some thought, I don't see any reason not to. "Alright," I agree, a little less enthusiastically this time. He's my husband, after all.

He reaches a hand out for me to take. I grin at him. Moments later, we're walking down the large staircase that leads to the main entrance.

"Will we drive?" I ask.

He shakes his head. "No. Can't believe I haven't really shown you before now. But we live close enough to walk, and it's a bright, sunny day." Even though I have permission to walk the grounds, I haven't gone much beyond the gardens that surround the estate.

We take a right at the stone walkway, the sea at our back, walking down a pathway that leads away from the mansion. He takes my hand and gives me a little tug so that I'm on the inside and he's on the street side. I have another vague twitch of memory, of him telling me that he'd do this, but then it fades as quickly as it came.

"So your Clan's mansion overlooks the sea," I say. "We'll walk away from the sea to head into town." I'm trying to get my bearings.

"Aye. Since that's the east coast of Ireland, we'll walk southwest to get into town."

"Makes sense. And your men? Where are they?"

"Behind us, but at a good distance to give us privacy. You won't even know they're there." Not sure I like that they're nearly invisible, but it serves my purpose well for now.

"Good," I say. I want privacy right now. "Because I want to tell you the memory I had a short bit ago."

He sobers and nods. "Go on."

I tell him about the memory of my parents, my sister, and how my parents made her watch her friend be tortured and beaten.

"Seems about right," he says grimly.

"You think that's alright?" I ask him. How could he think that okay? I try to pull my hand away, but he doesn't let me. He holds tighter, squeezing my hand tight enough so that I can't get away.

"I didn't say that, no," he says. "Aileen. Listen to me."

His voice hardens. I listen, though I'm still fighting anger.

"All I'm saying is that type of thing's common among the Martins. It's a shame the boy didn't have someone to tell him to stay clear."

"Many did, though," I tell him. Remembering, how we had so few friends when we were younger, because we weren't allowed, and once anyone knew who we were, they kept their distance. "It comes back to me when I talk to you."

He draws a little closer to me, as if shielding me with his body from the memories that threaten to hurt me. He can't though. Not even a big, muscular man like him can shield me from memories.

"Keep talking, lass," he says. "Just let it out. Sebastian says it's like lancing a wound."

"Oh, ew."

"Ach, you're a sturdy lass. You can take it."

"Sturdy, is it?" I ask, with mock effrontery. "Is that mob man speak for fat?"

"Don't you dare," he warns, but his eyes twinkle at me. "I meant sturdy mentally, silly girl. Not physically. When we get back we'll see how sturdy y'are *physically*."

I snort out loud. "Will we?"

"You have my word."

I like this, walking hand in hand with my husband. He may drive me crazy, but he's witty, and I enjoy him. Perhaps I'll learn to even more. God, but I hope so.

I crane my neck briefly, to get my bearings. It's a beautiful, sunny afternoon with a light breeze coming from the ocean and wisps of clouds painting the sky above. On the coast like this, it's often rainy and chilly, but today's a day to remember. Behind us stands the tall spire of a church, and further in the distance I can see the castle.

"Oh, I remember those," I tell him, turning back around, as if I just remembered the answer on a test. "Holy Family and Cold Stone Castle!"

"Aye. Good girl," he says with a smile.

The harbor sits below the cliffs to our left. Ships come and go, and several men and women drag large nets of fish to the shore. In front of us lies a small, cozy little place with a large, hand-painted sign out front that reads "Cottage Brew."

"What's that?" I ask.

"Local coffee and tea shop. Fancy a cuppa?"

"Aye, please."

He opens the door. I'm still a bit queasy, but a cup of tea might settle my stomach. He pulls out a chair, and leans in to whisper in my ear, "We'll see what triggers memories, aye? And if you need to tell me, do."

I nod. But as I look around the shop, it's unfamiliar. I'm not sure I've ever been in here before. It's small and classy and impeccably clean, with a long, glossy counter housing scones, breads, and biscuits, and a display of tea so impressive it nearly boggles the mind. Chai and herbals, mints and blacks, whites and fruity.

"Just a plain cup of tea, please," I tell Cormac. He goes

to the counter to order while I look around me, taking in every detail. At the counter, a petite, rotund woman with white hair piled on top of her head, ruddy cheeks, and tiny spectacles perched on her button nose, grins at him from behind the counter.

"Is that your wife, Cormac?" she asks with a grin. She knows him, then. I like that there's familiarity here for him. He has a home here. Even through my dim fog of memory, I know that I've never had anything like that before.

"Of course," he says. Several people sitting nearby are watching, though they're pretending they aren't. Seems the McCarthy brothers are sort of celebrities here.

The jovial woman reminds me of Mrs. Claus. She comes to the table with Cormac, holding a tray with two steaming cups and a plate of pastries. She slides it on the table and reaches her hand to me.

"So pleased to meet, you. Name's Isobel." She beams at Cormac. "Oh, isn't she a picture, lad?"

I smile to myself at her calling him *lad*.

"Aye," he says, unabashed. "She is."

I smile bashfully.

"Pleased to meet you," I say and point to the tray. "I'm Aileen. Your shop's lovely, and this looks delicious."

"Oh, go on with ya," she says, waving a hand but flushing with pleasure. "Now I'll let you two newlyweds to yer tea. Do come back?" She bustles away to serve more customers.

"She's a doll," I tell Cormac.

"Aye. One of the best."

I notice the people around us watch us with curiosity but keep a safe distance. Caitlin and Maeve have refreshed my memory, and I know now that he's one of the heads of the McCarthy Clan, an underground crime ring in Ireland. I also know that I came from a similar clan, the Martins. My memories do resurface in bits and pieces, but it's like a sketch made of chalk. The clearer, more concrete details are blurry. At times only shadows remain.

I lean in and lower my voice. "They know who y'are? What you do?"

His gaze sharpens. "And you do?"

"What do you think I've been talking about with Caitlin and your mam? Prams and nursery rhymes?"

He huffs out a laugh. "Aye. Figured as much. It's just as well. Would rather you know. And the answer is, aye, of course they do. I'll explain more later. Not here."

In privacy then.

He hands me a small plate with a scone and a cup of tea.

Chatter continues, but it seems as if everyone's more alert. It isn't lost on me that my husband is a dangerous man. Caitlin explained to me just today that the residents of Ballyhock aren't ignorant to the ways of The Clan, but because the McCarthy men take good care of their villagers, giving generously to the church and seeing to it that crime is mitigated, they turn a blind eye to their illegal dealings. Some do, anyway.

I can't believe how good it feels, just being out together like this. "What else is in town?"

"Oh, lots," he says. "There's the fishy. The Cheeky Mackerel, a bit down the road, but before you get there, down Main Street we have D'Agostino's Italian food. Pretty high end stuff, best calamari you'll ever put between your lips. Homemade bread and tiramisu that'll melt in your mouth."

"Mmm. Can we go there sometime?"

He smiles. "Absolutely."

"Today?"

He wags a finger at me. "Now you're pushin' it, eh?"

"You like that I like to eat so much," I say. "But it might not be so good for the fleshy face."

He snorts. "Give it a rest, Aileen. Your face is perfect."

I take a large bite of scone, and thank him around a mouthful. "Why, thank you."

"There's the Blimey Pub and Lickety Split Ice Cream Shoppe."

"Oooh."

"Crumb's Bakery, a laundry, and several little clothing shops."

"And I get to shop in any of them?"

"Aye."

"Can we go?"

He looks heavenward and releases a labored sigh. "To the shops? Sure."

"You look as if you'd rather I poke your eyes out with thumbtacks."

"Something like," he grimaces.

I giggle around another bite of scone, then wash it done with hot, strong tea. "Not a fan of shopping?"

"You might say that." He leans in and whispers in my ear. "But you could make it up to me tonight."

I grin. "I *could*. I'll think on it."

He growls, but just then the door to the shop opens. Cormac stills. His eyes have gone from jovial to murderous in the space of a second, so quickly my heart skips a crazy beat.

"McCarthy."

Awareness dawns. I know the oily voice behind me. It's one memory I wish I didn't have. I turn. Another memory triggers.

My brother. I have a brother. Blaine. His name is Blaine, and I hate him.

"Martin." Cormac nods. The tension in the little shop visibly heightens. He doesn't even look at me, but I know him. Visceral hatred boils in my stomach, making me nauseous like I was before. He's cruel and vicious. He's hurt me before, I know he has. He doesn't even look my way, but I stare at him. He looks bloody awful, his eyes sunken, his nose damp and reddened.

Cormac turns back to me as if my brother's of no consequence. "You ready to go to the shops?"

"Running, then," my brother says in a near whisper. *That* gets Cormac's attention.

"Cormac, no," I whisper, when he gets to his feet and draws himself to his full height. He's massively huge, much larger than my brother, and I have to admit it pleases me to see the wide-eyed fear that suddenly takes hold with my brother, the way he cowers and takes a step back. He's a weasel that's poked a lion.

Cormac stares my brother down, then walks to the counter in front of my brother. "Bag to go, will you?"

"Certainly," Isobel says. She looks nervously to Cormac. "Please, keep it civil, son," she whispers.

He nods. She hands him a paper sack and shoots daggers at Blaine. Cormac walks past my brother, ignoring him. I decide I'll do the same.

"We can take the rest with us."

"I'll take the shortbread in my hand," I say, rescuing it from the tray before he piles them in the bag. He grins.

We leave the shop without saying another word to my brother. I happily munch the shortbread. It's rich, mildly sweet, and delicious. Blaine won't hurt me anymore, not when the McCarthys are at my back.

"He's afraid of you," I say in a singsong voice, not even bothering to hide how this pleases me.

"Aye. He ought to be. Busted his arse a week or so ago."

"Would've paid to see that."

He laughs out loud. "I think you might've said the same when it happened. You remember, then."

"That my brother's a prick?" I sigh. "Aye."

He nods and smiles ruefully. "We'll have to make sure some of the memories you have are better."

I think for a moment before I reply. We're walking down the street toward a shimmering assortment of brightly-lit shops down the road. It feels so good to be out, in the sun, a light breeze stirring my hair and making me draw nearer to my husband.

"It would be nice if you could do that," I tell him. "Though I'm beginning to wonder how many I have?"

"Nice memories?"

"Aye."

He doesn't respond at first, but gives my hand a little squeeze. "We can remedy that."

We shop the rest of the afternoon, even though it looks as if it's almost physically painful for Cormac to endure. The third hour in, he's holding bags of things. Shoes and new knickers, a pretty little jumper, and a few wee things for baby Seamus.

"Alright," he says. "I've had quite enough of this now."

"Just one more place, the little—"

"*No.*"

I sigh, but I'm not really disappointed. I was only teasing him.

"Dinner," he says stoutly.

"Dinner," I repeat. A fair compromise.

"Italian?"

"Mmmm."

We get a table at D'Agostino's, and I feel a little underdressed. No, I feel a *lot* underdressed. The people around us wear cocktail dresses and suits, and I'm still just wearing my jeans and a top.

"Okay, this isn't good," I tell him with a frown. "I'll be right back."

I take one of my bags, go into the restroom, and emerge a few minutes later wearing a new dress and shoes. He blinks, and the corners of his lips quirk up.

"Did you just get changed in the jacks?"

"Aye," I say, picking up the menu.

He doesn't say anything at first, then just smiles and shakes his head.

"You're something else, Aileen McCarthy."

"Thank you?"

He snorts. "You're welcome."

We eat the calamari he raves about, though I happily give him the tentacles and stick to the little rings, thank you very much. I dig into a large platter of ravioli we share with delicious, fragrant pasta sauce swimming with garlic and herbs. We dip bread in fine olive oil and sip glasses of wine.

"This is so decadent and delicious," I tell him. "Thank you."

He's pleased, I can tell by the way he smiles at me.

"As I said…"

"I can thank you at home," I say, warming up to the idea on my second glass of wine.

He winks. "Aye, lass."

He tells me of his childhood, regaling all sorts of humorous stories until I'm snorting with laughter. Seems he and his brothers got into all sorts of mischief. I wish I could tell him stories of my own, but I have so few.

I think to myself, as I listen to him speak, his hands gesturing as he talks of many things, watching his eyes light up and his deep, rumble of a voice… *I could love this man.* I could.

We walk back to the mansion, hand in hand, as the sun sets in the distance.

"What a lovely date that was, Cormac McCarthy," I say, as we walk up the steps to the house. "I enjoyed myself immensely."

He pauses on the front steps, leans down, and cups my jaw. I know then that he's going to kiss me like this, right here, right now, bathed in the magical glow of moonlight like teenagers on a first date. And I know then that I want him to, that I'm falling in love with this man. My heart flutters, and he draws me closer, his warm, strong hand on my jaw. I close my eyes, as his mouth meets mine. I sigh into his mouth, inhaling his masculine scent, reveling in the strength of his touch, moaning when his tongue explores my mouth.

"Ahem." Someone clears his throat.

I jump, and Cormac growls, before we even see who it is. It's Nolan, standing against the top rail of the stairs on the little porch entrance, plumes of smoke rising upward from his cigar.

"Did you break curfew, son?" he asks, wagging his cigar at us.

"Shut it," Cormac says through tight lips, uttering a litany of profanity. I stifle a giggle.

"Told you to be sure you had her home before—" but he pauses, tipping his head to the side and looking out toward the garden. I follow his gaze, but see nothing. The teasing, playful look on his face vanishes in an instant. With a curse, he throws his cigar down, grinds it out with his heel, and takes off down the steps. We stand to the side to let him pass.

"Son of a bitch," Cormac mutters. He snaps his fingers, and it's as if the guard emerges from the shadows. How do they do that? Two large, uniformed men with comms in their ears approach us. I don't need to see the weapons they carry. Though they're concealed, I know they're heavily armed.

Is this to be my life, then?

Caitlin and Maeve accept it. Can I?

"Take her to my room," he orders.

I don't question it. My heart dances in my chest when two of his men flank my sides and escort me upstairs. He chases after his brother.

And as I sit in the room, memory after memory surfaces. I didn't have a guard, not like this. I had one guy who used me, and he's paid the price for that. I had no friends. No fellowship like they have in this clan. People hated my mother, but in this family, they love Maeve, our matriarch. Will I find that I belong here better than I did at home? Or will I remember things that taint this place, too?

I sit by the window in our room, looking out at the darkness below. Will it always be like this? Normalcy interrupted with the duties of The Clan? Will I ever feel at home?

Chapter 13

Cormac

Once Aileen is secured and I know she's in good hands, I take off after Nolan. His blond hair glints in the moonlight, and it's the only way I know where the hell he's going. He's faster than I am.

"Nolan!"

He doesn't respond, but I can hear him racing ahead of me, and another set of footsteps in front of him. Who the hell did he see? He shouts something, there's a crash, then a decidedly feminine scream. I almost trip on a tangle of limbs.

I stop short in surprise. Nolan's got someone in his grasp, but I can't see a damn thing. I pull out my phone and slide the flashlight on. The beam falls on Nolan wrestling a disheveled, furious redhead.

"Get it outta my fuckin' eye," Nolan growls at me. I

swing the beam away so it doesn't blind him. If it were a man he held, he'd subdue him in no time, but he won't use his fists or vicious force on a woman.

"You need help?" I ask, standing to the side.

"No," he snaps. "I've got this one."

"Let me *go*, or I'll call the police!" she howls, wriggling fruitlessly in his grasp. "I'll *scream!*"

He gets to his feet, and holds the woman to his chest, his arms like a straightjacket around her.

"Go ahead," he says with nonchalance. "Explain to the police how you trespassed on my property, will you?'

She huffs out in indignation.

"I'll tell them how you abused me!"

"Abused you?" he says, with the bored drawl of someone waking from a nap. "Go ahead, lass. I've got my brother as witness."

"I'll—I'll—"

"Make another threat and leave here with your knickers around yer ankles and yer ass reddened? Aye."

"How dare you threaten me!"

"You're the one issuing threats, doll," he says evenly. "I'm only tellin' you how this'll go."

He's walking her back toward the house. Dragging her, more like. I keep the light trained on the ground in front of him.

"You want me to call in anyone at all? Keenan?"

"Oh, no," Nolan says, and if I'm not mistaken, he's taking immense pleasure in overpowering the woman. "I'll see to her on my own, and will fill you in in the morning. You've a wife to see to, Keenan's got his own family. Little miss nosy and I will have a bit of a chat then she'll be on her way."

"We will *not*," she says.

"Aye," he says cheerfully. "But we will."

It finally dawns on me who she could be, the reporter he mentioned to Keenan that night in the club. "She the reporter?"

"Oh, aye," Nolan says when we reach the steps.

"Just doing my job," she says to me. "Tell him to let me go."

"Ah, no. Sorry 'bout that," I say. "Can't do that."

I can't see her in the poor light, save the masses of red hair.

"Aye, lass," he says. "And I'm just doing *mine*."

I open the front door and he drags her in. Several uniformed servants stand nearby, but no one even looks their way. They're used to us bringing folks in, and they're paid well to mind their own business.

"Night, then, Nolan," I say, and head for the stairs.

"Night, brother."

Aileen's waiting for me upstairs. I hope I have nothing else that draws my attention tonight. Nolan will sort out the spy we've got downstairs, and the few jobs I've got to do can wait until the morning.

Eagerness gathers low in my belly. I enjoyed the hell out of Aileen tonight. I intend on enjoying her even more later.

When I get to the room, I'm pleased to see my guard's waiting beside the door.

"Thank you," I tell them. "The lass is safe inside, then?"

"Yes, sir," they say in unison.

"Good job. Everything's fine. We had a spy, but Nolan's got it under control."

I open the door and leave them there. They'll stay the night and a new guard will come in the morning. I close the door behind me and listen for Aileen, but hear nothing. I kick off my shoes and walk into the bedroom. She's lying on the bed, a book in hand that's fallen to the side, forgotten. She falls asleep so easily, living life at full throttle, until she collapses in exhaustion. Her eyes are closed, her mouth hanging open. Christ, she's pretty as a picture, wearing the dress we bought only today that she changed into at the restaurant. Her shoes are kicked to the side, her hair hanging about her in golden waves.

I take the book out of her hand and lay it on the bedside table, and she wakes with a start.

"Did I doze off?" she asks in bleary-eyed confusion.

"Aye." I sit her up to help her undress, and she doesn't protest.

She yawns widely. "I'm so… so tired."

"Must've been the wine?"

"You think? Seems it's knocked me on me arse."

I can't help but smile at that. I love how unpretentious she is. What you see is what you get. I tug down her zipper, and she shrugs out of the top of the dress.

"Lay back," I tell her. "I'll help y'out of it."

"Course you will," she says coyly. "Isn't that what you do best?"

"Christ, I hope so."

She giggles and obeys, lying back and letting me shimmy the dress down her body. I stifle a groan when she's undressed. She wears a delicate, silky pink bra and matching knickers that dip low below her navel, just a wee scrap of a thing. She yawns and stretches her arms up over her head.

"Aren't you a sight," I murmur to myself. "Goddamn, woman."

"What?" she says. I fold her dress and place it on the bedside table, then kneel one knee beside her. I trace the delicate curve of her breast, just under the lacy bits. She bites her lip and watches me, her breath hitching when I slide my finger to the edge of her bra.

"You're absolutely gorgeous," I tell her.

"Curvy," she says with disdain.

"I fucking love those curves. I'll kiss every one of them and give thanks to the gods."

"Do it," she whispers with a grin. Her eyes twinkle at me as she bites her lip.

A challenge.

I lift her back and unfasten her bra. The fabric gives way and her breasts swing free. I groan and swallow.

"So *fuckin'* gorgeous."

I toss the bra up with her dress, then return to her. Kneeling on either side of her, I take hold of her knickers and drag them down over her hips. She lifts up to help me, watching as the thin fabric glides over and down her hips, her thighs, past her knees, then down to her ankles. I tug them off and fold them with her other clothes.

"You're still fully dressed," she says with a coy smile. "However will we do what we came here for like *that*?"

"Quite true," I say with mock seriousness. "Why don't you help me with that?"

She trembles a bit when she reaches for me, her voice low and husky when she responds. Christ, but the woman's as attracted to me as I am to her. "Happily."

She reaches for my collar and unfastens the button. One. Then two. Three, four fall away. I can feel the heat of her hand just inches from my chest. My cock strains against my trousers.

When she reaches my lower abdomen, she takes her time unfastening the buttons, gliding one hand past the shirt to my undershirt. Her hands span my waist, and her eyes meet mine.

"Whatever you do," she whispers. "To keep your body looking like *that*? Keep doing it."

"Aye," I say, amused. "You have my word."

She tugs first one shirt sleeve, then the other. I'm

bathed in her soft, feminine scent, her gentle touch, the way her eyes meet mine in unadulterated lust. My shirt falls to the floor. She tugs the hem of my t-shirt from my trousers, then tugs that off as well.

"God, Cormac," she breathes. "You're bloody hot."

She gets a kiss for that, a chaste brush of lips to cheek. She sighs when I pull away.

Next, she reaches for my belt buckle, unfastens it and pulls it through the loops. That falls to the floor, then she fumbles with my zipper. My cocks strains against the fabric when her hands reach my waist, her warm touch making me long for more.

Soon, we're both naked. My cock throbs, and the sweet, seductive scent of her arousal spurs me on. I lay on the bed beside her and draw her onto my chest. She hitches one knee up over my body, and drapes her arm over my chest.

"Come here," I whisper.

"Is this when you kiss me?"

"Aye," I say on a growl. I lift her and arrange her so that she's straddling me, then draw her closer with my hand on her lower back, bringing my mouth to her shoulder, and kiss her lush, velvety skin. She braces herself on my shoulders as I kiss lower, to the swell of her breasts.

"Gorgeous," I whisper. "And all mine."

I can tell she likes that, by the way she grinds herself against me and her eyelids flutter. I kiss each beautiful curve of her breast, then drag my tongue across her nipples on my way to her other shoulder. Kissing, licking, worshipping.

"Cormac," she moans. "Oh, God, don't stop."

"Sweetheart, I've hardly begun."

I roll her over onto her back and grasp her wrists in my hand, holding her in place while I continue my adoration of the curves, valleys, and slopes of her body. I kiss and lick my way down her chest to her belly, holding her in place. I love the way she squirms and moans when I kiss her nipple, lick her belly, trail my tongue down the fine line of hair that leads to her bare, shaved pussy.

I kiss the warm, damp place where her thighs meet until she pitches off into a pleased moan.

"Cormac, please," she whispers. "I want more. I want you."

I position myself above her and grind my hips against hers. The flush of her cheek and soft, labored breathing make me hard as hell.

I kiss her cheek. "Mine," I growl.

She tips her head to the side, and I kiss her neck. "Mine."

She pushes her wrists against my hold but I hold fast, bringing my lips to the valley between her breasts. "Mine."

I kiss the length of her body, down her full, vivacious curves until I get to the apex of her thighs. I kiss her bare pussy. "*Mine.*"

"Yours," she breathes. "Yes."

She's drunk on sex and arousal, and hell if that doesn't make me even harder.

I kiss and lick and bite and tease until arousal glistens on her thighs, her nipples point in hardened peaks, and her breasts swell with desire.

"Open your legs, lass," I whisper, before I bend to capture her mouth with mine. I glide my cock between her legs as I kiss her, gentle at first, then harder. Claiming. Owning.

I fucked up our first time together, and by some crazy twist of fate, she doesn't remember. I have another chance. An opportunity to do this right.

"Easy, sweetheart," I whisper. "Tell me if it hurts."

Gently, I press the tip of my cock at her entrance. She spreads her legs wider, begging for more. My cock throbs, but I hold myself back. I'm not going to fuck this up, not again. I glide in and out, gently at first, shallow strokes of my cock against her slick, swollen folds.

"Please," she says. "It doesn't hurt. I want you in me."

It's all I can do to hold myself back when she begs like that. I groan with the effort.

"God, woman," I groan. "Don't tempt me." I want to shove my cock in her, impale her until she screams, thrust in so hard and deep she knows to her very core that she's mine. But I can't. I won't. I have to ease her into this.

The first full thrust of my cock makes her moan and whimper a little.

"Does it hurt?" I ask her.

"Only a little."

"Let me make it better."

I kiss her cheek, then her lips, then suck the tender skin at her neck between my lips as I build a slow, steady, certain rhythm, thrusting in and out while the tight, hot walls of her sex clench. Christ, it's fucking brilliant.

"Yes," she breathes. "Oh God, yes."

I hold my body above hers, so I don't smother the girl. Her breath catches when I thrust, her hips rising to meet mine.

"Perfect," she moans. "Yes. Oh, God, yes, Cormac, just like that."

I rock my hips against hers, the slick arousal between us helping me build a rhythm that's harder and faster, until she's moaning on the edge of climax.

"Come with me," I command.

I chase my release and she's right there with me, her moans mingling with mine as we hit our stride, bliss rolling through me as her own pleasure consumes her.

"God, yes," she moans. "Cormac. Fuck, yes."

"Mine," I whisper in her ear, as I'm blinded by pleasure, her tight pussy milking my cock. We stay locked like that until our panting slows. I drop my head to her shoulder and close my eyes, granting myself this moment of perfection.

I had another chance, and this was exactly what I'd have wanted her first time to be like.

She drags her hand lazily through my hair.

"Beautiful," she says. "Was our first time together like that? I have this vague recollection of being nervous, then nothing..."

I won't lie, but I won't tell her the truth either. "This might as well have been our first time if you don't remember the actual first. First times are sometimes awkward and clumsy anyway."

She chuckles softly. "Cormac, you're many things, but awkward and clumsy at lovemaking isn't it."

"Why thank you," I say. With reluctance, I pull out of her and roll to the side. We lie in tangled sheets.

She reaches for my hand and entwines my fingers with hers. "Who was outside?"

"Fucking reporter."

"He trespassed on property?" she asks, shocked.

"*She.*"

"Ohhh. She. What did he... do with her?"

"Dunno. But I trust him."

She's quiet for a minute. "I'm assuming people aren't allowed to trespass on your property."

"Ah, no."

"And I'm... further assuming that... people who do regret it."

"Something like."

"Well I hope he doesn't hurt her." I don't respond.

"Cormac," she says, more insistent this time. "I hope he won't hurt her?"

"Depends on what you mean by hurt, sweetheart."

She smacks my shoulder and sits up in bed, her pretty eyes flashing. "Oh, come off it! You know exactly what I mean."

I hold her wrist. "Enough. Keep your hands to yourself, Aileen. Don't strike me again. *Ever.*"

She silently fumes, but after a brief moment of silent struggle, she concedes. "Fine. Let me go."

"Say please."

She growls and huffs, but finally says, *"Please."*

Once she's settled, I answer. "There are many ways we could hurt someone, Aileen. Now is it the same when one of my brothers gives a spy a beating to teach him a lesson, or when I take you across my knee for your smart mouth?"

She doesn't answer. My voice drops to a warning tone. "Aileen."

"Fine," she says. "No, it isn't the same. But do you really think Nolan will... strike her?"

"Lass, I've no *idea* what Nolan would do. But if it were me? I'd at least tie her up and interrogate her. I'd want to instill the fear of God in her, no matter what that took. Trespassing as a spy on Clan property is punishable by far harsher methods than he's likely to inflict on her. But the woman's trouble."

"How so?"

"She's been putting her nose where it doesn't belong

now for a good year, and it's about time she realizes that if she gets too close to fire, she'll get burned."

Aileen frowns. "Well, what's her problem, then? Why doesn't she just leave well enough alone? You deserve your privacy."

Seems she's changed her mind on which side to take.

"Aye. We do. We may skirt the law, but we keep peace in Ballyhock, and we keep the inhabitants of our little village well protected. The Clan is the very backbone of our economy, and it's because of us that half the village is employed."

"They work for you?"

"Some. But our entire strategy involves supporting local business. Heavily. And if she comes in and digs for dirt, she could upset the whole economical structure of Ballyhock."

Her pretty brows draw together in consternation. "Well *that's* not fair."

"Certainly not," I say with a nod. Now she's catching on. "But Nolan is a fair, just man. He isn't power-hungry like some other men I know. He'll get his point across with as little force as possible."

I tell her this to placate her, so she doesn't worry, but truth be told, I'm not at all confident he'll hold himself back.

"Alright, then," she says with a sigh. "Let me up to get ready for bed?"

"Aye." I release her with reluctance. I like having her beside me. I lean back on my pillows, one arm beneath my head, and watch her. She leaves the door open as she wets a washcloth and washes her body, then brushes her hair, removes her makeup, and does all the little steps she takes before she gets ready for bed. I like watching her. It's private and sweet, how she prepares for bed, with all her feminine routines. When she comes back to me, she wobbles on her feet a little and clutches her belly.

"Oooh," she says with a frown. "Bit nauseous again."

"Again? When were you before?" I get out of bed and reach my hand to her elbow to steady her.

"Before we went into town."

I lead her to bed and help her in. "You didn't mention anything to me."

"Didn't want to miss out going into town."

"Aileen." I don't bother to temper my stern tone. If she isn't feeling well, I want to know.

"I'm *fine*," she says, climbing under the covers. "Well, after a good night's sleep, I'll be fine."

"Don't do that again, lass. If you're not feeling well, you're to tell me. Sebastian says you could have residual symptoms from your head injury. Nausea's one of them."

"Mmm," she says sleepily, drawing the covers up over her shoulder. "Promise."

She sniffs. Is she *crying*?

"Are you alright, Aileen?"

"I just… I'm fine," she says through tears. "I'm just so thankful you take care of me. I don't know why I'm crying. *Again.*"

"Ahh. It's alright. A few tears never hurt anyone." I wonder if sex makes her emotional, or it's a side effect of the head injury. I've heard of such strange things before.

I get ready for bed myself, and climb in beside her. In silence, I hold her for a few minutes, until I realize in surprise that she's already fast asleep.

I check my phone. A text from Nolan to me and Keenan.

Nolan: Found the reporter on our property tonight. Sorted her out.

I'm glad Aileen didn't see that.

Keenan: Did she have any recording equipment with her?

Nolan: She did, she doesn't have it anymore.

Keenan: Good. Will she be trouble?

Nolan: Oh, I'm sure of it. I'll see to her.

Keenan: Did she tell you anything we need to know?

Nolan: Mentioned unrest with the O'Gregors but said she didn't know anything more.

I frown, and shoot off another text of my own. *She still on our property?*

Nolan: Aye. I'll escort her home in the morning, after I know she's understood my warning.

I delete the text thread so Aileen doesn't get her knickers all up in a wad again. We haven't seen the end of this.

I roll over and hold my wife to me. She's yet to learn the ways of our Clan. She's yet to remember who she is, and what her place is here. Will she take to it? Or will she fight it every step of the way? I hold her to me. I have her for now, just like this, soft and supple in my arms. And like that. I fall into a deep and dreamless sleep.

Chapter 14

Aileen

I'M TANGLED in sheets covered in blood. Cormac's naked and he's fucking me, but it isn't the sweet lovemaking of today. He's pinning me down and he's angry. I'm screaming, but no sound comes out. I try to push him off me, but it's no use, he's so much stronger than I am. Every thrust of his hips brings raw pain and rivulets of blood until I'm swimming in it.

"No!" I finally manage to say through the haze of silence that chokes me. *"No!"*

I wake suddenly, still tangled in the sheets. Cormac reaches for me.

"Easy, lass," he whispers.

I shove him away, still caught somewhere between sleep and terror.

"Leave me alone," I protest, slapping him away from

me and trying to get away. There's so much blood I feel as if I'm going to vomit. "Leave me alone!"

Still wrapped in the sheets that bind me, I try to get out of the bed, but he grabs me and yanks me over to him. Nausea rolls over me, and I struggle.

His voice is harder now. Louder. "*Aileen*. You were sleeping, lass. It was a dream."

"Let me go!"

But he doesn't. He holds me to him in an immovable grip. I struggle, but I'm no match to his strength. His deep, commanding voice makes me still.

"Relax, lass. You were sleeping. Easy, now."

The darkened room is bathed in moonlight from the open window. I blink, finally fully waking.

There's no blood on the sheets. They're as pristine white as they were before I fell asleep. I exhale and finally do what he says. I relax.

"Oh, God," I whisper. My heart still hammers in my chest, my nerves still fraught. The nausea I felt at the sight of the blood still lingers.

"Shhh," he says, holding me. "Sebastian said memories might come back like that. What were you dreaming?"

I don't want to tell him. Was that a memory? Or a nightmare?

"I can't remember," I lie.

He doesn't question me at first, just holding me.

"You were fighting me," he finally says. "Did you dream that I was hurting you?"

I sigh. "Aye. You were… God, you assaulted me. Like… like sexual assault."

"I raped you?" The tone of his voice should warn me, but I don't pay heed. Now that I've begun to tell him, I can't stop.

I nod. "And there was so much blood. Every time you —I would—" My voice trails off when my throat suddenly tightens. He growls, his eyes narrowed as if the very thought makes him furious. I don't like to talk about this at all. It's making me nauseous again. Bile rises in my throat and my mouth waters. "Let me go. I'm going to be sick."

He releases me and I race to the bathroom just in time. I heave the contents of my stomach into the toilet, too weak and sick to be embarrassed. He's by my side, a cool washcloth pressed to my neck, then cheek.

"Poor girl," he whispers. He's kneeling beside me, holding my hair. "No more wine for you, young lady."

"Isn't the wine," I protest, panting. I'm at least momentarily relieved that the nausea's passed. "I can drink wine. It's something else. Must've been something I ate. Damn calamari."

"You said you were sick before we went out, though."

He helps me to my feet and hands me a glass of water. I rinse out my mouth.

"Aye."

"Well, no need to diagnose this," he says. "Not now. You get yourself to bed."

He half-leads, half-carries me back to bed and tucks me back in. "Now rest, sweet girl. You need your sleep."

But sleep doesn't come, not at first. He lies beside me, brushing his fingers through my tangled hair.

"How do I know?" I ask him. "How do I know that what I dreamt was only in my mind, and not a memory?"

"I suppose you'd have to ask," he says. "I can assure you if you dreamt I raped you, that didn't happen."

"Of course not," I whisper.

But they're only words. How do I know? He's a man capable of vicious, brutal things. I know he is. The wisps of memory that come to me of my family are the same. Just tonight he admitted to his brother's casually delivering a beating, as well as retribution enacted on a woman. My own memory tells me my family were violent and vicious.

His is, as well.

I've married into a family of criminals.

What else have they done?

Can I love a man like him? A man I hardly know?

I finally fall asleep when the sun's rising, but only for a short time. I wake consumed with nausea again. Whatever it is hasn't abated.

I make it to the bathroom again, and he follows me. But this time, after I get back to bed, the nausea doesn't leave me. I roll and twist in the sheets, my stomach clenching with queasiness. Cormac dresses in a pair of pajama bottoms and calls Sebastian.

"She's sick. Says she didn't feel well yesterday, and it got worse throughout the night. We ate the same food, yes. I'm fine. And no, no one would've had a chance to slip anything."

It's an odd place for the questions to go, but I suppose it isn't out of the ordinary if you specialize in organized crime. My mind didn't even go there, that I was somehow poisoned. But given who I am and who he is, it isn't outside the realm of possibility.

Cormac's brows raise and he suddenly looks stricken. "Certainly. Aye. Most certainly possible. Yes, why don't you come up."

It dawns on me before he hangs up the phone.

Certainly possible.

My fatigue. The nausea. My unexpected tears and emotions I can't seem to check.

"Cormac."

He looks at me, his phone still in his hand. "Aye?"

"Am I pregnant?"

He blinks. "Sebastian's bringing up a test right now."

I sit up in bed.

"Why the long face?" he asks.

I blink and look up at him. "This is my serious, contemplating-life-choices face," I reply. A corner of his lips quirks up, and he turns and walks to my dresser. He tosses me a pair of pajamas.

"Put those on before he gets here." I blink. I'm still naked. Yikes.

I dress quickly, ignoring the way my stomach growls and churns, when a knock comes at the door outside.

Cormac answers it and comes back with the doctor I recognize from the day I woke up from a coma.

"Good morning, Aileen," he says pleasantly.

"Morning."

I wonder what he's seen. What he's done. If he's doctor to this crew of men, he's likely seen loads. What does he know? What secrets does he hold? Did Nolan hurt the reporter, and if so, was the doctor called in to see *her*?

"Tell me how you're feeling." I go over my symptoms with him, and he nods.

"Alright, then," he says. "Day of your last period?"

"Doctor, I hardly remember my last name or where I grew up, and you're expecting to remember the date of my last period? Not a clue."

Cormac snorts. "She was a virgin on our wedding night. If she conceived then, she'd likely have early signs now, no?'

Sebastian nods. "Likely." He turns to me. "I'll give you an early urine test, but if that doesn't show we'll do a blood draw. What other symptoms do you have?"

"I'm tired," I say, emphasizing my words with a yawn. "Very tired. And a bit weepy."

He nods. "Let's see what the test shows."

Cormac follows me to the bathroom. "Cormac McCarthy, I will not use the toilet in front of you."

"Fine," he says, rolling his eyes at me. "But you won't wait for the results of the test alone either, lass."

"Fine," I mimic. He narrows his eyes in warning and I slam the door.

I can hear the low murmur of their voices on the other side of the door while I do my business and pee into the little cup that came with the test. Out of sheer petulance and my husband's high-handed ways, I make him wait a full minute before I open the door to him.

"Alright. Come in."

He comes in, shuts the door behind him, and walks to the sink. He looks at the test. Nothing visible yet. He turns to me and reaches for my chin.

"Not a big fan of the smart mouth returning, Aileen," he says. "Pregnant or no, I'll expect you behave yourself."

I shrug him away. "Ack. I'm fine," I tell him. "No need for you to get all bossy and autocratic on me again."

He grunts. "We'll see about that."

He reaches for my hand and I begrudgingly allow him to take it. I'm not sure why I'm so out of sorts, but I can't seem to shake it.

"Would you look at that," he says, his brows rising. He lifts the thin test off the counter and shows it to me.

Two pink lines.

"Does that mean what I think it means?" I mutter, unsure of how I feel. I'm still tired and queasy, and now I've just found out my body's to be taken over by another. It's an odd feeling.

"It does," he says with unmistakable pride. He's fairly

grinning. "We're to have a son. The McCarthy swimmers have done their duty."

I snort. "First of all, that test doesn't say *son*, it says *pregnant*. Second of all, your swimmers hit fertile territory, so this wasn't all your doing."

He grins at me, lifts me, and crushes me to his chest. "A *baby*, Aileen. I can't believe it."

"Neither can I," I say. I think I may be in shock.

We head back into the bedroom where Sebastian waits, and Cormac waves the test at him. Sebastian smiles. "Well done, you," he says to Cormac.

I roll my eyes again. "Again, it's the McCarthy virile sperm we applaud."

Sebastian smiles at me, gathering his things. "Congratulations, Aileen. I suspected this might be the case, so if the nausea's still bad, I've got some medication for you."

I can barely stand through the waves that assault me, so I gratefully take the medication and swallow it down with some water.

"Anything that sounds good for breakfast, get it for her," Sebastian instructs Cormac. Cormac nods, wide-eyed and eager. "She can take the medicine regularly to help quell her nausea, but there are a few remedies I can send up as well."

"Thank you."

Sebastian takes his leave.

"Really, all that sounds good is some toast with marmalade." My mouth waters at the very thought. It's odd, since I've never liked the sweet yet bitter preserves.

"Anything else?" Cormac asks.

"Hot tea, please."

"Of course."

He orders my food, then takes a call from Keenan. He walks to the other room while we wait for breakfast, and I'm left with my own thoughts. Though I'm trying to be brave, this unnerves me.

I'm carrying the baby of a man who's virtually a stranger.

I don't know our history. I don't know his. Hell, I hardly know mine, though it comes back in bits and pieces. And now, this makes things so much more permanent than the mere band on my finger did.

I'm carrying the man's *child.*

I'm raising a child with this man.

With a man I hardly know.

I close my eyes and wait for the medication to kick in, and I think I may even drift off to sleep. I startle awake when I hear the door open, and a minute later Maeve comes in, carrying a large silver tray. She's already dressed for the day in a soft white sweater and slacks, her makeup perfect and her hair fixed just right. I feel frumpy and frazzled next to her.

"Cormac called me," she beams. "Congratulations!"

"Thank you," I say. "Cormac, could you give a girl some notice, first? I'm still in my pajamas, Maeve. Haven't even showered yet, so my apologies."

She waves a hand at me. "Pfft, go on with ya. Nothing I haven't seen before, and you're pretty as a picture just rolling out of bed as y'are."

I want to like this woman. I *do* like this woman. It's just that I don't know what my place is here, who I am. Who she is. If I should even like being part of this clan of people who seem nice, but then do things like capture reporters and… and all sorts of things, I guess.

"Sit up, love, and we'll get you sorted." She sits on the edge of the bed and looks at me with her kind eyes. "How are you feeling?"

"Bit nauseous."

Cormac snorts. "She's been riddled with nausea, she's utterly exhausted, and she—"

"Cormac! You're exaggerating. For goodness sakes, you act as if I'm an invalid."

He grunts to himself, but his phone rings, so he steps into the living room to take it.

Maeve leans in. "It's always the way with the McCarthy men," she says with a knowing smile. "Overprotective." She rolls her eyes and lifts the lid on my food tray. "He'll have you lying in bed and waited on hand and foot before you hurt yourself."

I frown as I take a slice of toast with butter and marmalade. My, but it looks good. "We'll see about *that*," I mutter.

She smiles and pours me a cup of tea. "Good girl. We will. But you're no pushover, Aileen. You give that son of mine a run for his money, and it's about time someone did."

Alright, then. Yes, I like her.

I eat the toast and follow it with the tea. "God, this is good," I say. The bread is thick and fresh, lightly toasted, slathered with creamy, rich butter. The marmalade is sweet with a pleasant tang, studded with liberal flecks of candied peel.

"Aye," she says with a smile. "Our chefs make it on site. Some of the best you'll find in all of Ireland."

The scalding tea washes down the toast, and between the food, tea, and medicine, I'm almost feeling myself.

"Goodness, I'm feeling better."

"Excellent," Maeve says. "I'm going to get you some ginger biscuits, an old remedy, and I'll be sure they're here if you need them. And if you need anything at all, you'll call me?" I can tell by the earnest look in her eyes that she hopes I do.

"Of course," I say with a smile.

"Get good rest," she says. "Eat small meals frequently, and we'll keep them nice and bland, but let's be sure it's something you want, okay?"

"Aye."

"Our staff makes some of the best ginger biscuits. Just nibble them with tea. If you *feel* like it, mind."

I nod. It's like she's been waiting for just this moment to mother me, like she's come into her own as matriarch of this family. I'm not complaining. I don't know if I've ever had anything like this.

"Wear good, loose clothing, none of those tight jeans and elastic bands around your waist," she continues.

"It'll help not put pressure on your tummy. We'll get you some nice leggings and things." Cormac steps into the room.

I suddenly remember something. I sit up straight in bed. "Cormac! I drank wine last night. My God! I could give the baby brain damage!"

He blinks, looking as stricken as I feel, but Maeve just rolls her eyes and clucks her tongue.

"Easy, you two. It's early on yet, and many have a bit of drink before they find out they're expecting. It'll be fine."

"How do you know?" I ask. "How do you *know*?"

"We'll call Sebastian back," Cormac says.

Maeve gets to her feet and pats my hand, and I don't miss the smile she tries to hide when she turns to go. "You do that, son," she says. "I'll go to the kitchen and be sure they make her a batch of the biscuits." She walks to the door. "I'll be back!"

Sebastian does indeed return, and he echoes Maeve's sentiments. There's nothing to worry about. He assures us the baby will be fine and leaves. I'm a little relieved.

"How's your tummy?" Cormac asks, sitting on the edge of the bed, his brows knit with concern.

I can't help but smile.

"What?" he asks.

"It's just funny, a big, burly, tough guy like you asking about my *tummy*. Do you say *owie* or *boo-boo* if I'm injured?"

He growls, but his eyes twinkle at me. "Wonder if yer ass is injured," he mutters teasingly.

"Now, Mr. McCarthy, we'll have none of *that*. I'm pregnant."

"Nice try," he says, his lips tipping upward. "Doesn't mean I can't have my way with you."

"You most certainly cannot!"

"Is that right," he asks, climbing onto the bed beside me. In ten seconds flat, he's got me pinned to the bed, his massive body pressed to mine.

"You can't—can't *spank* me and do all manner of torturous things to me, though."

"Can't I?" he asks, bringing his mouth to my ear and nibbling the lobe.

I make a noise that sounds something like, *"unnngh."* I close my eyes, losing myself to sensation as he licks and nibbles and teases.

"I'll have my way with you," he promises. "And you'd best behave yourself as well, or I'll be forced to find alternative methods of punishment."

Wetness pools between my legs, goddamn him. "Hmmph," I say, trying to pretend that I'm not turned on. I gather the scraps of my dignity.

"You act as if... you talk like..." my voice trails off. I'm at a loss for words.

"Like what, lass?" he says, bringing his mouth to my nipple, still covered in my pajama top. He nips me straight through the fabric. I gasp and keen with pleasure.

"Like you own me."

"But I do."

"I beg your pardon," I say, trying fruitlessly to wriggle out of his grasp. "But I—"

"You wear my ring," he says. "You bear my name. And now you bear my child. There's no getting away from me, Aileen McCarthy," he says, giving me a wolfish grin.

"Apparently not." I keep a haughty air, holding onto my dignity, even as his words excite me. I feel as if I should protest this further, as if I should fight for my autonomy, but when I'm under his heated gaze, I forget exactly why. The air's suffused with his ruggedly masculine scent, my wrists captured in his firm grip, the muted pain mingling with arousal a reminder of our lovemaking the night before. My whole world in that moment is Cormac.

He leans down and kisses first one cheek, then the next. I close my eyes when his lips meet mine, a gentle brush of warmth and possession, my body rising to meet his for a brief second before he pulls away.

"I know why you protest," he whispers in my ear. I shiver when the vibration of his voice glides over me. "And there was a time when I'd have taken my time with you. Introduced you to the ways of The Clan slowly. Given you space to really process who you are here with me, what your role is here." He brushes my hair off my forehead, bends down, and kisses my cheek. "But not when you bear my child, lass. You were mine to protect before, aye. But now it means so much more. You'll be the mother of my firstborn."

"It's hard for me to understand this, Cormac," I whisper. "I... I like how it makes me feel. I think? But it scares me, too."

"Aye," he says. He releases my wrists and joins me on the bed. He lifts his arm, and I scoot beneath it. He holds me to his side, and I close my eyes. I'm still tired, and it feels warm and comfortable here. He sighs. "I get that, lass. I do. You're still in a place where you don't know who you are, or where you came from, and I imagine that scares you a little, because what happens next is a mystery as well."

I nod. "Hmm. Didn't expect a guy like you to be so understanding."

He gives me a teasing pinch to the arse.

"What's that supposed to mean?"

I can't help but giggle. I sober quickly, though, at what I have to say next. "It comes back to me, you know."

"What does?"

"The memories. Who I am. Where I came from. How I got here."

"Aye," he says. "Kinda wish it wouldn't sometimes."

Well that's an odd thing to say. "Why not?"

"I want you to start fresh here. And the memories you take from your past aren't good ones."

I sigh. "Aye. What can you tell me about my parents?"

"You sure you want to have this conversation?"

"I do," I insist.

"Why now?"

"Why not?"

He chuckles. "Jesus, you're persistent. Alright. Truth be told, I don't know much about them. Your mam and dad had six girls and one boy. The girls were all given away to various clans, including the one you came from, as payment for various jobs."

I flinch. I knew this, I suspected it anyway, but to hear him confirm it makes me want to cry.

"Aye," I whisper.

"You were the last to go. Your parents profited immensely by giving your sisters to the Martin Clan to use. And this is why I won't allow you to go back home. This is why I tell you you're mine now."

I'm quiet for long minutes. I listen to his heartbeat and our quiet breathing in the stillness of the room. He gets a notification on his phone and swipes it aside.

"You have to go?"

"No."

"Who was it?"

"Just Keenan. Meeting."

"And you don't need to attend?"

"Actually, I do need to, but I'm having them come here. I'm not leaving your side. Not today."

I practically jump out of bed. "*Cormac.* I'm not dressed!"

He shakes his head. "You've got an hour, sweetheart. Don't get your knickers in a bunch."

I grunt under my breath.

"Mam says she's sending the biscuits up shortly," he says. "You need help getting to the shower?"

"I think I can manage," I tell him, but not surprisingly, he doesn't take my answer. He helps me into the shower and joins me.

We lather each other up. I love his powerful, muscled body, and revel in the way the warm water and soap help me glide my hands over his muscled shoulders, powerful back, the strong, chiseled planes of his body. When I reach his hips, I take his cock in my hand and stroke, watching as his eyes go half-lidded and he releases a low, guttural moan I feel right between my legs.

I love when he touches me, but I love when he gives me this control as well. I feel powerful, my own form of possession overtaking me as I stroke the length of his swollen cock. He braces himself on the shower wall and groans.

"God, that feels good."

"I'm glad," I whisper. The warm water cascades down the back of my head and my back. I brace myself by holding onto his shoulder, while with my other hand I continue to pump my fist with his cock, until he shudders and groans, throws his head back and comes. The pounding of the water drowns his groans as I stroke him to completion, the water washing me clean as quickly as I'm marked.

"Good girl," he whispers, pulling me soaking wet to him. "Jesus, that felt good."

"It did," I agree.

He holds me and kisses me, our steaming hot, soaked

bodies melding together. "I haven't even done anything to you yet."

"But you have," I say with a smile. "Just not this very moment."

"Is that right?" He cups my jaw and my heart flutters when he lowers his mouth to mine. I lose myself in the kiss, pressing my body up to his.

"Yes," I whisper.

"Get out of the shower," he whispers back. "Towel off. No clothes. Lie on the bed and wait for me, your knees parted. I want you to spread your legs for me. I want to taste you. I want to watch you come on my tongue."

"Right now?" I manage to whisper.

He grips my arse and cups it firmly. *"Now."*

I do what he says, step out of the shower and towel off, then go to the bed and lie on my back. I close my eyes, tired but eager, my body vibrating with need and arousal. He joins me a moment later, dressed in a pair of boxers.

"Good girl," he says. "Just like that."

He kneels before me, lifts my legs, and bends his head to kiss the fullness of my inner thigh. I'm longing for pleasure and release, to feel him take my body to orgasm once more. I shiver, holding my breath until I feel his mouth where I'm desperate to feel him.

I'm already aroused, already pulsing with need. With slow, masterful strokes of his tongue, he quickly takes me to the edge of climax. He grips my legs and suckles my clit, releases me and presses his warm, wet tongue upward. My head tips back, and I come.

He works me to completion, drawing out the last spasms of orgasm until I nearly collapse.

He stands, wipes his mouth with the back of his hand, and grins at me.

"Get dressed, sweetheart. My men will be up here in…" he glances at his phone. "About one minute."

Chapter 15

Cormac

AILEEN SITS UP IN BED, grabbing at sheets, her cheeks still flushed pink from climaxing. Her sweet, seductive taste still lingers on my lips, as I pull clothes on and she scrambles for her own.

"Why didn't you tell me what time it was?"

"Just did."

"But I'm not… I'm not *ready*," she stammers. "They're going to take one look at me and think 'sex-crazed.'"

I snort. "*What?*"

"I'm all pink and flushed and my heart's still racing, and I—"

I reach over to her, yank her to my chest, and press my finger to her lips. "None of them are going to know that I just made you come. And if anyone *does*, they'll know I'm only doing my duty as your husband."

She blinks. "Your duty?"

"Aye, lass. You belong to me. As mine, you ought to have your needs met. *That* is one of them."

"Right," she says, pinking at the cheeks again. She swallows hard. "I s'pose."

I tug a lock of her blonde hair and kiss her forehead. "*Go.* Get dressed." I pull out a light cotton dress, remembering what mam said about tight things around her belly.

"Alright, alright," she says.

"Wear *this*."

She pauses and raises her brows to me. "You're picking out my clothes?"

"What does it look like?"

She frowns, but a knock on the door has her squealing and running for the bathroom to get changed.

"Just a minute!" I shout to the door, dragging a t-shirt over my head and walking to the door.

Mam stands on the other side with a plate of biscuits, and behind her stands Caitlin and Megan.

"Ladies, we're having a meeting up here shortly," I say, exasperated. "It isn't what one might call a community meeting."

"I know," mam says, breezing past me. Caitlin gives me a sheepish look but follows. The door opens again, and Megan enters.

"You can't be here," I protest. I might be the Bonebreaker for the Clan, but I have no control over my mother.

"Now, Cormac, when a woman of the Clan's expecting, you can't expect us to leave her be," Megan says, walking right into the room with mam and Caitlin.

"I know, dear," mam says. "We'll shut the door and let you men do your thing."

"Is this about the reporter?" Caitlin asks.

"Ugh, that *bitch*," Megan mutters.

I want to shake the lot of them. "How do you know about her?"

"Well," Caitlin says, looking abashed. "I... she was bothering me yesterday, came into the garden and started asking me all sorts of questions about the baby and Keenan."

"And she had the nerve to take pictures of the baby!" Megan says, her bright green eyes flashing.

"When was that?" Aileen stands in the doorway of the bedroom. Her damp hair's twisted into a knot on the top of her head. She's wearing the dress I handed her, and she's barefoot, but she's the prettiest damn thing I've ever laid eyes on.

"We don't need you to get involved," I begin, but Caitlin answers her anyway.

"'Bout dinner time? I went to the garden with the baby, and she was there."

Aileen looks at me. "She was hiding a good long while then, wasn't she?"

"Aye," I say, when someone knocks on my door again. I

open the door to Keenan and Nolan, and before I close it, Tully, Boner, and Lachlan arrive.

"Okay, you girls off to the bedroom with Aileen," Keenan says but he snags a ginger biscuit off mam's tray first.

"Those are for her *nausea*, Keenan," she says, slapping his hand away.

"Honestly!" Caitlin says.

Keenan looks up at me, wide-eyed. "Nausea? There a reason for that, brother?"

Megan and Caitlin giggle.

"Aye," I say. I can't hide the pride I feel as I tell my brothers. "Aileen's expecting."

"Guess we don't wait around here," Aileen mutters. Nolan slaps my back, the others congratulate me, Boner proposes we celebrate at The Craic, and Keenan kisses Aileen's cheek. She flushes pink and thanks him.

The girls head off into the bedroom, and the men assemble.

"Well done, you," Lachlan says, giving me a grin. The youngest of our Clan, he only joined rank last year, after Keenan recruited him. He graduated St. Albert's, the finishing school where our men are trained, and quickly became one of the most loyal, dependable men.

Boner sits on the recliner in my living room and pushes it back.

"Alright, lads, now what's the story? Why'd you wake me out of a good, sound sleep, for a meeting?" he asks.

"To tell me Cormac knocked his wife up? Could've told you *that* myself."

"Fuck off, Boner," I tell him. I whip a pillow at his head, but the wanker catches it before it smacks him.

"No, we're here to talk about what happened to me last night," Nolan says. He leans back on the sofa and kicks off his shoes.

"Don't make yourself at home," I tell him. "After the meeting, I'm kicking you boys out of here so I can tend to my wife."

Tully and Lachlan give each other knowing grins. "Wish I could tend to a wife," Lachlan says. I give him a good-natured punch to the arm. He grins and rubs it out. Keenan sits on the sofa, leans forward, and rests his elbows on his knees. He clears his throat and the room goes quiet. We might give each other crap, but we know why we're here.

"Nolan caught a spy last night." No one laughs now. "Cormac witnessed as well. They were coming home from town, Nolan was on the front step. Both saw someone spying in our garden."

"How'd he get past security?"

"*She*," Nolan corrects. "A very good question."

Boner's eyebrows shoot up. Lachlan looks at Nolan sharply. To my surprise, Tully looks away.

Is he hiding something?

"Says she found the door unlocked and decided to pay us a visit."

"Unlocked?" Keenan says, his brows furrowed.

"Not unlocked, brother. Not when you look through footage on the security feed."

Tully looks paler than I've ever seen him.

"You got something to say, Tully?" I ask him.

He shifts uncomfortably on his seat and clears his throat. "No, why?"

Nolan sobers. "I think you do. Because I've already looked through the feed, brother."

The room goes quiet, and through the closed door to my bedroom, I can hear the higher-pitched, muffled feminine voices in the other room.

Keenan looks from Nolan to Tully. If Tully's in any way responsible for a security breach, he'd be smart to fess up now. It's a major infraction, on a level just below betrayal or theft from the brotherhood. We take security seriously.

When my father was Chief, one of his own left his wallet and keys in a woman's room after a one-night stand. I attended the punishment he received for it, witnessed Keenan delivering a beating I remember to this day. It was one of my first inductions into Irish mob life, one I won't forget.

Tully curses under his breath, then looks to Keenan.

"I'm sorry, sir," he says. "Slept with a girl from the club. Came home, found my keys missing."

"And you didn't tell anyone," Keenan says, his voice holding deadly calm.

Tully clears his throat. "No."

"Why not?"

"Thought I'd go by in the morning and get them," he said.

"You fucked her on your night on duty," Nolan says. His boyish grin is gone, his eyes flinty. "Sheena told all." He turns to Keenan. "Sheena's the reporter."

"Do I need to ask how you got the information out of her?" Keenan asks.

"No," Nolan says, and his lips twitch. "I did so thoroughly. Suffice it to say, the girl won't be back here anytime soon. I got what I needed."

Keenan nods. He trusts him.

"Would explain the call I got from Walsh," Boner says. He served time, and with his characteristic charm and wit, befriended several corrections officers and local police. He's the one that keeps their bellies and wallets full. It comes in handy having local law enforcement in our pocket.

"What'd Walsh say?" Nolan asks, a dangerous glint in his eyes.

Walsh is the head of the Ballyhock police force.

"Said a woman called to complain to him about seeing one of the men in our family manhandling a woman outside their estate."

Nolan snorts. "Didn't give a name?"

"No, but he traced it back to the bitch. Told her he'd look into it."

"I'll take care of her," Nolan says.

"Do it," Keenan says, his voice steel. "Or I will."

Keenan and Nolan lock gazes for a moment. Nolan knows Keenan's way of taking care of her will end her life. "You know the laws of The Clan when it comes to spying, Nolan."

"I do, brother," Nolan says. "But this particular spy may prove useful."

"She's got a nice arse, too, aye?" Lachlan says with a grin. He's young, nearly twenty years old, but he's a big lad, sturdy and fearless. "Might also prove useful."

Nolan narrows his eyes at him but the others guffaw.

"Shut it," Nolan says. "Her mighty *fine* arse has nothing at all to do with it."

We sober when Keenan clears his throat. "Lachlan."

As the newest member of The Clan, Lachlan's called on by Keenan to earn his place at times. He's still learning the laws of our order, the rules of brotherhood and fellowship.

Tully squirms, as if he knows what's coming.

Keenan continues to address Lachlan. "How would Malachy deal with one of you boys if you'd been responsible for a security breach by sheer negligence?"

Lachlan strokes his chin thoughtfully. "Well," he begins. "He taught us the order of the Clan, so we were held to those rules even as young lads."

"Aye."

"A breach against security puts the lives of everyone in danger," Lachlan says. His voice holds a tone of authority of an older man. He's a natural born leader. "Malachy is an old-fashioned sort," he says. "A minor infraction, anyone who did such a thing would likely lose privileges. No leaving school grounds, errand boy for the teachers at the weekend, that type of thing. But a more serious infraction would earn physical punishment. Hard labor. A brutal workout. A hard beating."

"Aye," Keenan repeats. He turns to Tully. "And what would you say's a proper punishment?"

As father figure to our Clan, Keenan holds everyone to high standards.

Tully clears his throat. "Whatever you think best, sir." Though we love each other like brothers, there's a distinct hierarchy we all adhere to. I observe Keenan's methods closely, as second-up to the throne.

Tully looks as if he might be sick. He's no wimp, and I've seen him fight with the best of them. A fellow strike force brother, he's had his jaw and nose busted. But it's one thing getting into a fight and getting your arse kicked, and quite another to be sentenced punishment by your Chief.

"Good answer," Keenan says. "It's by sheer luck the breach was something rather easily dealt with *this* time. Cormac will see to your punishment."

Christ.

He turns to Lachlan. "And Lachlan will capture it on video and send it to the girl you fucked."

My stomach tightens. I hate raising fists to my own brothers. But our rules are inflexible, and Keenan doesn't play games.

"The girl's best friends with Sheena," Nolan says. "It'll get back to her."

Keenan swings his gaze to Nolan. "Precisely."

"Will it please her, though?" I ask Keenan.

He shakes his head. "Depends on what we say when we deliver the message. I want her to know exactly who she's dealing with."

Tully stands and faces the group. "I'm sorry."

Keenan stands, nods to me, and accepts his apology with a grave nod. "You will be."

Several hours later, I come back to Aileen, work worn and tired. I did what I was ordered to, and Tully took it, not even raising his hands to block the blows I administered. Lachlan witnessed, Keenan signed off. Tully won't make that mistake a second time.

Aileen is sitting by the large window in the living room, a blanket on her lap and a cup of tea in her hand. She blinks when I enter the room.

"You didn't tell me you were going anywhere," she says matter-of-factly, the barest hint of reproach in her voice.

"I did," I tell her. "You didn't see the text I sent you?"

Her eyes go to my fists, lacerated and covered in blood, and she raises a hand to her mouth. I watch as her eyes widen, as she takes in my appearance.

"I didn't," she says. "Hell, I forgot I even have a phone. Why didn't you just tell me?"

"Would rather mam didn't know," I say with a sigh. "She hates it when we get violent among each other."

"You fought with a brother?" she asks, her eyes going even wider.

I sigh, cross the room, and sit on the couch opposite her. I go to scrub a hand across my brow but stop when I see the blood. I sigh. "No. I didn't fight him."

Her brows draw together. "Then why…"

"Retribution."

She frowns for a moment, then finally nods. "I see. Did someone break a rule or something?"

"Aye."

"And it's just that simple? You break a rule, this is the punishment."

"Aye."

She doesn't protest or ask any more questions, but sits back on the couch. Thoughtful. "And what about the woman Nolan caught last night? Is she alright?"

"She's home," I say.

"You didn't answer my question."

"I rarely will, lass. Not when it deals with the Clan."

She doesn't speak for long minutes. I finally stand and head to the bedroom. "I need a shower."

"So this is what I'm bringing a child into."

I turn back to her. "Come again?"

"This," she says with anger. "This… barbaric behavior. *This* is what I'm bringing a child into?"

I don't want to hear it, not now, not when I've just finished giving a man I'd give my own life for a beating that left both eyes swollen and shut and broken ribs he'll need mending. Bloody hell, I'd have rather fought him square and taken his fists myself than have him just fucking take it like he did.

So I don't take her bait. I don't answer. I turn and walk to the bathroom, stripping my clothes off on the way. I whip my dirty, bloodied t-shirt into the basket of laundry.

She has no choice in this. She bears my name and my child, and she was born into this life.

"Not now, Aileen," I tell her, fucking hoping she heeds the warning in my voice because I'm not in the mood for a fight.

"Is it?" she asks, her voice rising in pitch to match her temper. I turn back to face her.

"Is it what?"

"What I'm bringing a child into?"

"I said *not now*."

But she's on her feet, her hands on her hips. "No. Now. I want to have this conversation. I don't want you to hide this from me."

I turn to face her, my hold on my temper snapping like a twig in a hurricane.

Crack.

I stalk back to her. She doesn't back up or even widen her eyes, but narrows them on me. Waiting, without a trace of fear.

"Hide it from you?" I ask. "Hide fucking what? You reckon I have a secret life I don't share with you?"

"Aye," she says. "You *do*."

"I'm hiding nothing," I say, reaching her. "There are details you're not privy to, but you know who I am. What my job is. And how we operate."

We stand inches apart. Her chest heaves and her cheeks are bright pink with anger. My hands clench in fists. I could hurt her for this, for pushing me to the brink of anger when I'm at my lowest. I want to take her slender shoulders and shake some fucking sense into her.

"*Aye*," she repeats, angrier this time. "I. Fucking. *Do*."

I take her shoulders and grip, but I hold myself back. "Don't you dare. I told you I didn't want to talk about it. I fucking *told* you not to push me."

"Or what?" she says. She shoves my hands off her, then places her hands on my chest and pushes me away. "Or *what*? Are you going to beat me, too, then? Hmm? Pregnant and all?"

I fist her hair in my fingers and yank her head back. "You reckon because you're pregnant you get some sort of free pass, lass? Do you?"

She grits her teeth and doesn't reply. A part of me is happy she doesn't, because the truth is, she does have a pass. If she weren't pregnant, I'd stripe her ass with my belt for her cheek and insolence.

"No. I don't think I have a pass. All I want is the fucking *truth*."

I want to hurt her. To make her cry. But Christ, she's my wife, the mother of my child. So I hold myself back. I restrain the wild beast that threatens to attack, to hurt her.

"Fine, then," I say through clenched teeth. "I'll give you truth. Last night, Sheena, the fucking reporter, snuck onto our property. We don't know for sure what she saw or what she did. Nolan interrogated her and he got some answers, but how do we know if that's all?"

She blinks, her teeth still gritted, her nostrils flared.

"She got onto our property, because one of my fuckin' men banged her bestie. Left his wallet and keys. They had their fun. Played him for the fucking fool he is. It was a mistake that could've cost us lives." I tug her hair again. "And tell me, Aileen. You ought to know. Do you remember? Do you remember what happens to people who threaten the lives of the Clan? Or is *that* memory buried somewhere with the others?"

She blinks, then blinks again. The color drains from her cheeks, and I wonder if I've pushed too far. She remembers. She remembers why she hates me.

"Yes," she whispered. "You beat me before."

"I never beat you, lass," I whisper. "I punished you for running, yes. For jeopardizing the lives of many."

"And that's what you did tonight? Is there no one safe from the brutality you men inflict on others?"

I don't answer her.

I don't like the way her voice quavers. I don't like the way her eyes water, or how her look of anger has morphed into one of hatred. I don't like it at all. She blinks, and a lone tear rolls down her cheek. It makes my stomach turn sour.

What am I doing?

What the *fuck* am I doing?

I release her as if she's on fire. She stumbles and falls back onto the couch, shoving the heels of her hands into her eye sockets. Tears leak down her cheeks. I didn't hurt her, I know I didn't, but reminding her of the memories was a bad fucking idea.

She'd forgotten that I whipped her before we were married. That I fucked her ruthlessly on our wedding night when she asked me to make her bleed. She forgot all of that, and like a fucking douchebag, I remind her.

I should hold her. I should reach for her, comfort her. I should tell her she has a right to be upset, that brutality like this isn't right or good, and no, I don't like that I'm a part of this sometimes.

But I don't. I turn from her. I walk to the bathroom, finish stripping my clothes off, and turn the water on to scalding. It's so hot it burns, my skin aching beneath the onslaught. But it doesn't cleanse me. It doesn't cleanse me at all.

Chapter 16

Aileen

I SHOULDN'T BE SO angry. Or hell, maybe I should. God, I don't know.

I feel like my emotions are on a pendulum. One moment I'm up, the other I'm down. One moment, he's got me riding the highest of highs, sex-sated and eager to please him, hell, *cuddling*. Next minute, he's all full-on Neanderthal.

I hear the pounding of the shower, and I wish I could forgive him. I wish I could let this go. I wish I didn't have to push him when he was already at his lowest, or damn near to it.

But I remember. God, I remember, how he came into the room when I lived back home, masked and dressed in black. He whipped me for running. He humiliated me.

And then the night of our wedding…

The brutal memories I've kept hidden come pouring back with relentless, vivid clarity.

Lying over the table while he punished me to tears.

The bloodied sheets on our wedding night.

I remember. Oh, God, I wish I could forget.

It must be an hour later when I hear the shower turn off. I sit up and look around the room. It's darker, now, storm clouds rolling in overhead. I shiver, suddenly cold.

I need to get out of here to clear my head. I don't want to see him. These past days I've spent getting to know him, I thought he could be a good man. But I didn't remember what he did to me before.

Today, he beat his very own brother in punishment.

What will he do with me?

I open the door to the bedroom and walk blindly into the hall, barefoot, my eyes blurry. We're alone up here, all the men gone, Caitlin and Maeve gone as well. I wanted to talk to Cormac by myself, but now I hate the very thought of being alone with him.

I walk down the stairs and see a few servants. One gives me a curious look, but it's not out of the ordinary for me to be walking about alone. I feel a slight wave of nausea again, but the ginger biscuits and the medicine I took help. I pause and the nausea passes.

I walk quickly. I don't even know where I'm going or what I'll do when I get there, but I need to be away from Cormac for a little while. I walk out to the garden, forgetting that the clouds rolled in.

"Miss, it's raining out—" someone says behind me, but I let the heavy front door bang closed behind me. I don't care that it's raining. I don't care that within five steps of the house, I'm soaked to the skin. Lightning crashes in the sky above me. I probably should go back inside, but I can't bring myself to do it. I make it to the trellis in the garden and sit under the leaves that shield me from the torrent.

What am I doing? What will I do next? But above all, there's one question that has plagued me ever since I hit my head, and can't remember all that I need to.

Who am I?

I can't deal with memory after memory. My mother, my father, my sisters given away. Me, as a little girl, begging to go on a playdate and my mother sending me to my room for even asking. How I shunned all boys at school after seeing what my father did to the boys who came near my sisters. How I earned the name "bitch" because they thought me cold and detached.

I remember everything now, everything with such awful clarity I wish again for the lapse in memory. I had somehow built a resistance to the pain that tormented me, and now... oh, God. Now that it's flooding me at once, I can't handle the waves of pain and helplessness.

I jump to my feet when a large branch falls to the ground beside me. I step out of the trellis and let the rain cascade down my face. I close my eyes to it, but welcome the cold lashes of wind and water. They mingle with my tears, and I don't feel so alone. The only sound out here is the howling of wind and the slashing of rain on the ground. I'm frozen to the bone, but don't want to move. I belong here, right here, with the sodden earth beneath my feet and the sky above me.

I walk past the garden, down the stone steps that lead to the estate, to the large, wrought-iron fence that surrounds us. Several men stand in all black by the gate, wearing slickers, and their eyes immediately come to me.

"You can't be out here, miss," one says. "Mr. McCarthy will have my head if I don't bring you back inside." He steps toward me, but I'm half-crazed. I hold a hand up to him.

"Mr. McCarthy will have your head if you touch me," I warn him.

He holds both hands up in surrender. "Not goin' to touch you, ma'am. Just makin' sure you're okay."

The other man pulls out his phone and makes a quick call.

"Don't you dare," I tell him. He's going to call my husband. I know it.

But he dials anyway, ignoring my protest.

"Don't you fucking *dare!*" I scream. Nausea rolls through me in a sudden torrent that makes the world swim before me. *Damn it.*

"Christ, woman." I open my eyes and shield them from the rain when I see Cormac heading to me, wearing nothing but a pair of sodden jeans. He's barefoot and bare-chested, and he looks like he did in the bedroom, ready to throttle me.

"Go 'way." I say petulantly. "I don't want you right now." He waves his guards away to give us privacy, and they scurry like mice.

"Leave me alone, Cormac! I don't want you right now. I don't want anything to do with you."

"Aileen!" he has to shout my name to be heard above the roaring wind.

"Cormac!" I throw back at him.

"Get in the damn house!"

"Make me!"

We square off in the garden like that, my hands on my hips and his eyes shooting daggers at me, until he reaches me, yanks my hand, and pulls me to him.

"Let me *go*," I say, but it's fruitless. He's already got me wrapped in his arms.

"Impossible woman!" he seethes. "What the fuck am I going to do with you?"

"You could—" I begin, but his mouth slams down on mine and silences me. He slams his hand on my lower back and shoves me to him as he claims me with his mouth, his tongue sliding against mine. God*damn* him, my body flames beneath the onslaught of his mouth, and I can hardly stand. He reaches down and hoists me up until my legs wrap around him. He kisses me until I'm melting, until I can no longer feel the rain at my back, and my whole body's light and warm with the feel of his lips on mine.

We're panting when he pulls away. I drop my forehead to his.

"It's fucking raining," he says.

I laugh out loud. "Good thing I've got you to enlighten me," I tell him. "Not sure what I'd do without that."

He playfully smacks my arse straight through the sodden fabric and holds me to him.

"I love you, you crazy woman. You know that?"

"How can you?" I ask him. How can you love someone you just met? How can you love me all crazy and unpredictable like this?

"You're my wife. You bear my child. How could I not?"

"Pretty easy," I say. "I mean, I could list five reasons right off the top of my head."

He shoots me a lopsided grin that does wicked things to my heart, for he never grins like *that*.

It feels good to be held like him, good to be kissed, but I know I'm just being weak. I'm letting him seduce me.

Don't fall for it, my mind warns me. But I'm cold and lonely, and I want him to love me. I want *someone* to.

"Come back inside," he says. "And I'll warm you up."

With a sigh, I nod. What choice do I have? I'm surrounded by guards, and if I tried anything foolish, he'd stop me.

Where would I go, anyway?

I go in with him, and he does just that, warms me up.

He takes off my wet clothes and helps me into clean ones, tucks me back into bed when the nausea overtakes me again, and when the queasiness passes, we make slow, beautiful, languid love until the sun sets and it's dinnertime.

I didn't tell him I loved him back. I accept that he loves me. But my heart is guarded.

Am I so weak that I let him bring me back to him? That a kiss, an orgasm, and the promise of protection makes me fold like a cheap tent in a gust of wind?

No, I tell myself. I'm not weak. I have to get through this early stage of pregnancy, get my bearings and my feet under me. I can't make any moves until then.

Chapter 17

Cormac

I DON'T KNOW what to do with the woman.

I take the best care of her I can. She sleeps for long hours, but she's troubled even then. When she wakes in a cold sweat, or worse, in tears, I hold her. I get her the medicine that helps her nausea, feed her the food she craves that keeps her at an even keel.

But she's closed off to me. She doesn't open up.

I wish she'd let the demons that plague her out. That she'd tell me what it is that torments her. She's a troubled soul, but I can't do anything to slay her dragons if I don't even know what they are. And hell, I'm so busy with my work that I can't devote every minute to her like I wish I could.

We still haven't found who's responsible for nearly killing her and the others. Keenan's convinced the

O'Gregors had something to do with it, but I'm not so sure myself. I wouldn't put it past her brother.

I wake before she does most days, and this morning it's my phone that wakes me. I grab it off the table beside me. The door to the bathroom's closed and she isn't in bed. Sometimes she still gets queasy, poor lass. I answer the phone.

"Yeah?"

"Mornin', Cormac."

It's Tully. We're good now. Hell, in some strange way, I think we're closer than we were before, as if what we went through solidified us.

"Morning."

"Saw something strange last night at the club."

"Did you?"

He's gone back to the club with Boner and Nolan, but I haven't been in weeks. I'm a married man now. And even though Aileen and I have a ways to go, I'm determined to remain faithful to her.

"Can you come down to breakfast today?" he asks.

"Aye."

I hang up the phone and call out to Aileen over my shoulder. "Heading downstairs for breakfast, need to meet with Keenan. Call me and I'll bring up what you like."

I leave the room, and something troubles me. I don't really know what it is, but my instincts are warring with me. To stay with her. Not to leave. But I can't be with her every second of the day, so I appease my conscience by making sure the guard is outside the door, and my phone is on.

I go downstairs to the dining room, my mind elsewhere, and nearly run smack into mam at the foot of the stairs.

"Y'alright, son?" she asks, her brow furrowed in concern.

"Aye," I tell her, leaning in to give her a kiss on the cheek. I don't want her to share the concern that bothers me. "Just distracted is all."

"How's Aileen?" she asks. She gathers freshly-picked flowers in her arms from the garden. She likes to put them around the house in little vases.

"Fine," I say, too quickly. "Still nauseous but she's getting along now. Got to go, mam."

I turn to walk away, but she stops me. "Can I take her to the shops today, Cormac?"

No.

I don't want to let her out of my sight, not when whoever's responsible for hurting her's still at large.

I shake my head. "Not today."

Mam purses her lips. "Ya can't keep her under lock and key and expect her to be happy, you know."

Happy. Goddamn it.

I didn't ask her advice, and I'm not in the mood to take it. I shake my head. "True, but I'm also not letting her out into the wild with people out there who still want to hurt her."

What I don't tell her is that a part of me fears if I let her go, she won't come back. She isn't happy here, and I know it.

"Cormac, she's come from Irish mafia and married Irish mafia. There will always be a time when someone wants to hurt her."

I stare at her for a moment, unsure of how to respond. Does she feel that way, even now? That her life is always endangered? I'd be a fool to say she doesn't speak truth.

"No shops without me," I insist.

Mam frowns. "Then come with us."

I groan. "To the shops?"

"Aye."

"Could use a new bag that goes with yer outfit, brother." I turn to see Boner, bouncing on the balls of his feet, prepared to duck my blow. I fake one with my left, and when he ducks, I get him with my right. He doubles over and howls with laughter, even as he gasps. I smack the side of his head before he dodges another smack and races off to the dining room.

Mam rolls her eyes and doesn't even wince.

"Right, then, I'll see she's ready to go and we'll head out after breakfast," she says.

"Mam," I say with a groan. "I've got business to attend to."

Her voice is laced with steel when she responds to me. "And part of that business you've got to attend to is seeing to the needs of your wife, son. Now what'll it be? You can come with us or double the guard." She smiles pleasantly.

"Anyone ever tell you you're meddlin'?" I mutter.

Keenan comes around the corner, baby Seamus tucked up to his chest. "Wait 'til you've got a baby."

"Go on with you," she says, flushing, but I can tell with the smile she hides that she's pleased. It's the highest of compliments to tell her she's meddling.

"Go," Keenan says. "We'll discuss what we need to at breakfast, and you'll have the day ahead of you."

Mam beams.

He leans in and says in my ear. "And she's right. There's something to be said for bein' sure you've tended to the needs of your wife."

"By going to the feckin' *shops*?" I groan.

Keenan nods with chagrin. "Tell me about it."

"Alright, then."

With a smile, mam trots upstairs to see to Aileen.

I head to the dining room and find most of the inner circle of the Clan waiting. Tully and Sullivan, Lachlan, Nolan, and Boner. Even Carson and Brady, Clan bookkeeper and detective, sit at round tables, drinking steaming cups of tea and eating scones, eggs, and bacon.

"Full house here, today," I say to Keenan.

"Aye. Haven't had a proper meeting in a while."

I take my place beside Keenan at the table. Nolan

hands me a full plate of food, and one of our waitstaff fetches me tea.

"What is it, lads?" I ask Tully. "You mentioned the club."

"Aye," Tully says. "I've been looking to see if Blaine would show his damn face again."

I grunt in response. Fucking Blaine.

"And?"

"And he showed up last night with a woman." I frown into my tea.

"Oh?"

"A redheaded woman," Tully says, looking with interest toward Nolan, who suddenly sits up straighter.

"Did you see her face?" he asks.

"No. She was masked."

"Sheena?"

"Don't know, but she was with her mate." We all know who he's talking about, the one who snuck Sheena onto our property.

Nolan can't mask his fury. Nostrils flaring, eyes blazing, he glares at Tully as if he's responsible. "What the fuck was she doing with that prick?"

Tully shakes his head. "No idea, mate. But Blaine had his way with the pair of them, right there where anyone could see."

Nolan looks as if he wants to whip his cup of tea across the room.

"Anything else?" Keenan asks. He stands at the head of the table, rocking the baby, who's fussing and squirming in his arms.

"The girl passed us and said something about the paper," Lachlan says.

I look at him sharply. "Since when do you frequent the club?"

His eyes darken and he purses his lips. "Ages ago," he snaps. "Why?"

I think of him as my younger brother, too young for the shenanigans at the Craic.

"He's of age, Cormac," Nolan says with a note of pride in his voice. "Needs a bit of a mentor."

"And you fancy yourself his sensei, do you?"

"Aye," Nolan says with a grin.

"Right." One word, and Keenan's got the attention of everyone. "Lachlan's plenty old enough to be going to the Club. In fact, he'd be an asset if these two ever get their arses in a sling again." He tips his chin to Nolan and Boner.

Boner grins. "True, that."

Keenan turns to Lachlan. "What'd you see, Lachlan? You notice anything?"

"Noticed lots, sir," he says to me. "Noticed the redhead speaking into her phone and using an earpiece. Her mate kept looking at Nolan, and Blaine seemed happy as a pig in shite."

Nothing new there, then.

"Thought you taught Sheena a lesson?" Keenan says to Nolan, who gives him a grim smile.

"Seems the lass is a slow learner."

Boner snorts. "Feckin' crime, you'll have to teach her."

But Keenan doesn't smile. "She's interfered enough," he says. "If she were a man you know what we'd have already done."

Nolan narrows his eyes. "Aye. Not sure why you're warning me. The lass means nothing to me."

Keenan holds his gaze. "See to it that's true, Nolan," he warns. "Wouldn't want any of your feelings to get in the way of what must be done."

His words hang in the room while we all sit in silence for long moments. We may be brothers, and we may have a code we abide by. But spies aren't allowed to interfere, be they woman or man.

"Aye," Nolan grunts. "I'll reach out to our friendly reporter today, make sure she's behaving herself."

Mam and Caitlin enter the room. Mam walks to Keenan, and reaches for the baby.

"Sorry to interrupt, boys," mam says. "Cormac, where's Aileen?"

I blink in surprise and shake my head. "She's in the room. She was in the jacks when I came downstairs."

Mam rocks the baby on her hip while the men talk about what they need to do. Nolan and Keenan are in a bit of an argument, but I hardly hear them.

"She wasn't there when I went up, son," she says. "Guard says she went for a walk."

I'm on my feet. Tully and Lachlan look my way.

"Relax," mam says. "Likely just needed a bit of fresh air is all. Did you see her in the bathroom before you came down?"

I shake my head. God, I'm a fuckin' idiot. I assumed she was in there because the door was closed, like a goddamn novice.

I call my guard. Pat answers on the first ring.

"Where's my wife?"

"Said she was going to the library early this morning, sir."

"And you let her?" I'm exiting the dining room. Mam's beside me and Caitlin follows.

"Yes, sir. Didn't know I wasn't supposed to, sir." He's right, but I still want to throttle him. She's allow to roam the premises. She lives here, for Christ's sake.

"Relax, Cormac," mam says, but I wave her off, heading to the stairway that leads to the bottom floor, the workout rooms, the library. The interrogation rooms.

I dial Aileen, but it just goes to voicemail. She never has her phone with her anyway. We need to have a talk about that.

I trot down the steps, and head first to the workout room. Empty. Next, the library. I hear someone rustling through papers on the right side of the vast room, but when I turn the corner, I only see one of our staff with a dust cloth in her hand, her eyes wide.

"Have you seen my wife?"

She nods. "Aye, sir. An hour or so ago?"

"Where?"

"She was down here for a bit. Did some reading, then went off that way." She points her cloth to the door that leads to the exit. And to the interrogation rooms.

I've never brought her in here before. She's allowed to roam our grounds freely, but she's never been to where we interrogate. Windowless and soundproof, the door's closed except on days the ground floor is cleaned. Like today.

Damn it.

"Cormac." Mam's in the doorway to the library, still holding baby Seamus. "Take it easy, son. Probably went for a bit of a walk is all."

"Stop telling me to relax," I tell her. "She hasn't been herself. Something's on her mind."

"Of course there is," mam says, shaking her head. "The woman's carrying your baby."

"Exactly." My body tightens.

"Cormac," Caitlin says next. She clears her throat, and her cheeks turn pink when I look her way. "We talked last night, Aileen and I."

My tone sharpens. "Did you?"

"Aye," she says with a smile. "She's just trying to find her place here is all. It's hard enough carrying another human in your body. Complicates things a bit when that baby belongs to a man you've only just met, doesn't it?"

"She can worry about the baby in her belly all feckin' day, so long as she does it where I can see her."

I stalk past them, ignoring the look that passes between them. They don't understand. They don't know how she's been. How she's walled off apart from me. How things have changed since her memory's returned.

I walk to the interrogation room, my stomach clenching. I don't want her in here. It's where we perform some of the more base interrogations. It's where I punished Tully days ago. Where we taught Lachlan the ways of the Clan, where he trained.

Soundproof, it's where criminals come to die. It's no place for a woman. No place for my wife.

I yank the door open, half expecting to see her, both hoping and dreading seeing her wide blue eyes and long blonde hair.

But it's vacant. I turn to leave, when something catches my eye. I turn back toward the exit. This room can be entered either from the connected rooms on this floor, or from an outside exit, a useful construction when we have to drag a suspect in, or hell, a body out. We keep it tightly secured, and only inner circle members even have a key to access this room. Today, the exit's left ajar, just slightly enough for a sliver of light to shine through.

I hear mam and Caitlin behind me, but I walk toward the exit.

"Everything alright, Cormac?" mam asks.

"I think so," I tell her. "But I'm going to find out."

I leave them both and head out the door. Just beyond the exit to this room lies the pathway to the greenhouse on the other side of our house, the pathway nearly hidden in shadow. I pause, frowning, and turn back to the door. Something's amiss. I'm eager to get to Aileen, to find her, so I don't investigate now, but make a mental note to come back to it.

Little pebbles line the walkway toward the greenhouse, and nearby, stacks of freshly-chopped wood wait for the late night fires we'll build in the backyard, under the stars and moon, on a chilly spring evening. Some of the best nights of my life were spent under those stars. How I long to sit beneath that blanket of heaven with my wife and child. How I wish I could make her happy, bring her peace.

I walk past the greenhouse and garden, past the gate that keeps us apart from everyone else, down to where the rough, craggy rocks of Ballyhock lead to the cliff's edge. Is this where she's gone? If not, where else could she be?

Goddamn anywhere.

I grit my teeth and keep walking, when the sound of a lonesome song drifts my way. Hauntingly beautiful, I would know that voice anywhere, though I can't make out the lyrics. My heart gives a great lurch at having found her, then squeezes at the pain in her voice.

Ahead of me lies the sea, tumultuous but beautiful, flecked with foam. The swirl of blue-green holds power and grace. Like my girl. My wife.

She stands on the cliff's edge, staring at the water below. If she sees me approach, she doesn't show it, her lilting voice now carrying the words that haunt me.

. . .

He quickly ran to her

And found she was dead

And there on her bosom

Where he soaked, tears he shed

MY HEART SQUEEZES. She sings the song of Molly Ban, a tragic story of accidental loss and new love that ends in tragedy.

I want to call to her, to reach out and drag her back to me, but she stands too close to the cliff's edge. If I startle her, she could fall.

I clear my throat to get her attention.

"Aileen."

"Mmm."

She closes her eyes as if to drown me out, and gives me a slight nod. All the anger I had at her disappears evaporates when I go to speak to her. My throat is strangely clogged. Maybe it's because of the song, or the blessed relief that floods me when I see that she's okay, but my voice comes out softer than I intend. I can't remember the lecture I planned on delivering or the warning I wanted to give her, how she shouldn't scare me like that, or risk her safety, or go wandering alone where I can't find her. Instead, my tone is gentle when I speak.

"Y'alright, sweetheart?"

She doesn't open her eyes, but nods. It's then that I

notice she's carrying something, holding it close to her chest.

"I'm fine," she whispers. She's anything but.

I take a few steps toward her, careful not to startle her.

"Are you?" I ask. "Why are you out here all alone, lass?"

Wordlessly, she holds the folded newspaper out to me. "Found this," she whispers, her gaze still fixed out at the sea. The paper falls from her hands, and a gust of wind swirls, but I snatch it just in time. If I were a superstitious man, it'd feel like an omen.

I take the paper from her, and within seconds, the calm I felt for a moment while looking out at the sea has vanished.

T*AKEN*

*D*AUGHTER *of one of the most powerful men in all of Ireland, Aileen McCarthy may be used to the ways of the Irish mob, as it's the only way she knows how to cope, but it doesn't mean she's had it easy. Aileen represents a small, repressed group of women under the thumb of the underworld of Ireland: the vicious mob that rules with an iron fist.*

Taken from the comfort of home, leaving behind her family and friends and all that matter to her, when the ink hadn't yet dried on her college diploma, Aileen was bought by rivals and taken to be bred like her mother before her. Forced to marry Cormac McCarthy, to carry his baby, she now ignores anyone who questions her. She insists she's a McCarthy and has no ties to the family she left.

A tragic loss, and hard to imagine that modern day Ireland still hearkens back to traditions from our forefathers, the women sold into mob life have no will of their own, no personal opinions save what their husbands believe, no say in their future. Mindless muppets under the control...

AS I READ ON, my blood boils. I glance at the name of the writer of this article and don't recognize it, but note fine print below the title.

Information in collaboration with Sheena Hurston of News Republic.

Has the woman no fear? No shame?

"Careful, Cormac," Aileen says, her light blue eyes cast to the sea in front of her. "You're liable to pop a blood vessel."

It's then that I realize my hand is shaking and I've clenched the paper so tightly it's crinkled like elephant's skin.

"Where did you get this from?"

"I found it," she says with a sigh, pulling her shawl tighter around to shield herself from the wind, but I imagine she's shielding herself from me.

"Where?" She didn't find it randomly. This was planted. Someone wanted her to see this.

She turns to face me, her eyes icy blue. Cold.

"In the library," she says, her lips pursed. "Naturally."

I want to shake her, until her pretty blonde hair comes loose from the knot on top of her head and tumbles onto her shoulders, until she loses that haughty, icy look of anger.

"You were in the library," I state stupidly, still clutching the goddamn paper.

"Yes. I went down there this morning before you got up." She sighs and looks back out at the sea. "Then I found the torture room."

"The torture room?"

She purses her lips and shakes her head. "Don't pretend you don't know what I'm talking about," she says through clenched teeth. "The room where you do evil things."

The interrogation room. We met in a room just like that.

"This is nothing but bloody lies, Aileen," I say, shaking my fist at the sea. I'd toss the paper to the cliffs, but I need to bring this to Nolan.

"Is it?" She turns to me so sharply, I'm afraid she'll fall. I reach a hand out to steady her but she backs away to avoid me. Her foot catches on a loose pebble. With a shriek, she stumbles, falling. My heart takes a great leap but I move on instinct, reaching a hand out to grab her. I grasp fabric and skin and hair as I yank her back to me and we fall to the rocky ground. She bangs her head on my shoulder, and I hold her to me.

"Are you okay?" I ask, holding her shoulders to look into her eyes. "Did you hurt yourself? God, did you hurt the baby?"

She grimaces, reaching a hand to her head. Closing her eyes, she whispers, "No. God. I'm fine. And the baby's fine." But she can't hide a tear that rolls down her cheek. She swipes it angrily away.

"Aileen," I say. I draw her to me. Holding her. I hate that she's hurt, that they've done this to her. "This doesn't matter. None of it does, lass. They publish lies, and we ignore them."

"Do they?" she challenges.

"Of course they do. You know that article isn't true. It's meant to sensationalize, but they don't know about the real workings of our family."

How devoted I am to her. How I'll devote the rest of my life providing for her needs, and the needs of my family. How I'll do anything within my power to keep her safe, protected, well cared for.

She nods with a sigh. "I'm hungry, Cormac," she says in a little voice that tugs at my heart. "Can we go back?"

I nod. "Mam and Caitlin want to take you to the shops."

Her eyes light up. "Oh?"

I stand take her hand, and lift her to her feet. "Only one condition, lass."

"What's that?"

"I come with you."

Chapter 18

Aileen

JUST WHEN I think for one moment that I'm starting to heal from all this... that I can forget the past that haunts me, and welcome the present, accept this as my lot in life... something happens to remind me how wrong I am.

I wonder if I can leave, how that will go. What would Cormac do? Would he find me? Would he come for me? We're bound together with this child growing in my womb, and yet still, I wonder...

Where would I go? Would I have the freedom I long for if I left this place? Is it even Cormac and Ballyhock I want freedom from?

He's been good to me, I can't deny it. At night when I wake from a terrible dream, the damn things that *will* keep coming, he's there. He holds me. At first I didn't understand it at all. Why would a man who's so stern and domineering be all kind and gentle when it comes to me? I don't know if I can trust it, trust *him*. I wasn't sure, at first. I didn't really get it.

Then Caitlin and Maeve took me out for a walk by the cliff one day and explained. They told me how seriously the men of The Clan take their responsibilities toward their women. The way Maeve talks about her late husband—a man I never met, but a man Cormac refers to with honor and reverence—makes me long for that type of earnest, heartfelt love that most women only dream of.

Maeve wears a thin locket around her neck and her wedding band, thick, solid gold with a Celtic knot dead center, to this day. When she talks of her husband Seamus, she spins that ring and talks in a distant voice, as if part of her heart was buried with him.

And Caitlin's love for Keenan is nothing short of adoration. The way she speaks about him, you'd reckon the man hung the bloody moon. But he's fallible. They all are. He's good to her, though, just like Cormac is to me and Seamus was to Maeve. I'll never want for anything. I know this.

"'Tis a matter of honor, lass," Maeve said over hot tea in the library one afternoon. "He'll never let you go without. Your every need will be met. But in turn, they have expectations."

"Aye," I said bitterly. "Don't step a toe out of line, eh?"

She smiled. "No, love. Not quite. You're allowed to speak yer mind and have your say, of course. But in time you'll learn when and how to speak your mind. It's all in the timing."

"Right," Caitlin said. "For example, when he's lying in after a good night's... sleep?" Her cheeks flushed pink as her eyes darted between me and Maeve, indicating it isn't a good night's sleep she's thinking of. "Good time. On his way to do a job or mete out punishment to someone who's defied the Clan or disobeyed an order? *Not* the right time." She took an extra long pull from her tea to hide her flaming hot cheeks.

"Quite right," Maeve said with a snort of approval.

I like these two. There's a kinship between us I never had before. I miss my sisters, but these two fill a void in my heart.

Maeve smiled. "Life is like a cup of tea, lass, as the old saying goes." She lifted her mug and took a long draught before finishing her sentence. "It's all in how you make it."

It's all in how you make it.

Do I like it sweet and soothing, comforting and warm, so it slips down to my toes and warms me through? Or will I make it bitter and cold, tainted by bitter regret and anger?

I'm trying. God, I'm trying, but the weight of a child in my womb and his ring on my finger makes everything seem that much harder.

I'm eager to get out of here, to go with Maeve and Caitlin and work a little retail therapy out of my system. And yes, to see the way my husband's eyes go dull and sullen when I drag him around the shops. I giggle to myself at the memory. Cormac McCarthy is many things; a shopper is not one of them.

I wish I could get that damn article out of my mind. It

hounds me like a thorn in my heel, aching with every step that I take. If there weren't truth in the article, it wouldn't rankle so much.

But I bury it. I put it down. I'm here with my newfound family, and even though the pain I carry taints my interaction with them, I have to admit, I'm starting to feel as if I belong here.

"You ready to go to the shops?" Caitlin asks from the landing. "Megan wanted to come, but she had a shift at the hospital."

Megan's recently been hired as a nurse. It pleases Keenan, who thinks her services could come in handy. I'm disappointed I don't get to see as much of her.

"Pity she couldn't make it," I say. I join her on the bottom floor. Cormac told me to go ahead and plan where I wanted to go with Caitlin and Maeve. I think he has some sort of foolish notion that if we plan ahead we'll be quicker, but the truth is, planning ahead just means we'll have more shops on the list to go to than we can possibly fit in.

"We'll have to plan another outing with Megan as well." I like the brass, friendly cousin. And she knows things about the boys, having been raised with them. She tells us stories Maeve's too classy to repeat, and they're too proud to tell us themselves. A McCarthy by blood, she has an in with the Clan even Caitlin doesn't.

Caitlin smiles. "She demanded you send her every picture of every outfit you buy. You know how she is about clothes. Look what she got baby Seamus."

I bend down to the pram to see she's got baby Seamus all dolled up in a little sailor outfit.

"Oh aren't you the cutest little thing?" I croon at him. He's got the McCarthy family wide green eyes above rosy cheeks. He shoots me a full, toothless smile. I turn when I hear Cormac coming down the stairs behind me, and the baby squawks to get my attention again. I turn back to the baby quickly. "What was that?"

"His father's taught him well," Cormac says. "Don't let the lady's attention wane. He's got you trained already, auntie."

I roll my eyes, and he bends and kisses my cheek, then leans into the pram and gently tweaks baby Seamus' nose. "Aren't you a cute little bugger? Good thing you inherited your mum's good looks, lad, and not your crooked-nose father's."

"Cormac!" Caitlin chides. "Keenan's nose is *not* crooked in the least."

Maeve joins us, gives Cormac a playful smack on the shoulder, and we're off.

He holds my hand and guides me to his side, so he's nearest the road. I don't question it. I remember what Maeve and Caitlin have told me, how the men of The Clan need to feel as if they can protect their women. He needs to be needed, I think.

But as we walk along the street toward the shops, I wonder.

What do I need?

What do I really, truly, need?

A good home. A place where I'm safe and welcomed. Something I never had growing up. Family to care for me, to tend to me... to love me.

Could the McCarthy family be that for me?

Could Cormac?

I shove the questions out of my mind.

Within an hour, I've got a bag with new shoes in one hand and a scone in the other hand.

"You'll be needing some maternity clothes next, Aileen," Maeve says.

"True," Caitlin says. "They'll be more comfortable soon."

Cormac's shoulders slump, and he stifles a yawn, but the man soldiers on.

"Having fun, are you?"

"Time of my life," he mutters. I can't help but giggle when his eyes go wide at the maternity racks.

"Really?" he asks, holding out a pair of trousers with an enormous stretchy cotton pocket where the belly goes. "Do they really need them *that* big? Is it for twins, then?"

"Darling, not everyone is as tiny and pixie-like as your wife," Maeve whispers in his ear.

I snort. "Hardly. I must've packed on twenty pounds already, and heavens, I think it went straight to my arse."

Cormac's mouth comes to my ear. "Don't you dare

make a comment like that again, lass. You're utter fucking perfection."

His comment makes me flush, so I step away from him toward the fitting room. "Be right back," I murmur.

"Where are you going?"

"Right there," I tell him, waving in the general direction of the room. "I need to try these on." I need to take some pictures and send them to Megan, too.

I'm not paying attention to where he's going, so when I turn and find him nose to nose with me in the tiny room, I stifle a scream.

"What are you doing in here?"

"Helping you try clothes on."

"In *here*? There's hardly room for one, let alone two."

"I'm not letting you do any of this alone."

"Has anyone ever told you you're smothering?"

"Has anyone ever told you you've got a smart mouth?"

I growl. He growls louder.

I glare.

He stays.

With a sigh, I pick up the first top and I look at the price tag. I wince. Lord, I've never spent this much money on clothes. "Oh, ouch. I can't believe they gouge pregnant mums like that. It's too much."

He rolls his eyes. "I don't care about the price tag, sweetheart. I care about getting you home. Do you understand me?"

"I ... suppose so. So it isn't too much?"

"Course not. Buy whatever you want."

"Seriously?"

He reaches for the top, tears the price tag off, and throws it to the floor. *"Seriously."*

I can't help but laugh at that. "Haven't even bought it yet."

"I can already tell I love it. Buy it."

"Did anyone ever tell you patience isn't one of your virtues, sir?"

"You just did. And call me sir again, I'll let you buy the shoes, too."

I smile to myself. God*damn* it, if he keeps going on like that, the man'll win my damn heart despite my misgivings.

I stare at the top. It's hard to wrap my brain around the fact that I can buy whatever I want.

"Are you going to try it on, or do you want to continue to chat in this room that's too small for me to even scratch my arse?"

I give him a look that doesn't even ruffle his feathers. "Would be more room in here if you weren't here, you know." I bend over to kick my shoes into the corner when he playfully smacks me across the arse.

"Hey!"

"Hey yourself. Get changed before I strip your clothes off myself."

"Always trying to get me outta my knickers," I mutter

to myself, but I strip and try on the clothes. The top is perfect. It instantly accentuates my curves, hides the lumpy bits, and the soft ivory fabric's as soft as butter.

"Love it," he mutters, tossing it in the pile. "Go on, now."

As I keep trying things on, I've got an odd feeling, even with him with me. It takes me a moment to realize it's the familiar feeling that someone's watching me.

I shake my head and turn back to changing, slipping into a pair of jeans and a red top.

Was that my imagination? Cormac's phone rings and he scowls at it.

"Goddamn it," he says. "I have to take this." He gestures for Maeve or Caitlin, but they're too far away. The baby's crying and they're trying to soothe him.

"Take your call," I say. "I'm fine. For goodness sakes, there isn't a soul in here." The only other person in this section of the store is a clerk in the back, rustling about unpacking boxes.

"Fine," he says, scowling at the changing room as if he expects someone to materialize out of the mirror or something. So damn overprotective. I roll my eyes when he finally leaves and takes the call.

I glance at myself in the mirror, at my slightly rounded belly and fuller breasts. How much will my body change? It seems like some sort of foretelling of things to come. The recent days I've spent wondering who I am, begging the question... where do I belong here? Who am I now?

I grab the hem of my shirt to take it off. This one will

come home with me, thanks to Cormac's generous plastic. Maybe I'll get two.

I get dressed in the clothes I came in and look around for my bag. Where the hell is it? I open the door to the changing room and look around. Cormac's by the door near Maeve and Caitlin, speaking angrily into his phone with it tucked up against his ear.

He looks my way and I give him a quick wave. *I'm fine. We're fine.*

He points outside, and I nod, waving my hand for him to go. The door to the shop shuts, I turn back to the changing room and go to gather my belongings when I feel someone tug my arm.

Before I can open my mouth to scream, I'm tugged back into the changing room by a woman with flaming red hair.

She slams the door to the room and puts her hand to my mouth. I try to shove her off. What the hell is she playing at?

"Hush. It's about your sister!"

I blink. "Let *go* of me." I yank my arm away from her. "Who are you?"

"Get Cormac to take you to the club," she hisses. "I've got vital information to relay to you but we aren't safe here."

"Which club?" I ask her. "What are you talking about?"

"He'll know," she says, looking over my shoulder, but the door's shut fast. "He'll know exactly what I mean. Ask him to take you to the club, tonight. I'll meet you there, and tell you what I need to. It's about your mother. She needs your help. It's about your future."

She puts her hand on the door and turns it. "Now go, go out and pretend like nothing ever happened, and meet me at the club tonight."

"Aileen?"

Her eyes widen at Cormac's voice right outside the door. "Go," she mouths.

I open the door and stumble out. He's standing by the entrance, shaking his head, distracted. "Y'alright?" he asks. I walk out of the changing room toward him, blindly handing him the items I want to buy.

For one moment, I consider opening the door and telling him what she did, but he'll cause a scene in here. And what if my sister sent her? I'm disoriented and confused, and need to think about what she just told me.

Was she following me? She knows who I am, clearly. Who is *she*? And what does she have to tell me?

"Aileen," Cormac repeats. "Are you ok?"

"Fine," I lie. I was just accosted by a woman who told me to get to the club tonight. If I tell him, he'll find her, and then what? I won't know what she's talking about, what she means, unless I go.

And what is this club, anyway?

I have too many questions to ignore what she's said. Still, I feel a bit nauseous and unsettled about all of this. I shake my head and walk with him.

"Was everything okay?" I ask, speaking quickly, so he

doesn't suspect anything. "You took that phone call and left so quickly."

"Fine," he says. "But I'll have to get back home soon."

Maeve comes up to me and admires the little dress and tops I picked out. I ask Caitlin if I can hold the baby, and she gives me a smile as she hands me the little one. He's wrapped in a baby blue blanket and has finally fallen asleep. I hold him to me, to soothe my pounding heart and my fraught nerves, and my mind teems with questions, with no rhyme or reason.

Will I be a good mum?

Who was that woman, and what does she know?

What is this club?

But the one that plagues me above all else... *do I care if my sister needs me?*

I'm distracted with the rest of the day's festivities. We eat baked goods from Miss Isobel, and eat lunch at D'Agostino's. I eat my ravioli and dip my bread in oil. It's delicious and makes my belly feel good, but I don't really listen to what they're saying, my mind occupied with what I have to do.

Someone was responsible for the attack that caused the three of us to be hurt. Someone was here, spying on us, and caused Cormac to leave in the middle of the night to do whatever it is the men of the Clan do. Someone knows more about me than I do myself, as evidenced by the article I saw this morning. And someone wants to talk to me. Alone.

"Aileen." Cormac calls my name from across the table.

I look up at him quickly to find his eyes on me narrowed and sharp.

"What?"

"You're a million miles away, lass," he says, his words gentle but his tone hard. "You're still thinking of that article you read, aren't you?"

I shake my head.

"What article?" Maeve asks.

He explains, and she rolls her eyes heavenward.

"I hope it's not that that's got you troubled," she says. "It's a form of induction, as it were. None of us are true members of the Clan until the media's dragged us up."

"Aye," Caitlin says, patting the baby's back over her shoulder. "Happened to me as well."

"I don't like it," I protest, pushing my plate away. "Don't we get any privacy?"

"Aye," Cormac growls. "I'll see to it you do."

"Don't make promises you can't keep, son," Maeve warns. "She'll learn to let it slide off her is all."

"Is that what you were on the phone about?" I ask him.

He grunts in reply. "Aye."

He would lose his *mind* if he knew I was approached in the fitting room.

We get our check and walk back to the house. Maeve and Caitlin walk ahead of us, Maeve pushing the pram, making plans for the baby's baptism, and Cormac and I linger behind.

A part of me wants to tell him, what I was told, and what she asked me to do. But I know if I do, I'll never find out what she needs to tell me. He'll go all overprotective and brooding, probably call his whole force out, and hunt down the woman who came for me.

No. I want to find out.

"Cormac," I say, trying to frame my conversation just right.

"Mmm?"

"Will you take me to the club?"

He stops short. "What club?"

I have to play this just right. "You know what club."

"No." His body's taut, his voice rigid. "I'm not taking you to that club."

All pretense aside, I'm a little angry he's taking this stance. How is this okay? "You frequent a club without me, and you think it okay not to take me?"

He holds my hand to prevent me from walking, so there's more distance between us and the others. "Aye," he says. "But correction, lass. I *used* to frequent a club I'll no longer go to. I'm a married man now, and I have no business in a sex club."

My heart twists, and for one moment, the feelings that blossomed for him, that I've buried in my weeks of misery and confusion, surface again. He's dedicated to me and to me alone. The men of my father's clan have no such compunctions, taking mistresses and girlfriends and cheating on their wives. But not this man. Not Cormac. He won't even share a pint with his brothers at a club where he could be tempted toward infidelity. And God, but I love that. How could I not?

And then my mind catches up to what else he just said.

A sex club? *Oh.* My heart races a little faster. I swallow hard. "What does one do at a sex club?"

He snorts, his voice lowers, and he rolls his eyes. "Exactly what you'd think, lass."

"Oh. Oh, my."

Okay, so now I *really* want to go.

"Cormac, you know what they say about pregnant women," I begin.

"I don't," he says, and his lips twitch. "Why don't you tell me?"

"Supposedly after the nausea and such die down, they need loads and *loads* of sex."

He raises his eyebrows, reaches for my hand, and gives me a little squeeze.

"Is that what they say?"

"Aye."

"I take it then your nausea's better, hmm?"

"Oh, much." And I'm not playing at this. Just the strong, warm, masculine feel of his hand in mind is doing strange things to my body. I once confessed a fascination with sex of a kinky nature to him. What would it really be like if this man unleashed his full potential? My heart flutters in my chest.

"You've been too easy on me, Mr. McCarthy," I say coyly. And I'm not just play acting. The mention of a sex club, and the thought of my sexy, devoted husband doing wicked, wonderful things to me, has me all kinds of aroused.

"Have I?" he asks in a low rumble I feel straight between my legs.

I swallow hard. "You have. Now what's the harm in taking me there if you're with me? I'm assuming the other men of the clan go as well?"

"Aye. Some."

If he finds out I'm manipulating him into going, I might regret goading him into not being so easy on me. I haven't forgotten the way we met.

"Who?"

Now I'm back to digging for information. "Nolan. Boner. Carson sometimes, and Lachlan. Most of them."

"Will they be there tonight?"

"If I ask them? Aye. But there's something you need to know, lass."

"What's that?"

"Your brother frequents the club as well."

It's as if he poured ice water straight over my head.

"Fucking Blaine." I hate him. The thought of being anywhere near him again makes my skin crawl.

"But," Cormac says with a grim smile. "Your brother

damn near shite his trousers last time he saw me, and I s'pose he'll keep well enough away."

I love you, I think.

The words bubble to my lips like sea foam, and just as quickly, pull back with the tide. I don't speak them. But I'm not immune to the pull of seduction over the simplest of things. And knowing he's punished my tormentor and won't let the man ever touch me again does all sorts of irrevocable things to my heart.

"Christ, woman," Cormac mutters, tugging me a little closer. Once more it's not lost on me that I'm on the inside of the street, and he stands between me and any threat on instinct.

"What?" I ask, unsure of why he's suddenly gotten strange on me.

"You've been apart from me, Aileen." He stands still, and pulls me closer to him, pinching my chin between his thumb and forefinger to prevent me from looking away. My heart beats faster.

"Oh?" I swallow hard.

"You have," he whispers. Stars twinkle above us, embedded in the sky like crystal-studded velvet. A cricket chirrups nearby, and in the distance, the sound of waves lapping on the shore brings a strange sort of comfort. And for the first time since he made me his bride, a deep, abiding sense of belonging pervades me.

"You've been up here," he says, releasing my chin long enough to gently tap his index finger to my temple. "With your worries and fears and your anger. And I wondered how I could get you back."

Tears prick my eyes. "For a big bear of a man, you're surprisingly perceptive," I whisper.

He grins at me, and his eyes crinkle around the edges. How have I never noticed that before? My heart does a somersault.

"Careful, Mr. McCarthy," I whisper.

"Why?" he whispers back.

"Because a girl could lose her knickers over a grin like *that*."

He snorts. Damn, he's cute. "Doesn't matter," he replies. "Already knocked you up."

I close my eyes the second before his lips meet mine. I want to remember this. I want to feel this again, to lose myself in his touch, his scent, his taste. He slides one hand to my lower back and draws me near, so the heat of his body suffuses me. Deepening the kiss, he swallows my moan and slides his tongue into mine. Plundering. Owning.

My heart races, my pulse accelerating. When he pulls back, his forehead meets mine. Maeve and Caitlin are long gone, and the two of us are alone.

"Tonight," he says. "I'll take you to the club. But you have to do exactly as I say. Understand?" The commanding tone of his voice excites me. I swallow hard.

I almost forgot about the damn club there for a minute.

I nod.

"You're mine, and as such, you'll not go near another man."

"Of course not."

He snorts mirthlessly. "You say that, but you don't know how these clubs operate."

"I'll wear a burka if it pleases you."

"You'll wear no knickers and a dress of my choosing," he says. "*That* pleases me."

Oh *my*.

I give him my most fetching grin, caught up in the moment of scoring what I want and sincere eagerness for what we'll do tonight.

Chapter 19

Cormac

I'D DO anything to see that beautiful smile of hers. It seems she's been mired in misery for days on end, but something's shaken her out of it. I wish I knew what, so that I could keep her here.

How did she hear of the club?

A part of me hates the idea of bringing her to that place, but I have to admit, I'm not totally opposed to the idea. She's confessed fantasies of being dominated before. What else lingers in that mind of hers?

I tell Nolan I want to take Aileen to the Craic. He's eager to go, and we quickly round up a crew to meet us there.

"What do I wear?" Aileen says, standing barefoot in front of her closet. She stares into the depths and twists a strand of her hair around her finger. "What do people wear to sex clubs?"

"Black leather and latex," I say, turning back to the mirror to brush my teeth.

She snorts from the other room. "Tell me you're joking."

"Half joking. People do wear those sort of things, but there's no way in hell *you* will."

"Right. Burka it is," she mutters. "Or perhaps a dress?"

"One could argue a burka's a dress."

"You would think that," she says, but she's smiling. "You know, Mr. McCarthy, I like the fact that you're unapologetically possessive of me. Most of the time, anyway."

"Damn right," I say, placing my toothbrush back. "Now what shall *I* wear? A black t-shirt to show off my manly physique, or a leather jacket to scare off the twats that look at my wife?"

She holds a light green dress in her hand and tips her head to the side. "Not sure I like anything drawing attention to my *husband* either," she muses.

Something stirs low in my belly at that. Every time she calls me her husband, every time she gets that possessive look about her. I like that she's jealous. I cross the room to her. I need to feel her, to hold her. I gather her in my arms, and kiss her. She responds instantly, melting into my arms and kissing me back.

"I love you," I whisper to her. "You don't have to say it back. Give it time, lass. Let me prove myself to you."

She blinks hard, as if trying to stop herself from crying.

"That's about the best thing you could tell me right now," she whispers. "You know that?"

I shrug. "I get a good idea every once in a while."

She grins, gathers my face in her hands, then pulls my face down to hers so she can plant a kiss on my forehead.

"Go on with you," she says. "Let me get dressed before you're balls deep in me and we never make it to the damn club."

I give her arse a smack and let her go.

We dress and get our ride downstairs. We're in the back of the same car that took us home from our wedding. It seems so long ago now.

"We're going alone?" she asks.

Why does she seem suddenly nervous?

"Aye. The others will meet us there. You'll see, there's a sort of anteroom in the front, but the real fun takes place in the back. Members-only."

She stills. "My brother goes there?"

"Aye. But don't worry about him, lass. He gets one look at me or my brothers and he turns and goes the other way."

It doesn't appease her, though. She frowns and doesn't reply.

"We'll get a drink in the front and I'll introduce you to the others. Then when you're ready, I'll take you to the back."

She nods slowly. "Do people have… rules and things?"

"Aye. Club's safeword is flagon, but you won't be using that."

She nods.

"No drink for you either," I continue. "For obvious reasons."

"Mhm."

I take her hand, kiss her fingers, then tug her closer. "But you'll have rules of your own as well."

She swallows. "Will I?"

She likes this. I'll use that to my advantage.

"Aye."

She swallows again. Her eyelids lower, and she squirms a little.

"You'll do nothing without my permission. If you have a question for me, you'll address me as *sir*, and you'll stay by my side. And whatever happens, you're not to come without my permission."

"Aw, fuck," she says in a throaty whisper. My cock twitches at the sound.

"What?"

"That's hot as fucking hell," she groans.

I slide my hand up her thigh and squeeze, letting my thumb graze the heated vee where her thighs meet. She pulls closer to me.

"Good girl," I say. "You remembered no knickers."

"Mhm." She closes her eyes when I stroke between her legs. Sighing, she drops her head to my shoulder.

"That's a girl," I whisper. "Open your legs, sweetheart."

She parts her legs obediently. Holding her to me, I drag my thumb along her thighs, before I gently stroke between her legs.

"Fuck, woman," I groan. "You're so damn wet."

I haven't even taken her to the club yet, and she's damn near ready to come. Keenan told me she might be like this, starving for sex and easily turned on. She'll get no complaints from *me*.

"On your back," I whisper.

"Cormac, the driver—"

She gasps when I slap her thigh. "On. Your. Back."

The way she bites her lip as she obeys makes my pulse race. Leaning back in the car, she lets her legs fall open. I kneel in front of her and kiss her inner thigh, preparing her. I drag her dress up so it's around her waist. With tinted windows and a screen between us and the driver, no one will see. I'll protect her modesty, but damn if it isn't hot thinking they could.

"Cormac, really," she says in a high-pitched squeak.

"Quiet," I tell her. "Or we'll begin the night with you over my knee."

"You can't spank a pregnant woman," she says, but her eyes are half-lidded, and when I quirk a brow at her, she bites her lip and swallows.

"Says who?"

"I… well, you know…"

"I have it on good authority from the doctor himself that kinky pleasure's absolutely permissible for an expecting woman."

She flushes. I kiss her inner thigh again, and her legs begin to tremble.

"Pleasure?" she whispers.

"Aye," I say, my cock lengthening at the arousal laden in her voice. "Do I need to demonstrate?"

She groans. "Maybe."

I grin at her, lower my mouth to her pussy, and drag my tongue through her folds.

"Just imagine," I say, letting my hot breath graze her private parts. "You're draped over my knee for being a naughty little girl."

"Mmm," she says, her head falling back as I kiss her sweet spot. Her hands fly to my hair when I suckle and lick.

I lift my head and whisper, "You squirm and kick beneath the weight of my palm."

"Cormac."

She groans when I lick and suckle again.

"I could make a proper spanking pleasurable for you."

"I…" she pants, gripping my hair, fueling my desire for her. "Believe that."

I give her pussy a parting kiss.

"Good girl," I say approvingly. "Now you're good and primed for the club."

"Cormac," she groans, reaching for me, but I grasp her wrists and move her away from me.

"Aileen."

"You're not going to just… to just *leave* me like this?"

"Certainly not all night," I tell her. "Just for now."

"You can't—"

"I can," I remind her, my tone hardening. "Now be a good girl or you'll give a taste of that spanking before we even exit the car."

She pouts, but the faint pink flush of her cheeks tells me she'll respond well to what I have planned for her tonight. After a huff and whine, she finally nods her head. "Fine. Alright then." Drawing in a deep breath, she gives me what I'm looking for. "Yes, sir."

I drag her over to me, kiss the sweet spot on her neck, and suckle the tender skin there. I pull her to me, my cock pressed up to her body. "Good girl."

"Someone likes having his way," she mutters with a teasing smile.

She has no fucking idea.

We enter the club, and at first she looks disappointed. I bring her to the bar and we order drinks. I won't take her to the other part of the club until the others arrive.

"Is this it?" she asks, frowning as she sips her virgin cocktail.

"Well, you can't have alcohol for now," I tease.

She rolls her eyes. "You know what I mean. Not the drink. Thought you said there was another room."

I grin at her, but tug a lock of her hair. "Don't roll those eyes at me, woman. And the answer is no. This isn't it. But I'll take you to the good part after my brothers arrive."

She sips her drink and looks around the tame interior. Rafferty approaches us and smiles.

"You must be Cormac's wife," he says, extending his hand out to greet her. "Pleased to meet you."

"I am," she says with a smile. "And thank you."

He pulls another pint for me. "Brother's Blaine, right?"

My body tenses when her face pales and she stammers, "Right. Yes, that's my brother. You haven't seen him, have you?"

Rafferty pushes the pint my way and I give him a warning glare he misses.

"I have," he says. He looks to me. "Been coming back on the regular since you haven't been coming." He frowns and jerks his head to the back. "I'll notify you if I see him tonight?"

"Aye," I say. "We're not on good terms."

He nods, wiping the counter down. "Don't blame you. Man's a fucking prick."

Aileen hasn't taken another sip of her drink since Rafferty mentioned her brother, but I'm glad he did. I want him to tell me if he sees him. I want to be prepared. Even with my brothers arriving soon, I don't like being unprepared for whatever Blaine does.

Why the fuck did I bring her here tonight?

"I don't care, Cormac," she says, lifting her chin with

that stubborn, fierce determination I've come to love about her.

"Good girl," I say approvingly. "You know I won't let him hurt you." I also won't let him intimidate her, or have her scared of showing her face anywhere he is. So tonight, we'll stake our claim. We won't cower because of fucking Blaine.

She nods. "I'm good for a solid kick to the bollox myself if need be."

I clink my glass to hers. "Aye. The way to bring a man to his knees is *always* through a solid kick to the bollox."

She grins. "Good to know. Cheers."

Nolan arrives with the others, and after brief greetings, I take Aileen's hand.

"Let's go," I tell her. "It's time."

I'm eager to get her to the club, to see how she responds.

And then to get her the fuck *home*.

"What's the story, brother?" Boner asks. He sips his pint and walks on my left, Nolan to the right of Aileen.

"My wife was curious about the club, so I'm showing her, but you know I don't trust her brother. Rafferty says he's back since I haven't been coming."

"He here tonight?"

"No, but that could change."

"I'm not going to hide from him," Aileen says tightly, her eyes cast ahead of her.

"Of course not," I agree. "I just don't fancy having to dole out another beating when I could be doing far better things with you."

"Oh, I'd help you with that," Nolan says, then quickly amends. "The *beating* part, not the wife part. For Christ's sake, keep yer knickers on. I'd pay to get a chance to break the man's nose."

Aileen smiles. "'Tis probably deviant to take pleasure in such a thought, but I won't deny it pleases me."

We get access to the private part of the club. I hold Aileen's hand tightly in mine as we enter. Something unsettles me tonight. I didn't recognize the men at the door, and it's much more crowded there than I ever remember seeing before. There are men dressed in black at the exits, men and women, singles and couples, roaming the darkened interior.

"Is it always this dark in here?" I ask Nolan. I don't like it. I've half a mind to gather her up and head back home before we've even begun.

"No," Nolan says. A muscle twitches in his jaw as he sweeps his gaze across the room. "Shouldn't be so dark in here. It isn't safe."

"Tell them to put the damn lights on, then."

Boner shakes his head. "You twats, it's soirée night."

"What the fuck is that?" I ask.

"Themed night at the club?" he says. "Dimmed lights. Fancy dress. Cocktails." He snags an hors d'oeuvre from a waitress passing by as if to show us what to do.

"Relax, Mr. McCarthy," my wife says with a charming grin. "I'm sure you'll keep me so close to you that even the dim lights won't interfere. Oh my God, is that a curry spread?" She takes three mini toasts off the tray a waitress holds and devours the food. I grin at her. I sometimes forget what a hearty appetite she has.

I take her hand and lead her around, finding every cocktail waitress with a tray we can find. When she's filled her belly with crudité, grilled potato skins, mini egg rolls, and bacon-wrapped scallops, she collapses on a nearby bench still nursing her drink.

"Aren't you going to eat, Cormac?" she asks, daintily wiping a napkin across her lips.

"Aye," I tell her. I tug her onto my lap and kiss her.

"Don't you even say what you're thinking," she says, crossing her legs as if that will actually prevent anything. I tug her forward to straddle my lap, my cock pressed hard against her arse.

I lean in and whisper in her ear. "I've still got the taste of your pretty pussy on my lips. It's ruined me for anything else."

She gasps and squirms. I raise the hem of her dress and rest my thumbs on her inner thighs. I tease her, lightly brushing my fingers near her secret spots. She wraps her arms around my neck and squirms, wriggling her arse so she draws closer to me.

"Pinch your nipples," I whisper in her ear.

"Cormac!"

"Do it, before I spank you."

"You wouldn't dare. You can't—"

Ah, the classic female protest. I easily arrange her over

my knee, her pert little arse raised high in the air, and give her a little pat.

"Can't I?"

"People will... how can you... Cormac!"

I inhale the sweet, seductive scent of her arousal, lift the hem of her dress, and place my palm beneath the fabric. I squeeze.

"Cormac," she repeats on a moan.

I lean in and whisper in her ear, "Do you need a spanking, young lady?"

"No, sir," she says stoutly, but the flush of her cheeks and the way she bites her lip tells me another story.

"Oh, I think otherwise." It's so crowded and dark in here, not a soul looks our way as I lift my hand and give her a good, hard slap. She's more than safe here, over my knees, with her belly well supported. Sebastian assures me some kinkier times could actually be beneficial as long as we're careful. Something about raising hormone levels and blah blah blah.

"Now," I tell her, my hand poised above her arse. "What did I say to do?"

"Pinch my—you can't *mean* it," she protests. I underscore exactly what I do mean with another hard smack. She bucks and squirms but reaches for her breasts and with her eyes squeezed shut, pinches her nipples to tight peaks.

"Good girl," I say, with another approving hard smack. "Just like that."

I wonder if she's forgotten where she is. She certainly

doesn't look like she cares anymore. Her protests die on her lips as she pinches her nipples through the thin fabric and I continue the slow, deliberate spanking I've been eager to deliver.

"Pinch them."

Smack. My dick throbs. She moans.

"Again."

Smack.

"Oh God." She's panting in earnest now, while I give her one hard swat after another, pausing between strokes of my palm while she works her breasts.

"Good girl," I whisper. "Just like that." I lift her back onto my lap upright, facing me. "Keep going," I tell her. I lift the edge of her dress and slide my hands beneath it. Still, not a soul looks our way. She could be giving me a lap dance for all they know. I touch her swollen pussy and finger her clit. The first stroke of my fingers has her throwing her head back. The second, she's gasping for breath.

"Come," I breathe in her ear. "Let yourself go. Come for me, sweetheart."

She moans, losing herself to ecstasy. Her head rolls backward, her eyes closed tightly, and beneath my fingers she pulses against my hand. I savor every moan and gasp, loving the way she spasms on my lap while she milks her pleasure.

"Good girl," I say. "Just like that, love. Come for me."

I stroke her until she slumps against me, spent and sated, and it's the most beautiful fucking thing I've ever seen. Her pale, soft skin flushed pink with pleasure. Thick black eyelashes against her cheeks, her eyes closed in bliss. Her golden hair tumbling about her shoulders, fragrant and silky. Her gorgeous body limp with pleasure.

"Christ, you're so beautiful it kills me," I say to her. She smiles, leans forward, and burrows into my chest. Instinctively, I wrap my arms around her and hold her. Warmth floods my chest. I know she's just come, that she's still high on endorphins, but it pleases me that she trusts me like this. That she seeks my comfort and closeness.

She places one hand on my chest. I lift her palm to my lips and kiss her, fold her fingers over, then tuck her hand back onto her chest.

"A kiss to take home?" she whispers.

"Aye."

She smiles. "Never would've taken you for a sentimental man, Mr. McCarthy."

"Seems there's something about a beautiful lass wearing my ring and bearing my child that does strange things to me."

I hold her, nestled in my arms, all soft and warm, as the music plays on and couples mill about in various stages of dance and erotic foreplay. The air is pungent with the scent of sex and drink, as I plan on where I want to take her next.

Nolan's a few meters ahead of me, laughing and drinking with a woman dressed in red. To his right I see Boner and Tully sitting at a table with a few girls. I scan the room, always on the lookout for Blaine, when something catches my eye.

I narrow my eyes and look harder. Mother of God. Though she's dressed in all black and her hair's tucked into a wig, I swear to God that's the redheaded reporter. Doesn't she know we frequent this place? Does she have no shame?

"What is it, Cormac?" Aileen sits up and peers at me. "I could feel your body go all still like. Something amiss?"

"Aye," I growl, gently pushing her off my lap. But before I can even get to my feet, there's a commotion ahead.

Jesus. Three blokes approach Nolan all at once, and I can tell by the way they carry themselves they're after him.

"Stay with me," I say to Aileen. I can feel her at my back as I head to Nolan. I have to warn him before they attack him without notice.

I get to him seconds before one of the men pulls a knife. Son of a bitch wants to stick him without anyone noticing.

"Nolan!"

He looks my way. There's no time to warn him. I tackle him to the floor as the man attacks. Boner and Tully are at my side. Fists are flying, women screaming. Glass breaks, and something hot and sticky covers my hands.

I blink in surprise when I see someone's cut Nolan. There's a savage laceration across his forehead. Blood drips into his eyes.

"Motherfucker," he mutters, trying to see who attacked

him. I catch the prick by the back of the shirt, tackle him to the ground, then knock him out with a solid blow. Security officers swarm us, and seconds after we've got his attackers under wraps, I look around me for Aileen. She was just there, just at my back.

Son of a bitch.

"Aileen!" I shout. "Aileen!"

But she's nowhere to be found. She's fucking gone.

Chapter 20

Aileen

I FOLLOW BEHIND CORMAC, certain that something's wrong. Does this have anything to do with why I'm here? Why I was summoned? Goddammit, I let myself get seduced by my own husband and damn near forgot why I came here to begin with.

Has Blaine come into the club? It's so stifling in here, crowded and dim, that I'm surprised Cormac saw anything at all. In any other place, the crowd would've noticed the sudden disturbance, but it seems as if we're the only ones aware that anything at all is wrong.

But just as Cormac reaches his brother, someone calls my name.

"Aileen! Help!"

The sound of a high-pitched feminine voice in distress

makes my pulse spike. I freeze and spin around, trying to find the source of the voice. Who called me?

I swing my gaze wildly around me, and at first I see nothing amiss, when red hair catches my attention. She's dressed in black but being dragged to an exit by two strong men. I can't see the men, but when she sees me looking her way, she screams again.

"Aileen!"

I turn back toward Cormac, and gasp when I see someone pull a knife. I look to him, and then back to her. I can't help both of them. Tully and Boner and another man I don't know show up beside Nolan and Cormac. Those men can hold their own. My decision's an easy one.

He's going to throttle me for running away, but I hope he understands why I did. I race toward the exit where they took the woman.

It's impossibly darker down this corridor. I don't know what to expect, so come short when I find door after door, lit only by one dim lightbulb overhead. Which room did they go into? I try first one knob, then the next, but they're all locked, like I'm in some sort of fucked-up labyrinth. I wring my hands, and try to think of another plan, when I hear a high-pitched scream come from the door at the furthest end of the corridor. I run to it, yank the doorknob, and it opens.

I shove the door open. I don't have a plan except to help her. She's the one that told me to come here tonight, the very one they've taken. I can't let anything happen to her.

The room's cloaked in darkness save one eerie greenish-yellow light at the furthest end. Her screams grow louder. I've come to the right place, but now that I have I feel as if my feet are made of lead.

"Stop!" I shout. "Leave her alone!"

I step into the room, and the door slams behind me. I look wildly about me, but no one is there. Someone shut this door from the other side. I yank the doorknob but it's locked.

We're in a small bedroom that looks as if it's a hotel room straight out of a porn flick. I stand in the small, narrow entrance, a bathroom to my left with a sink and mirror, but I can only see narrowly in front of me because of the passage. One bed sits in the center of the room, complete with rings and chains, a mirror at the head. My redheaded visitor's tied fast to the chains, stark naked. Tears stream down her face.

Panic floods me.

"I'm sorry," she says. Dark black mascara trails down her cheeks, as she quietly sobs. I stand still, taking everything in. The bed, made up in gray bedding, the blanket neatly folded and pillows plumped, as if prepped by a maid for tonight's events. The cold metal cuffs around her wrists. A whip coiled on a nearby table, a hideous-looking mask, a vicious knife, a thick metal bar that makes my skin crawl.

"Why are you sorry?" I ask. I don't move toward her. We've been set up here, and I don't know why or how.

She sniffs. "They told me to find you. They told me to lure you here tonight. They told me if I didn't they'd kill my mother."

Icy cold fear trickles down my spine. I swallow hard. I have to keep my senses about me. I was set up, but I'm not alone. My husband and his men are right here in this club. They can help me if I need them. Hell. I'm going to need them.

"Who?"

"They were sent by your brother, but it isn't him," she begins. Her face contorts in pain and she writhes in her restraints, her eyes flitting to a wall I can't see yet from my narrow vantage point. I blink in surprise. How are they causing her pain when we're the only ones in the room? I take a step toward her.

"Don't!" she screams. "Don't! If you come any closer, they'll—"

Her words drown in screams once more. Someone's punishing her for warning me. How?

I freeze. I look back toward the door that's locked. There's no escape there. She's warned me not to come closer. If I do, someone's liable to do something terrible, I know it.

"Go on." A cold voice comes from inside the room. She's not alone.

I reach for the door knob again to find it still shut tight, and I make up my mind. I can't leave, and I'm not going to turn around in fear. I walk toward her. She screams and tries to warn me, but I'm going to find out who the hell is behind this. I'm going to defend myself if they hurt me, and then I'm going to call my husband.

"Don't come nearer," she pleads. "Please."

I don't heed her warning. Where else am I going to go? I'm not the girl who cowers in fear in a fucking hallway. I walk past the bathroom, march straight into the room, and the second I do, sharp pain erupts across my skin. I scream, raising my hands as if to ward it off, but I can't do anything to stop it. My skin's on fire, everything in my world blinding, searing pain.

I drop to my knees when it stops as suddenly as it started. I'm braced on the floor, my hands in front of me, panting in relief, when a cold, hard, nasally voice I recognize sounds behind me.

"Aileen."

I look up from the floor to see Blaine sitting placidly in a chair, one foot crossed on his knee, his hands clasped.

"Blaine." My words are tight with anger. He brought me here. He lured me.

But she just said it wasn't my brother.

"What are you doing here?" I ask him. "What have you done? Who made you? I know you're not capable of doing anything on your own."

"Fuck you." His lip curls in a snarl and he's on his feet. He hits a switch in his hand and pain explodes in my senses once more. I'm twisted in pain, my own screams drowned out by the other woman's. The sadistic son of a *bitch*. I'm writhing in pain, my whole world blackness and vivid agony, as if someone's found a switch to my nerves and set them on fire.

"Enough." A sharp command comes somewhere in my periphery. The pain instantly stops.

I look at Blaine, whose face is still contorted in anger. Someone told him to stop. Who?

I look around the room. No one else is in here, yet somehow, someone just commanded him.

"You weren't supposed to go to the McCarthy clan," the woman pants from her restraints. I freeze, staring at her, afraid that one more word will have her tormentor torture her again. But maybe this was part of the plan. "They had me come to you, had me get you in the shops and lure you here." More tears. "I couldn't let them get my mum. Please forgive me."

"Who?" I demand. "Not my brother, then who?"

"The man who was supposed to marry you," my brother says. "You don't pay attention, do you? Not the fucking man who's name you carry. You were promised to another, and Martin fucked up. I tried to stop him. I warned him."

What the hell is he talking about?

Another voice carries through the room as if spoken through overhead speakers. The voice behind the curtain, as it were. "Did you get the McCarthy's attention, then?"

"Aye," Blaine says. "But I'm not letting them in to get her quite yet."

"You'll do whatever the fuck I tell you, or you know what happens."

Blaine winces and rubs a hand across his nose. How could I have not noticed before? My brother's a goddamn addict. Does the man who commands him now get him his fix?

301

I was so damn ignorant. And what does he mean, Martin promised me to another? I stare at the mirror, at my own reflection, Blaine's twisted face and the other woman's naked, tortured form. Something's wrong with it. I blink, trying to understand what's off about it, and it finally dawns on me. I'd bet anything it's a one-way mirror. This room is meant for voyeurs, the exhibitionist's delight. On the other side of that mirror sits the man talking to Blaine.

"Who are you? Are you too cowardly to show your face, then?"

Pain shoots through my limbs. They're sending some type of electric shock. I remember with a sudden stab of fear that I'm pregnant. What if the pain they're causing me will hurt the baby? I begin to tremble but try to hide it.

I close my mouth. I can't provoke them.

How will I notify Cormac? How do I alert the men of the clan where I am?

First, I have to stop the pain. The controller in Blaine's hand is like a switch. When he flicks it, I'm in agony. I have to get to that first.

"Fine," I say, dropping my head to the floor. "Please, stop. I've done nothing."

"Nothing but play along with every fucking order Martin sent you."

"Then your gripe is with him, not with me."

"Believe me. My gripe is with both of you. McCarthy knew you were promised to another and he acted on it anyway. Said it would bring peace to the clans." Cold rage takes over his voice. "Fuck him and the cart he rode in on. Fuck his brother. Fuck all of them. Blaine, start recording."

I have to get to Blaine. If I can stop the device in his hand, I'll be able to control myself better. I can scream for Cormac. Cormac will come.

How will I get to Blaine? Then I remember the teasing words Cormac spoke to me not thirty minutes ago.

"The way to bring a man to his knees is always through a solid kick to the bollox."

I make my plan.

I turn to him and start to speak in a placating voice.

"Blaine. I'm your sister. I know you hate me, but—"

"Shut up." His face is red and blotchy with fury.

I'm slowly edging closer.

"I know that you—"

"I said shut up!" he's on his feet, the device in his hand. I lunge at him. Pain explodes through my body, but I've met my mark. I'm at his feet. With a savage scream, I butt him between the legs with my head. With a howl of rage, he topples to the floor, clutching his bollox, but I've got him now. He can't cause pain anymore without the damn device. I step on his hand until I hear bone crunch.

The man on the other side is howling in rage. I have seconds. I turn to Blaine and kick him one more time. He's clutching himself in agony, unable to chase after me. I run to the woman bound, but she shakes her head at me.

"Don't worry about me. Break the mirror. He can't hide behind it anymore, and Cormac will hear." She jerks her head at the table. "Get the bar. Smash it!"

I look wildly about the room and see the table with tools. I lift the bar, run to the mirror, and slam it. The glass splinters into web-like lines. I have to hit harder. I hit it again, and again. But before I can take in details, someone grabs at my ankles. Fucking Blaine. I kick at him, when the wall of the mirror topples fully to the ground. I was right. We aren't alone.

Dermot sits on the other side, his eyes narrowed on me.

"I thought you were dead."

"Would've been convenient for you, wouldn't it?"

I freeze. He's pointing a gun at me.

"Not another word," he says. "You bought it all, didn't you? The bumbling fucking fool without a brain?"

What?

"You didn't know Martin had promised you to *me*. Told me if I found you, you'd be mine, and McCarthy could fuck himself. But no. You thought you could manipulate me, just like you manipulated everything else, didn't you?"

He's out of his mind. I knew nothing about this, and yet he blames me. How will I escape?

"Thought I answered to your fucking brother, you slut." His hand shakes on the gun.

I hear shouts in the hallway, and my heart gives a jolt of hope. Is it Cormac? Has he heard anything?

"Now, Dermot," I say, trying to distract him. "You know it was nothing personal."

His eyes narrow on me.

"Call his name, and I'll shoot," the man says in a voice of deadly calm. "Go ahead. I dare you." He heard them, then.

I don't speak.

Someone's at the door. They're pounding on it, trying to get in. Blaine grabs my feet and I kick at him, but it's no use. He's got me.

"Fucking bitch," he growls, dragging me to the floor.

"Let her go, Blaine," Dermot orders. "She comes to me unharmed. Let her go or you get nothing."

"Fuck you," Blaine says. "Fuck your blow. I'm not letting this bitch get away."

I scream when he pushes the device and pain shoots through me. I'm panting with fear and pain, the world around me dim and hazy. A gunshot rings out as the door breaks down. I see Cormac and Nolan and Tully enter the room.

"Cormac!" I scream, when gun shots ring out again and bright red blossoms across his chest. "Cormac!"

Tully lunges at the mirror, and Nolan throws his body at the woman in restraints. It's confusion and red-hot pain as Blaine pulls the trigger relentlessly. I reach for him, but can't get to him.

Cormac's stumbling toward me. Oh God, oh *no*. He's hurt. My husband. Shot.

He falls to his knees but cocks the gun in his hand.

"Let her fucking go."

But a gunshot rings out before he does. Tully slumps to the ground, shot by Dermot. Cormac takes the opportunity and pulls the trigger on Blaine, who screams and twitches on the ground. More men rush into the room, men with badges and uniforms. There's pain and confusion, blood and screams. I'm in Cormac's arms, and they're tight around me. He's covering me like he did in the greenhouse, his body over mine.

"Lay still," he whispers, his voice contorted in pain. "Stay right there." Blaine lies on the ground, unconscious, in a pool of blood.

"Brave lass," Cormac whispers in my ear. "Such a good, brave lass."

"Someone help me!" I scream, my voice tattered in pain and fear. "Please, help me. My husband. He's shot! Nolan!" I look to see him holding the woman in his arms, covered haphazardly in a blanket, tucked up against his chest.

"Stay strong, Aileen," Nolan says. "He'll be alright. Stay strong, lass."

In the end, they have to take me with them, in the ambulance that goes to the hospital. I won't let him go. We fought for this. We fought through this. They're not taking him away from me. No one will.

I've never seen my husband so pale and wan. He's strong as an ox. He'll pull through this.

"Stay with me, Cormac," I whisper. "Stay with me, and the baby." I don't know if he even hears me. I close my eyes, the wails of the sirens speaking the song of my heart.

Chapter 21

Cormac

BRIGHT LIGHTS and hazy vision are for the fucking birds.

I rub a hand across my brow, and blink to clear my vision, but it's not working. Bloody hell.

"You should go home." It's Keenan. He's to my left, and he's standing by Aileen, speaking to her. My vision begins to clear.

"No," she says stoutly.

"For Christ's sake, woman, you listen to the Chief," Keenan growls.

"You're not my Chief," she says staunchly. "You can't make me."

I smile even though it hurts to, my heart swelling at the sound of her stubborn voice. I love this fierce, headstrong, beautiful woman.

"Feisty lass," I mutter. My voice doesn't sound like my own.

"Cormac!" She's on her feet and rushing to my side before I can catch a breath, but she stops right before she launches herself at me.

"My God, I thought they'd killed you. I was half ready to wake them from the dead and kill them all over again."

I look down at myself. "Eh, shot through the feckin' shoulder, they'd have to try harder than *that*."

"Aye," she says, her beautiful eyes brimming with tears. "My God, you scared the hell outta me!"

"Scared the hell out of both of us," Keenan says grimly. "And brother, I'd appreciate it if you'd get yourself better so you can tame this woman of yours. Escaped her own fuckin' room barefoot in a hospital gown to find you, hasn't listened to a doctor's orders, damn near killed herself waiting for you to wake."

"Silly girl," I say, taking her hand. "You've got to take care of yourself."

"Ach, go on with you," she says, shaking her head at Keenan. "He's exaggerating. I put shoes on."

Mam enters the room, takes one look at me, covers her face and bursts into tears.

"Jesus, Mary, and Joseph," she weeps. "Just when I think I get a handle on you men, you go and do something like *this*. I'm done, I tell you, *done*."

"Go on, now, Mam," Keenan says soothingly. "He's alright. You know Cormac. Has to throw himself on the frontline for his girl, but he'll heal and move on."

"You'd bloody better," she says, giving me a look I haven't seen since I was an errant teen. "You've got a wife and child to look after!"

I look quickly to Aileen. I swear her belly's more rounded.

"The baby isn't hurt, then?" I ask, sitting up so quickly in bed pain shoots through my shoulder and I wince.

"Get back on those pillows," Aileen orders, wagging a finger at me. "The baby's fine." She turns to mam. "He'll be fine, Maeve." She reaches for my mother's hand and gives it a squeeze. "I'll see to it he doesn't do anything stupid to jeopardize himself again, alright?"

"Will you, lass?" I chuckle. "Near death experience freed your tongue, aye?"

"I'll tie him to the damn bed if I have to," she says, ignoring me. "Make him rock the babe, and do the midnight feedings. I'll exhaust him so he collapses into bed at night and can't go off chasing the bad guys."

Keenan snorts at "the bad guys."

"Don't need a babe to do *that*," I mutter. "Already exhausts me."

I can't wait to get her alone again, to hold her in my arms and kiss her. To hear her lilting voice sing the songs of our people. To tug that golden hair. To school that mouth of hers, with pleasure.

"You're both alright, then?" I ask.

Aileen pours me a glass of cold water from a pitcher on the table beside me. "Drink, Cormac," she says, the edge in her voice softening now. I take the glass and drink. She nods approvingly before she answers. "Aye.

We're fine. The baby's strong as an ox. Should know the sex next week, if you're so inclined."

"Told you," I say, teasing her. "Will be a son."

She rolls her eyes heavenward. "Because that's what this family needs is more testosterone."

Mam laughs out loud. "Damn right. We need another woman to balance off the sexes. More lavender and pink."

Keenan groans.

I look around the room and realize I'm in the hospital wing at home. "So who's going to tell me what happened then?"

Keenan looks to Aileen, and the symbolism of his deferring to her is not lost on me. As Clan Chief, it's his job to keep me abreast of what happens, but he's giving her space to do so, recognizing our relationship as husband and wife.

And it seems as if the ordeal has helped Aileen, too. She fought this. She fought *me*. She fought our union, and bringing a child into this family. But now it seems she's assumed her role with grace and strength, and hell if I don't love her the more for it.

"Seems the man who worked for my father, the damn bodyguard who stood right outside my door back at home, had a hand in the coke trade. Supplied my brother by skimming off the top of shipments, as it were. I thought Dermot was killed for letting me go, but he wasn't. He joined up with the O'Gregors in the north, held my brother by the bollox with the coke, set the fire on the greenhouse for vengeance. When that didn't work, he had other plans."

"Motherfucker," I mutter. "Where's he now?"

"Jail," Keenan mutters. "Club security called it in before we could get to him. Blaine is, too."

"Son of a bitch survived then." I turn to Aileen. "And how do we know all this? I'm guessing Dermot didn't confess to anything."

"Sheena," she says. "The redheaded reporter?" She grows a little sheepish and looks at her hands. "She was the one who lured me to the club to begin with."

"What's that? What do you mean?"

She looks at me, then mam and Keenan. It's the first time she's told anyone, I'm guessing.

"That day we were shopping," she says. "She came to me in the dressing room. Told me I had to get to the club, that my sister was in trouble."

My hands clench into fists as she tells me the story, and I steady my breathing to calm myself.

"And you didn't tell me."

"She told me I couldn't," Aileen says. "Look, I know how stupid that was now, but at the time, I wasn't thinking straight."

Maybe a good, hard spanking will help her think straight.

"Don't blame her, Cormac," mam says. "Sheena's the one to blame."

"And even then," Keenan says. "The lass was blackmailed by Dermot and Blaine."

"How do you know this?"

"She fessed up to Nolan."

"Aye."

I pinch the bridge of my nose together to help me think straight.

"And we've been in touch with Martin," Keenan says. "Shouldn't have to do anything on our end, brother. You and I both know peace between the clans is of the utmost importance to him. He'll take care of Dermot and Blaine."

"Aye, but I wish I could get out of this bed and take care of them myself."

"Of course you do," Aileen says softly, her hand on my arm. "I know you'd probably like to break their legs, or bust their heads, or put bullets through their pasty white temples, mmm?"

I grin at her. "You talk about vicious, brutal violence like you're telling me a bedtime story."

She smiles at me, leans down, and kisses me. I'm enveloped in her soft, feminine scent. "And this, my love, is why you and I were meant for each other."

Something warms in me at that. She's changed. Whatever wall that divided us before has crumbled to dust. I squeeze her hand, and she places her head on my chest. I can't move my left arm easily, but tuck her against me with my right.

"That's a good girl," I whisper. I inhale her scent and hold her to me. It isn't until I feel the gentle tremble of her shoulders that I realize she's crying.

"I thought you were gone," she says through her tears, her voice choked with meaning and pain. "You bled so much. They had to bandage you up and they moved so damn slow. You passed out on the way, and I thought... I thought..."

"Shh, sweetheart. It's alright. You're a good lass to see me through this. But I'm fine. And you're alright?"

"*Fine*. They used a goddamn electric shock thing to keep me and Sheena in line. Seems the sick fucks at the club use it for fun, hmm?"

I shake my head. "Not me," I tell her. "I prefer--"

I look to mam and stop. Aileen groans.

"We'll leave you two," mam says, looking from me to Aileen with a sort of wistfulness. "She's a good woman, Cormac. You see to it you treat her right."

"The very best," I agree. "Course I will."

As soon as Keenan and mam leave, Aileen climbs straight into the hospital bed beside me. I lift my arm and she crawls under it, burrowing her head on my chest and draping her arm around me.

"I love you, Cormac McCarthy," she says, her vivid eyes still shining with tears, but laced with conviction. "I love you so much it hurts right here." She takes my hand, makes a fist, and places our hands together on her heart. "I knew when I was in that room that you'd come for me. That you'd protect me, no matter what. That you'd do anything for me. I knew it in my heart, and I knew when they took you from me that I wanted that. I wanted you. I wanted *us*."

"I would have," I say. "Done anything to protect you. And I will yet."

"I know it," she whispers. "I'm—I'm sorry I..." her voice trails off.

I shake my head. "You'll not offer any apologies, Aileen. You've been through hell, but you've come through it stronger. This is no fairy tale. It's bloody and messy, but in the end we have each other, and that's what matters. We'll build a family together, you and I. You're one of us now."

"And God, I love that," she says, her voice trembling again. "So much, Cormac. Your mother and your brothers and Caitlin and Seamus. I've never had the love of family like I do here. And I'll do my best to be as good to all of you as you are to me."

"You're already enough, lass."

She leans up and kisses my cheek. "You're very sentimental when you're all drugged up."

"That what it is?" I say. "Thought it was the near death experience—"

"Near *death*, is it?" she says, the fire returning to her eyes like a match to tinder. "Just a moment ago it was nothing, now it's near death because it suits you?"

"Something like," I grin.

She grins back. "Something like," she says softly. "And now you've gone and done it, Mr. McCarthy."

"What's that, lass?"

"Stolen my damn heart," she says.

"About goddamn time," I mutter. I weave my fingers through her hair. She giggles and sighs, two of the sweetest bloody sounds I've ever heard.

"First the ring, then the baby, then the heart," she says. "You've gone about this all wrong, you know."

"Aye," I tell her. "But you're an unconventional lass, so it only suits that I won you in an unconventional way."

She laughs her pretty laugh and burrows deeper into my chest.

"Am I hurting you?" she asks.

"Nah, you're fine."

"Good," she says. "Because I'm not going anywhere either way."

"You'd better not," I tell her. "You're here to stay."

She closes her eyes, inhales deeply, and when she lets her breath out, a sort of peace settles over her. "Here to stay," she whispers. "I like the sound of that."

EPILOGUE

SEVEN MONTHS LATER

I've experienced pain in my life, but nothing, *nothing* beats this.

"Oh my God," I scream, sitting up in the middle of the night. A contraction grips me so hard and fast that I lose my breath. I grip my belly, and Cormac damn near jumps straight out of the bed.

"It's the baby!" he says. "The baby's coming?"

He stumbles around in the dark, nearly tripping on his trousers while he pulls them on.

"Aye," I say, panting between contractions. "But relax, they don't come in seconds, you know."

I didn't tell him contractions were coming all day long, several hours apart. I'd been getting them for weeks, and Sebastian says it's normal. Caitlin said she had pre-labor contractions for six weeks before baby Seamus came, and I didn't see the need to tell anyone. But as the night wore on, the contractions came stronger and harder. I texted Megan, and she's been keeping watch with me on the phone, making sure I got as much rest as I could.

"Call your mother," I say. I want her by my side before I want Sebastian. The doctor can come in when I'm ready to push. "Sebastian can wait."

He opens his mouth to protest, then shuts it again. Though he's a bossy sort and certainly wears the pants around here, it seems he thinks differently when it comes to telling a woman in labor what to do.

Five minutes later, Maeve and Megan are in the room.

"Oh, it's time, isn't it?" Maeve asks, resting her hand on my belly when another contraction grips me.

"Breathe, love," Megan says. She holds my hand through the contraction. "Come here, Cormac. Let her squeeze your hand while I get some things ready for her."

He looks stricken but determined when he comes to my side. I breathe through the contraction, and it finally fades.

"Two minutes apart," Maeve says. "How far dilated were you at your last check-up?"

"Four centimeters."

Maeve grins. "Ah. We'll have a McCarthy baby by daybreak, I think."

Thirty minutes later, Sebastian's joined us, but Maeve and Megan do the bulk of the work. They feed me ice chips and put a cool cloth on my forehead, and Cormac's gotten over his momentary panic. He's my rock. I squeeze his hand when I contract.

"That's my brave girl," he says encouragingly. "So strong and brave. You can do this, lass."

"You're all too good to me." Apparently, labor's made me weepy. But I've never had anything like this before, and even through the pain of labor, it brings tears to my eyes. Cormac's love and attention, Maeve and Megan's guidance, they're the family every girl wishes she had. And they love me.

It's five hours and forty-seven minutes of intense, brutal labor, but in the end, Maeve proves prophetic. We bring sweet baby Naimh into the world as the sun rises. I'm sweaty and exhausted when Megan hands me the wee babe, wrapped in a light pink blanket. Her eyes are closed, her lips parted in sleep.

"Welcome into the world," I whisper.

"Reckon being born tuckered her out," Cormac says, his voice thick with emotion. "Tuckered you both out. If you need me to hold her while you get some rest, I will."

I give the little bundle a kiss and hand her to her daddy. "Aye," I tell him. "I'm exhausted." I am, but I could hold her all night long and not get weary of it. I just want to let him hold her.

Watching him hold our baby to his chest, the wee thing dwarfed by his massive frame, my heart squeezes.

"Can't wait to dress her up and plait her hair and sing to her," I say, resting my head back on the pillow. "But tonight, I need rest."

"You did so well, lass," Cormac says, rocking the baby

in his arms. "Never met a stronger woman than you, you know that?"

I smile at him. "A man like you needs a strong woman, Mr. McCarthy."

He grins at me, and even though I'm still aching with the pain of delivering his child, that grin would make me lose my knickers all over again.

The baby and I recover quickly, under the doting attention of the staff. After the second week, Cormac allows my mother to pay a visit. The visit's brief and uneventful. She shows little interest in the baby, and more interest in the house and my clothes.

"Very posh it is here," she says with a sniff.

I give her a tight smile. "Aye," I say. I'm grateful when she leaves, having paid her respects. "Didn't even come with a single guard."

He shakes his head. "Typical. Shows where their loyalties and concerns lie. But anyway, now that she's gone and done what she had to, hopefully we won't need to see her again for a while."

Maeve shakes her head. "'Tis a shame," she says. "I'd have done my best to get along with her."

"Of course you would've," I say. "But she's of a sort that won't try."

Maeve looks at me and smiles. "I'm glad you're one of us now, lass. The daughters my sons have brought home to me are my pride and joy."

I love this woman. She makes the pain of my past fade with every day that passes.

Maeve takes her leave. Cormac shuts the door behind her and sits in the chair by the window. A muscle ticks in his jaw.

"I've got something to tell you," he says.

"What is it?"

"Trouble at the school," he says. "Nolan and I'll have to pay a visit at the weekend."

I nod. Trouble comes and goes for them, and I've come to expect it.

"Seems the redheaded woman's causing more trouble."

"No," I say. "Sheena? Are you kidding me? Hasn't she learned her lesson?"

He grins. "She's the sort that seems to enjoy a lesson."

"Oh, lord," I mutter.

He snorts. "You wouldn't know anything of that, now, would you?"

"Nothing at all," I say with a smile. I busy myself with buttoning the baby's little romper.

"But Sheena's brought us news that hasn't hit the press yet, and I thought it best I tell you myself."

"Has she?"

"Aye." He clears his throat. "Mack Martin put a hit on Blaine and Dermot. Both found dead in prison not an hour ago."

Even though we expected this, the news still hits me in the gut. I swallow hard. At the very same time, it brings me unfathomable relief.

"I'm glad," I whisper. The baby sleeps in my arms, and I brush a tiny strand of hair off her forehead. "I hate that these things happen, but I'll rest better at night knowing we're raising our daughter in a world without those two."

Cormac swallows hard and nods. "Absolutely." He stands and walks to my bed, bends and kisses my forehead. "You alright, sweetheart?"

I rock the baby, take his hand, and hold it to my cheek.

He bends and kisses me, wrapping his arm around the baby, a little huddle of peace and togetherness in this crazy world we live in.

"I always wanted to be part of a family that cared for me," I tell him. "And now look at this. Look at *us*. We are that family."

His eyes crinkle around the edges as he smiles at me. "We are."

From the author: I hope you've enjoyed reading Cormac: A Dark Irish Mafia Romance.

I am so grateful for your support! Please read on for previews of my other books you may enjoy.

PREVIEWS

Keenan: A Dark Irish Mafia Romance

PREVIEWS

Keenan

I WATCH from where I sit on the craggy cliffs of Ballyhock to the waves crashing on the beach. Strong. Powerful. Deadly. A combination so familiar to me it brings me comfort. It's two hours before my alarm goes off, but when Seamus McCarthy calls a meeting, it doesn't matter where you are or what you're doing, the men of The Clan answer.

I suspect I know why he's calling a meeting today, but I also know my father well enough not to presume. One of our largest shipments of illegal arms will arrive in our secured port next week, and over the next month, we'll oversee distribution from the home that sits on the cliff behind me. Last week, we also sealed a multi-million-dollar deal that will put us in good stead until my father retires, when I assume the throne. But something isn't right with our upcoming transactions. Then again, when dealing with the illicit trade we orchestrate, it rarely is. As a high-ranking man of The Clan, I've learned to pivot and react. My instincts are primed.

The sun rises in early May at precisely 5:52 a.m., and it's rare I get to watch it. So this morning, in the small quiet interim before daybreak and our meeting, I came to the cliff's edge. I've traveled the world for my family's business, from the highest ranges of the Alps to the depths of the shores of the Dead Sea, the vast expanse of the Serengeti, and the top of the Eiffel Tower. But here, right here atop the cliffs of Ballyhock, paces from the door to my childhood home, overlooking the Irish Sea, is where I like to be. They say the souls of our ancestors pace these shores, and sometimes, early in the morning, I almost imagine I can see them, the beautiful, brutal Celts and Vikings, fearless and brave.

A brisk wind picks up, and I wrap my jacket closer to my body. I've put on my gym clothes to hit the workout room after our meeting if time permits. We'll see. My father may have other ideas.

I hear footsteps approach before I see the owner.

"What's the story, Keenan?"

Boner sits on the flat rock beside me, rests his arms on his bent knees, and takes a swig from a flask. Tall and lanky, his lean body never stills, even in sleep. Always tapping, rocking, moving from side to side, Boner has the energy of an eight-week-old golden retriever. My younger cousin, we've known each other since birth, both raised in The Clan. He's like a brother to me.

"Eh, nothing," I tell him, waving off an offer from the

flask. "You out of your mind? He'll knock you upside the head, and you know it."

If my father catches him drinking this early in the day, when he's got a full day of work ahead of him, heads will roll.

"Ah, that's right," he says, grinning at me and flashing perfect white teeth, his words exaggerated and barely intelligible. "You drink that energy shite before you go work on yer manly *physique*. And anyway, get off your high horse. Nolan's more banjaxed than I am."

I clench my jaw and grunt to myself. *Fuck*. Nolan, the youngest in The Clan and my baby brother, bewitched my mother with his blond hair and green eyes straight outta the womb. Shielded by my mother's protective arms, the boy's never felt my father's belt nor mine, and it shows. I regret not making him toe the line more when he was younger.

"Course he is," I mutter. "Both of you ought to know better."

"Ah, come off it, Keenan," Boner says good-naturedly. "You know better than I the Irish do best with a bit of drink no matter the time of day."

I can toss them back with the best of them, but there's a time and place to get plastered, and minutes before we find out the latest update of the status of our very livelihood, isn't it. I get to my feet, scowling. "Let's go."

Though he's my cousin, and I'm only a little older than I am, Boner nods and gets to his feet. As heir to the throne and Clan Captain, I'm above him in rank. He and the others defer to me.

He mutters something that sounds a lot like "needs to get laid" under his breath as we walk up the stone pathway to the house.

"What's that?" I ask.

"Eh, nothing," he says, grinning at me.

"Wasn't nothing."

"You heard me."

"Say it to my face, motherfucker," I suggest good-naturedly. He's a pain in the arse, but I love the son of a bitch.

"I *said*," he says loudly. "You need to get fuckin' *laid*. How long's it been since the bitch left you?"

I feel my eyes narrow as we continue to walk to the house. "Left *me?* You know's well as I do, I broke up with her." I won't even say her name. She's dead to me. I can abide many things, but lying and cheating are two things I won't.

"How long?" he presses.

It's been three months, two weeks, and five fucking days.

"Few months," I say.

He shakes his head. "Christ, Keenan," he mutters. "Come with me to the club tonight, and we'll get you right fixed."

I snort. "All set there."

I've no interest in visiting the seedy club Nolan and Boner frequent. I went once, and it was enough for me.

Boner shakes his head. "You've only been to the anteroom, Keenan," he says with a knowing waggle of his eyebrows. "You've never been *past* there. Not to where the *real* crowd gathers."

"All set," I repeat, though I don't admit my curiosity's piqued.

The rocky pathway leading to the family estate is paved with large, roughly hewn granite, the steep incline part of our design to keep our home and headquarters private. Thirty-five stones in the pathway, which I count every time I walk to the cliffs that overlook the bay, lead to a thick, wrought-iron gate, the entrance to our house. With twelve bedrooms, five reception rooms, one massive kitchen, a finished basement with our workout rooms, library, and private interrogation rooms, the estate my father inherited from his father is worth an estimated eleven million euros. The men in The Clan outside our family tree live within a mile of our estate, all property owned by the brotherhood, but my brothers and I reside here.

When I marry—a requirement before I assume the throne as Clan Chief—I'll inherit the entire third floor, and my mother and father will retire to the east wing, as my father's parents did before them.

When I marry. For fuck's *sake*. The requirement hangs over my head like the sharpened edge of an executioner's blade. No wedding, no rightful inheritance. And I can't even think of such a thing, not when my ex-girlfriend's betrayal's still fresh on my mind.

I wave my I.D. at the large, heavy black gate that borders our house, and with a click and whirr, the gates open. When my great grandfather bought this house, he kept the original Tuscan structure in place.

The millionaire who had it built hailed from Tuscany, Italy, and to this day, the original Tuscan-inspired garden is kept in perfect shape. Lined with willow trees and bordered with well-trimmed hedges, benches and archways made from stone lend a majestic, age-old air. In May, the flowers are in full bloom, lilacs, irises, and the exotic violet hawthorn, the combined fragrances enchanting. The low murmur of the fountain my mother had built soothes me when I'm riled up or troubled. I've washed blood-soaked hands in that fountain, and I laid my head on the cold stones that surround it when Riley, my father's youngest brother and my favorite uncle, was buried.

We walk past the garden, and I listen to Boner yammer on about the club and the pretty little Welsh blonde he spanked, tied up, and banged last night, but when he reaches for his flask again, I yank it out of his hand and decidedly shove it in my pocket.

"Keenan, for fuck's—"

"You can have it after the meeting," I tell him. "No more fucking around, Boner. This is serious business, and you aren't going into this half-arsed, you hear?"

Though he clenches his jaw, he doesn't respond, and finally reluctantly nods. I'm saving him from punishment ordered by my father and saving myself from having to administer it. We trot up the large stairs to the front door, but before we can open it, the massive entryway door swings open, and Nolan stands in the doorway, grinning.

"Fancy meetin' you two here," he says in a high-pitched falsetto. "We won't be needin' any of yer wares today."

He pretends to shut the door, but I shove past him and enter the house. He says something under his breath to Boner, and I swear Boner says something about me getting laid again. For once in my life, I fucking hope my father assigns me to issue a beating after this meeting. I'm so wound up. I could use a good fucking fight.

"Keenan." I'm so in my head, I don't notice Father Finn standing in the darkened doorway to our meeting room. He's wearing his collar, and his black priest's clothes are neatly pressed, the overhead light gleaming on his shiny black shoes. Though he's dressed for the day, his eyes are tired. It seems Boner isn't the only one who's pulled an all-nighter.

"Father."

Though Father Finn's my father's younger brother, I've never called him uncle. My mother taught me at a young age that a man of the cloth, even kin, is to be addressed as Father. It doesn't surprise me to see him here. He's as much a part of the McCarthy family as my father is, and he's privy to much, though not all, of what we do. It troubles him, though, as he's never reconciled his loyalty to the church and to our family.

Shorter than I am, he's balding, with curls of gray at his temples and in his beard. The only resemblance between the two of us are the McCarthy family green eyes.

Vicar of Holy Family, the church that stands behind my family's estate, Father Finn's association with the McCarthy Clan is only referenced by the locals in hushed conversation. Officially, he's only my uncle. Privately, he's our most trusted advisor. If Father Finn's come to this meeting, he's got news for us.

He holds the door open to my father's office, and when I enter I see my father's already sitting at the table. He's only called the inner circle this morning, those related by blood: Nolan and Cormac, my brothers, Boner, Father Finn, and me. If necessary, we'll call the rest of The Clan to council after our first meeting.

"Boys," my father says, nodding to Nolan, Boner, and me in greeting.

My father sits at the head of the table, his back ramrod straight, the tips of his fingers pressed together as if in prayer. At sixty-three years old, he's only two years away from retirement as Chief, though he keeps himself in prime physical shape. With salt and pepper hair at his temples, he hasn't gone quite as gray as his younger brother. He jokes it's mam that keeps him young, and I think there's a note of truth in it. My mother ten years his junior, they've been wed since their arranged marriage thirty-three years ago. I was their firstborn, Cormac the second, and Nolan the third, though my father's made mention of several girls born before me that never made it past infancy. My mother won't talk of them, though. I wonder if the little graves that lie in the graveyard at Holy Family are the reason for the lines around my mother's bright gray eyes. I may never know.

I take my seat beside my father, and pierce Nolan and Boner with stern looks. Boner's fucking right. Nolan's eyes are bloodshot and glassy, and I notice he wobbles a little when he sits at the table. Irishmen are no strangers to drink, and we're no exception, but I worry Nolan's gone to the extreme. I make a mental note to talk to him about this later. I won't tolerate him fucking up our jobs because he can't stay sober. I watch him slump to the table and clear my throat. His eyes come to mine. I shake my head and straighten my shoulders. Nodding, he sits up straighter.

Cormac, the middle brother, sits to my left and notices everything. Six foot five, he's the giant of our group, and, appropriately, our head bonebreaker. With a mop of curly, dark brown hair and a heavy beard, he looks older than his twenty-five years.

He nods to me and I to him. We'll talk about our concerns about Nolan later, not in the presence of our father. Or any of the others, really.

"Thank you for coming so early, boys," my father begins, scrubbing a hand across his forehead. I notice a tremor in his hand I've never noticed before and stifle a sigh. He's getting older.

"It came to my attention early this morning that Father Finn has something to relay to us of importance." He fixes Boner and Nolan with an unwavering look. "And since some of you haven't gone to bed yet, I figured we should strike while the iron's hot, so to speak."

I can't help but smirk when Nolan and Boner squirm. When Boner's father passed, one of the few gone rogue in our company, my father took Boner under his wing and treated him as one of his own. I love the motherfucker like a brother myself. Though he's got a touch of the class clown in him, he's as loyal as they come and as quick with a knife draw as any I've seen, his aim at the shooting range spot-on. He's an asset to The Clan in every way. When he's fucking sober, anyway.

Now, under both my gaze and my father's, he squirms

a little. My father keeps tabs on everyone here, Boner no exception.

"I think it best I let the Father speak for himself, since he needs to leave early to celebrate mass." None of us so much as blink, the Father's duties as commonplace as a shopping list. We're used to the juxtaposition of his duties to God's people and to us. We have long since accepted it as a way of life. He has a certain code he doesn't break, though, and out of respect for him, we keep many of the inner workings of The Clan from him. We give generously to the church, and though God himself may not see our donations as any sort of indulgence, the people of Holy Family and Ballyhock certainly do.

Father Finn sits on my father's left, his heavy gray brows drawn together.

"Thank you, Seamus." He and my mother are the only ones who call my dad his Christian name. Finn speaks in a soft, gentle tone laced with steel: a man of God tied by blood to the Irish mob.

My father nods and sits back, his gaze fixed on his younger brother.

Father clears his throat. "I have news regarding the... arms deal you've been working on for some time."

My father doesn't blink, and I don't make eye contact with any of my brothers. We've never discussed our occupations with Father so out in the open like this, but like our father, he sees all. The church he oversees is sandwiched between our mansion that overlooks the bay to the east, and Ballyhock's armory to the west. Still, his blatant naming of our most lucrative endeavor is unprecedented.

Though we dabble in many things, we have two main sources of income in The McCarthy Clan: arms trafficking and loansharking. Though neither are legal, Father Finn's insisted we keep out of the heavier sources of income our rival clan, the Martins from the south, dabble in. They're known for extortion, heroin imports and far more contracted hits than we've ever done. Rivals since before my parents married, we've held truce ever since my father took the throne. Both his father and our rival's former chief were murdered by the American mafia; the dual murders formed a truce we've upheld since then.

"Go on," my father says.

Father Finn clears his throat a second time. "There's no need to pretend I don't know where you're planning to get your bread and butter," he says in his soft voice. "Especially since I've advised you from the beginning."

My father nods, and a muscle ticks in his jaw. His brother takes his time when relaying information, and my father's not a patient man. "Go on," my father repeats, his tone harder this time.

"The Martins are behind the theft of your most recent acquisitions," he says sadly, as he knows theft from The Clan is an act of war. "Their theft is only the beginning, however. It was a plot to undermine you. They fully plan on sub-contracting your arms trafficking by summer. They have a connection nearby that's given them inside information, and I know where that inside information came from."

Boner cracks his knuckles, ready to fight. Nolan's suddenly sober, and I can feel Cormac's large, muscled body tense beside me. My own stomach clenches in anticipation. They're preparing to throw the gauntlet, which would bring our decades-long truce to a decided and violent end.

"Where would that be?" I ask.

Finn clears his throat again. "I'm not at liberty to give you all the details I know," he begins.

Boner glares at him. "Why the fuck not? Are you fucking kidding me?"

The Father holds up a hand, begging patience.

"Enough, Boner," I order. There's an unwritten rule in my family that we don't press the Father for information he doesn't offer. I suspect he occasionally relays information granted him in the privacy of the confessional, something he'd consider gravely sinful. Father Finn is a complex man. We take the information he gives us and piece the rest together ourselves.

"I can give you some, however," the Father continues. "I believe you'll find what you need at the lighthouse."

I feel my own brows pull together in confusion.

"The lighthouse?" Nolan asks. "Home of the old mentaller who kicked it?"

"Jack Anderson," the Father says tightly.

The eccentric old man, the lighthouse keeper, took a heart attack last month, leaving Ballyhock without a keeper. Someone spotted his body on the front green of the lighthouse and went to investigate. He was already dead.

Since the lighthouses are now operated digitally, no

longer in need of a keeper, the town hasn't hired a replacement. Most lighthouse keepers around these parts are kept on more for the sake of nostalgia than necessity.

The man we're talking of, who lived in the lighthouse to the north of our estate, *was* out of his mind. He would come into town only a few times a year to buy his stores, then live off the dry goods he kept at his place. He had no contact with the outside world except for this foray into town and the library, and when he came, he reminded one of a mad scientist. Hailing from America, he looked a bit like an older, heavier version of Einstein with his wild, unkempt white hair and tattered clothing. He muttered curse words under his breath, walked with a manky old walking stick, and little children would scatter away from him when he came near. He always carried a large bag over his shoulder, filled with books he'd replenish at the library.

Father Finn doesn't reply to Nolan at first, holding his gaze. "Aren't we all a little mental, then, Nolan?" he asks quietly. Nolan looks away uncomfortably.

"Suppose," he finally mutters.

The Father sighs. "That's all I can tell you, lads. It's enough to go on. If you're to secure your arms deals, and solidify the financial wellbeing of The Clan, and most importantly, keep the peace here in Ballyhock, then I advise you to go at once to the lighthouse." He gets to his feet, and my father shakes his hand. I get to my feet, too, but it isn't to shake his hand. I've got questions.

"Was the lighthouse keeper involved?" I ask. "Was he

mates with our rivals? What can we possibly find at the lighthouse?"

Inside the lighthouse? I've never even thought of there being anything inside the small lighthouse. There had to be, though. The old man lived there for as long as I can remember. There's no house on property save a tiny shed that couldn't hold more than a hedge trimmer.

My father holds a hand up to me, and Cormac mutters beside me, "Easy, Keenan."

Father Finn's just dropped the biggest bomb he's given us yet, and they expect me just to sit and nod obediently?

"You know more, Father," I say to him. "So much more."

Father Finn won't meet my eyes, but as he goes to leave, he speaks over his shoulder. "Go to the lighthouse, Keenan. You'll find what you need there."

READ MORE

Preview:

BEYOND MEASURE: A Dark Bratva Romance (Ruthless Doms)

Tomas

I SCOWL at the computer screen in front of me. As *pakhan*, the weight of everything falls onto my shoulders, and today is one day when I wish I could shrug it off.

A knock comes at my office door.

"Who is it?" I snap. I don't want to see or hear anything right now. I'm pissed off, and I haven't had time to compose myself. As the leader of the Boston Bratva, it's imperative that I maintain composure.

"Nicolai."

"Come in."

Nicolai can withstand my anger and rage. Over the past few months, he's become my most trusted advisor. My friend.

The door swings open and Nicolai enters, bowing his head politely to greet me.

"Brother."

I nod. "Welcome. Have a seat."

When I first met Nicolai, he wore the face of a much older man. Troubled and anguished, he was in the throes of fighting for his woman. The woman who now bears his name and his baby. But I've watched the worry lines around his eyes diminish, his smile become more ready. While every bit as fierce and determined to dutifully fill his role as ever, he's grown softer because of Marissa, more devoted to her.

"You look thrilled," he says, quirking a brow at me. Unlike my other men, who often quake in my presence, having been taught by my father before me that men in authority are to be feared and obeyed, Nicolai is more relaxed. He's earned the title of *brother* more readily than even my most trusted allies.

"Fucking pissed," I tell him, pushing up from my desk and heading to the sideboard. I pour myself a shot of vodka. It's eleven o'clock in the fucking morning, but it doesn't matter. I've been up all night. "Drink?"

He nods silently and takes the proffered shot glass. We raise our drinks and toss them back together. I take in a deep breath and place the glass back on the sideboard before I go back to my desk.

"Want to tell Uncle Nicolai your troubles?" he asks, his eyes twinkling.

I roll my eyes at him.

I made an unconventional decision when I inducted Nicolai into our brotherhood. The son of another *pakhan*, Nicolai came here under an alias, but I knew he had the integrity of a brother I wanted in my order. I offered him dual enrollment in both groups, under both the authority of his father and me, and he readily agreed. We've come to be good friends, and I would trust the man with my life.

"Uncle Nicolai," I snort, shaking my head. None of my other brothers take liberties like Nicolai does, but none are as trustworthy and loyal as him, so he gets away with giving me shit unlike anyone else. "It's fucking Aren Koslov."

Nicolai grimaces. "Fucking Aren Koslov," he mutters in commiseration. "What'd the bastard do now?" He shakes his head. "Give me one good reason to beat his ass and I'll take the next red-eye to San Diego."

He would, too. Nicolai inspires fear in our enemies and respect in our contemporaries. Aren falls into both categories.

"Owed me a fucking mint a month ago, and hasn't paid up," I tell him. I spin my monitor around to show him the number in red. "And you don't need me to tell you we need that money." As my most trusted advisor, Nicolai knows we're right on the cusp of securing the next alliance with the Spanish drug cartel. Our location in Boston, near the wharf and airport, puts us in the perfect position to manage imports, but the buy-in is fucking huge. We have the upfront money, but the payout from San Diego would put us in a moderately better financial position.

Nicolai leans back in his chair, rubbing his hand across his jawline.

"And you have meeting after meeting coming up with politicians, leaders, and the like."

I eye him warily. Where's he going with this?

"It's easy to say you need money. But that isn't what you need, brother."

I roll my eyes. "I suppose you're going to tell me what I need."

"Of course."

"Go on."

"You know what you need more than the money?" he asks. I'm growing impatient. He needs to come out with it already.

I give him a look that says *spill*.

"You need a wife," he says.

A wife?

I roll my eyes and shake my head. "Sometimes I think

your father dropped you on your head as a child," I tell him. What bullshit. I look back at the computer screen, but Nicolai presses on.

"Tomas, listen to me," he says, insistent. "Money comes and goes, and you know that. Tomorrow you could seal a deal with the arms trade you've been working, and you know our investments have been paying off in spades. But a good wife is beyond measure, and Aren has a sister."

"You've been married, for what, two fucking days and you're giving me this shit?" I reply, but my mind is already spinning with what he's saying. I never dismiss Nicolai's suggestions without really weighing my options. Aren is one of the youngest brigadiers in America and has a reputation that precedes him everywhere he goes. He commands men under him, and I'm grateful he hasn't risen higher in power.

He grunts at me and narrows his eyes. "I've loved Marissa for a lot longer than we've had rings on our fingers."

"I know it, brother," I tell him. "Just giving you shit. Go on."

"Aren's sister is single, lives with him on their compound. Young. I don't know much about her, and haven't seen a recent picture, but I met her years ago when I first came to America. And she was a beauty then. I imagine she's only grown more beautiful."

Seconds ago, this idea seemed preposterous, but now that I'm beginning to think about it, I'm warming to the idea.

"You think he'd let her go to pay off his debt?"

"With enough persuasion? Hell yeah. And a good leader needs a wife. You've seen it yourself. There's something to be said for having a woman to come home to. The most powerful men in the brotherhood are all married."

He's right. Just last week, I met with Demyan from Moscow and his wife Larissa. He brings her everywhere with him. The two are inseparable. And he's risen to be one of the most powerful men the Bratva has ever known.

"And face it, Tomas. You're not exactly in the position to meet a pretty girl at church."

I huff out a laugh. The men of the Bratva rarely obtain women by traditional means.

I lift my phone and dial Lev.

"Boss?"

"Get me a picture of Aren Kosolov's sister," I tell him. Our resident hacker and computer genius, Lev works quickly and efficiently.

"Give me five minutes," he says.

"Done."

I hang up the phone and turn to Nicolai. "I want to see her first," I tell him.

"Of course."

"How's Marissa?"

He fills me in about home, his voice growing softer as he talks about Marissa, but I'm only half-listening to him. I'm thinking about the way a woman changes a man, and how he's changed because of her.

Do I need a wife?

The better question is, do I want Aren Kosolov's sister to be the one?

My phone buzzes, and Nicolai gestures for me to answer it. A text from Lev with a grainy picture pops up on the screen, followed by a text.

There are no recent pictures. This was from a few years ago, but it should give you a good idea.

Still, it's a full profile picture. I murmur appreciatively. Wavy, unruly chestnut hair pulled back at the nape of her neck, with fetching tendrils curling around her forehead. Haunting hazel colored eyes below dark brows. High cheekbones, her skin flushed pink, and full, pink lips. She's thin and graceful, though if I'm honest, a little too thin for me. The women I bed tend to be sturdier and curvy, able to withstand the way I like to fuck.

I don't want to have this conversation via text. I call him and he answers right away.

"Background?" I ask.

"Never went to college. Under her brother's watchful eye since her father died."

"Lovely," I mutter. He might not give her up easily.

"Temperament?" I ask, aware that I sound like I'm asking about adopting a puppy, but it fucking matters.

"Not sure, but she has no record on file at school or legally. Perfect record. Graduated top of her class in high school." He snorts. "Volunteers in a soup kitchen in San Diego and attends the Orthodox Church on the weekend."

Ah. A good girl. Points in her favor. Sometimes the good girls fall hard, and sometimes they're tougher to break, but they intrigue me.

"Boyfriend?"

"None."

"Name?"

"Caroline."

"Caroline?" I repeat. "That isn't a Russian name."

"Her mother was American."

I nod thoughtfully. Caroline Koslov.

She would take my name.

Caroline Dobrynin.

I drum my fingers on my desk, contemplating. I nod to Nicolai when I instruct Lev. "Get Aren on the phone."

READ MORE

The Bratva's Baby (Wicked Doms)

Kazimir

THE WROUGHT IRON park bench I sit on is ice cold, but I hardly feel it. I'm too intent on waiting for the girl to arrive. The Americans think this weather is freezing, but I grew up in the bitter cold of northern Russia. The cold doesn't touch me. The ill-prepared people around me pull their coats tighter around their bodies and tighten their scarves around their necks. For a minute, I wonder if they're shielding themselves from me, and not the icy wind.

If they knew what I've done... what I'm capable of... what I'm planning to do... they'd do more than cover their necks with scarves.

I scowl into the wind. I hate cowardice.

But this girl... this girl I've been commissioned to take as mine. Despite outward appearances, she's no coward. And that intrigues me.

Sadie Ann Warren. Twenty-one years old. Fine brown hair, plain and mousy but fetching in the way it hangs in haphazard waves around her round face. Light brown eyes, pink cheeks, and full lips.

I wonder what she looks like when she cries. When she smiles. I've never seen her smile.

She's five-foot-one and curvy, though you wouldn't know it from the way she dresses in thick, bulky, black and gray muted clothing. I know her dress size, her shoe size, her bra size, and I've already ordered the type of clothing she'll wear for me. I smile to myself, and a woman passing by catches the smile. It must look predatory, for her step quickens.

Sadie's nondescript appearance makes her easily meld into the masses as a nobody, which is perhaps exactly what she wants.

She has no friends. No relatives. And she has no idea that she's worth millions.

Her boss, the ancient and somewhat senile head librarian of the small-town library where she works won't even realize she hasn't shown up for work for several days. My men will make sure her boss is well distracted yet unharmed. Sadie's abduction, unlike the ones I've orchestrated in the past, will be an easy one. If trouble arises eventually, we'll fake her death.

It's almost as if it was meant to be. No one will know she's gone. No one will miss her. She's the perfect target.

I sip my bitter, steaming black coffee and watch as she makes her way up to the entrance of the library. It's eight-thirty a.m. precisely, as it is every other day she goes to work. She arrives half an hour early, prepares for the day, then opens the doors at nine. Sadie is predictable and routinized, and I like that. The trademark of a woman who responds well to structure and expectations. She'll easily conform to my standards... eventually.

To my left, a small cluster of girls giggles but quiets when they draw closer to me. They're college-aged, or so. I normally like women much younger than I am. They're more easily influenced, less jaded to the ways of men. These women, though, are barely women. Compared to Sadie's maturity, they're barely more than girls. I look away, but can feel their eyes taking me in, as if they think I'm stupid enough to not know they're staring. I'm wearing a tan work jacket, worn jeans, and boots, the ones I let stay scuffed and marked as if I'm a construction worker taking a break. With my large stature, I attract attention of the female variety wherever I go. It's better I look like a worker, an easy role to assume. No one would ever suspect what my real work entails.

The girls pass me and it grates on my nerves how they resume their giggling. Brats. Their fathers shouldn't let them out of the house dressed the way they are, especially with the likes of me and my brothers prowling the streets. It's freezing cold and yet they're dressed in thin skirts, their legs bare, open jackets revealing cleavage and tight little nipples showing straight through the thin fabric of their slutty tops. My palm itches to spank some sense into their little asses. I flex my hand.

It's been way, way too long since I've had a woman to punish.

Control.

Master.

These girls are too young and silly for a man like me.

Sadie is perfect.

My cock hardens with anticipation, and I shift on my seat.

I know everything about her. She pays her meager bills on time, and despite her paltry wage, contributes to the local food pantry with items bought with coupons she clips and sale items she purchases. Money will never be a concern for her again, but I like that she's fastidious. She reads books during every free moment of time she has, some non-fiction, but most historical romance books. That amuses me about her. She dresses like an amateur nun, but her heroines dress in swaths of silk and jewels. She carries a hard-covered book with her in the bag she holds by her side, and guards it with her life. During her break time, before bed, and when she first wakes up in the morning, she writes in it. I don't know yet what she writes, but I will. She does something with needles and yarn, knitting or something. I enjoy watching her weave fabric with the vibrant threads.

She fidgets when she's near a man, especially attractive, powerful men. Men like me.

I've never seen her pick up a cell phone or talk to a friend. She's a loner in every sense of the word.

I went over the plan again this morning with Dimitri.

Capture the girl.

Marry her.

Take her inheritance.

Get rid of her.

I swallow another sip of coffee and watch Sadie through the sliding glass doors of the library. Today she's wearing an ankle-length navy skirt that hits the tops of her shoes, and she's wrapped in a bulky gray cardigan the color of dirty dishwater. I imagine stripping the clothes off of her and revealing her creamy, bare, unblemished skin. My dick gets hard when I imagine marking her pretty pale skin. Teeth marks. Rope marks. Reddened skin and puckered flesh, christened with hot wax and my palm. I'll punish her for the sin of hiding a body like hers. She won't be allowed to with me.

She's so little. So virginal. An unsullied canvas.

"Enjoy your last taste of freedom, little girl," I whisper to myself before I finish my coffee. I push myself to my feet and cross the street.

It's time she met her future master.

READ MORE